The Magic Fix

The Magic Fix

Mark Montanaro

Elsewhen Press

The Magic Fix
First published in Great Britain by Elsewhen Press, 2020
An imprint of Alnpete Limited

Elsewhen Press, PO Box 757, Dartford, Kent DA2 7TQ
www.elsewhen.press
British Library Cataloguing in Publication Data.
A catalogue record for this book is available from the British Library.
ISBN 978-1-911409-63-2 Print edition
ISBN 978-1-911409-73-1 eBook edition

Printed and bound by CPI Group (UK) Ltd, Croydon, CR0 4YY

Contents

Dedicated to Catherine – she asked first

The Known World

N

Trolls

Furmah

Elves

The Oracle

Tulden River

Carlom

Lapthyp

Arqyen

Stonem

Ogres

Humans

Orthica

Wanlock River

Peria

Rubin Kraw

Galvera River

Turner River

Daqmah

Madesco

Nuberim

White Castle

Goblins

Pixies

Lothia

10 20 30 40 50
Miles

Chapter 1

"Did we win the battle?" asked King Wyndham.

"Well it depends how you define winning," answered Longfield, one of the King's royal commanders. "Some would define it as simply losing fewer soldiers than the opposition, others would base it on how much territory is gained or lost."

"Personally sire," interrupted Godrich, "I prefer not to focus on results. Instead I think it is important to consider individual battle technique and overall tactical quality."

"Indeed," said the Lord of War; the man sat opposite the king with a blank yet slightly smug look on his face. It was the kind of look that a knight might give you if he had forgotten to take his sword to battle, but was trying to convince you that he preferred to use his fists anyway.

"It was a most tactically sound performance from our men, and our fighting technique was quite simply breath-taking. My breath was indeed taken on many an occasion."

"And the new armour plating for the swordsmen really did look divine," added Longfield helpfully.

"Enough," said the King forcefully. "I have no doubt that our men looked very nice in their uniform and rode their horses very well. But unfortunately this is war, and not a circus performance. So for the last time, did we, in any real sense of the word, win the battle at Carlom?"

"We..." began the Lord of War again, before realising there was little point in trying. "Alas no, on a strictly winning by results basis I would have to concede that we lost."

The King let out a heavy sigh.

"How many men?"

"Close to a thousand I would estimate sire. Only around two hundred were able to make it back to the Fortress."

A fairly long silence followed. Neither the Lord nor his commanders could think of anything positive to say at this point. King Wyndham was a reasonable man; he was not here to point fingers. Nevertheless the tension in the room was growing, you could almost cut it with a Lothian broadsword. And those things were pretty rubbish.

"And the Trolls?" said the King at last. "Did they sustain any casualties?"

"Some, yes," replied the Lord "I could not give you a number, truth be told it was not nearly as many."

The King rolled his eyes. 'Truth be told' seemed a fairly ironic phrase, given most of what he heard from his Lord of War.

"You all said we fought with breath-taking technique and excellent tactics. So tell me then, why in all the Gods' names did we get beaten to a pulp by an undisciplined army of savages?"

"Well..." started the Lord of War, deliberately speaking slowly in the hope that someone else would butt in. Luckily someone did.

"Numbers," said Godrich. The King and the Lord both turned their heads to face him. "Numbers is a key reason. We must have been outnumbered two to one."

"What?" replied the King, turning back to his Lord. "You told me you expected roughly even numbers on both sides!"

"Well there were at the start," continued Godrich, not realising it was probably his turn to be quiet. "But by the end of the battle it was definitely about two to one. And the more people they killed, the more they outnumbered us."

"A vicious circle really," chipped in Longfield.

"All right," said the King. He was evidently not in the mood for this. It was bad enough that he had lost a thousand good soldiers today, but right now the worst of it was that these two buffoons of commanders were not among them.

"From now on, only people with 'Lord' in front of their name are allowed to speak."

There was a short silence, as the Lord of War looked quickly at his two commanders as if taking a second to realise that he was the only one left. Cecil was the Lord's name, though he insisted on being called the Lord of War by anyone whom he outranked, which was basically anyone but the King. He was a pale man, dark haired and very skinny. He certainly did not have the appearance of a tough soldier like his two comrades sitting either side of him, which was not really a problem given that he never had to do any fighting.

Growing up he had always been small for his age, and also very weak. He liked to claim that having such a tough childhood just used to make him more determined to become a success, and it was the reason why he had risen to become one of the most important people in the Kingdom; some people argued that being the first-born son of the previous Lord of War probably had something to do with it, especially given the only way to get the title was to inherit it. Finally he spoke.

"The Trolls were undisciplined as usual, and we used the terrain well; we had altitude on our side."

The King nodded, hoping that they were finally getting somewhere.

"But we just couldn't stand up to the dragon."

"Dragon?" retorted the King. "Where did a dragon come from?"

"We think it flew there, sire. It was flying around while we were there. And of course swooping down and killing a lot of our soldiers."

"Just our soldiers?" replied King Wyndham.

"Well mostly, yes," said the Lord of War. Dragons were wild creatures, living in the far corners of the Known World. They never ventured near the Realm of Humans, but in the far-reaching places like Carlom they often seemed to rear their scarily ugly heads.

The King turned to look at Longfield who was nodding ferociously, evidently attempting to remain an active participant in the meeting without being able to speak.

"Well this is simply too much," said the King. "It is hard enough to maintain our fortress at Carlom against the swarm of Trolls. But with dragons suddenly turning up and attacking us; how can we possibly fight against that?"

"We can't sire, not until we learn how to tame the unicorns."

Unicorns. The King sat back in his chair. There was no point in even asking this question but he asked it anyway.

"Any progress on that?"

"Not that I'm aware of sire. You'll have to ask the Lord of Science; he could tell you the latest."

Unicorns were certainly interesting animals; that was something that everybody in the realm of Humans agreed on.

This was mainly because nobody knew anything about them, so in the end rather than arguing about whether they were shy, wild or dangerous animals, and whether they were more closely related to horses, birds or one-horned goats, people generally just accepted that there was not much point in arguing. They agreed that they were interesting and moved on to talk about the weather.

However both the Lord of War and the Lord of Science thought there was more to it than that. These animals could fly, yet in a lot of ways they resembled horses. If only they could figure out a way of taming them and riding them, finally they might be able to fight the dragons in the air.

The Lord of War estimated that one unicorn in the air was worth about a hundred horses on the ground, although given that no unicorn had ever been used in a battle this estimate was not considered wholly reliable. The Lord of War did not like to expand on his estimate, although it was believed to be based on a number of parameters. These included wingspan, airspeed trajectory and a dream the Lord had had a few weeks earlier.

The King had nevertheless commissioned a great deal of research into this idea. Stage 1 of which involved a group of the land's finest scientists getting together and running experiments. However given that the unicorns were usually flying far out of reach, most of the experiments involved staring up at the sky and writing down whatever it was they observed.

They did, once, manage to catch a unicorn with the use of an apple and a very high-pitched song, but the unicorn escaped before they could even confirm that it had the expected number of legs. They were pretty sure it did. Stage 2 of the research was due to begin shortly, which is expected to involve more scientists, more apples and hopefully at least one more unicorn.

"To be honest sire, I don't expect there has been much progress in the last few days. Most of the research takes place outdoors, and the recent weather has simply been awful," continued the Lord of War, still sitting facing the King with the same half-smug look on his face. "I don't think we can even consider the unicorns as an option at this moment in time."

"I quite agree," said King Wyndham. "But I fear that we are running out of options to consider. The Trolls are growing stronger, and angrier. Right now our fortress in Carlom is looking about as weak as a baby in a jousting match. And with a thousand soldiers gone, we simply can't afford to reinforce it right now."

"You're probably right there Sire, although of course the Lord of Gold might well have a different opinion," replied the Lord of War.

"How could he? There is no gold. What is even the point of having a Lord of Gold when there is none?" said the King.

"That's why I hope the war will never end," the Lord of War replied, and luckily the King found it funny. "In all seriousness though, I think we have to consider abandoning that fortress, and withdrawing our men out of Carlom entirely."

The King nodded slowly, still trying to think things through given that this was such an important matter.

"There is another option of course. What if the Elves were willing to send in reinforcements?"

"I think that's about as likely as a two headed unicorn," replied the Lord, fairly sure that unicorns generally only had one head. "But nevertheless it may be worth a try."

"Indeed," King Wyndham replied. "I should meet with the High Elf at once, or at least with one of his Ambassadors. Can you arrange a royal visit to Lanthyn as soon as possible?"

"Yes sire," said the Lord of War. "Although really that's a job for the Lord of Peace."

Chapter 2

Samorus quickly picked up another glass bottle and started to fill it. This was very intricate work, but now was not the time to be careful. After another long seven hours he was finally almost done. Another full batch of healing potion would soon be complete, and another monotonous day's work would be over.

Healing potion was a highly magical substance; at least it seemed magical to anyone who had never actually tried it. For the people who had tried it the results were somewhat mixed; many seemed to find it actually made them worse rather than better, which was really the opposite of its intention.

Most however reported that they didn't notice any change whatsoever after drinking it; but that they at least had a few minutes of enjoyment from the fact that they might.

A fair number of Pixies now argued that the real magic of the product was its ability to make people continue to buy it, despite it serving no useful purpose whatsoever. They didn't tend to mention this fact outside of their own lands; after all healing potion still remained one of their biggest exports.

Finally it was the end of the day for the old Pixie. He put the final bottle on the shelf and let out a long sigh. Pixies are only about two thirds of the size of a typical Human, and their voices tend to be higher. Nevertheless this sigh was as heavy as one that could come from any Human.

He sat down at the side of the chamber, and while his assistant Petra was still cleaning up the apparatus he took a moment yet again to think about how he had ended up here. There was just no money to be made in real magic these days, which is why so many wizards had to settle for work in research, chemistry and, of course, potion making.

Samorus did not consider himself a potion maker; he was still a wizard dammit and if he couldn't get paid for it he would still be a wizard in his spare time.

"How are you feeling?" he asked Petra, now that she was

finally putting the last of the equipment away. She was a very clever girl and a great assistant, though unfortunately she was also very enthusiastic and this annoyed him no end. There are only so many times you can clean a conical flask without getting bored out of your mind, and yet somehow she always seemed to be able to find new ways of making it interesting. Cleaning it for a third time also never made it any cleaner, but that never seemed to stop her from doing so.

She was young, dark haired and slightly taller than the average Pixie. A fair few people would probably do anything for the chance to gaze into those bright green eyes, though Samorus was obviously not one of them.

He did not choose his protégé based on appearance, in fact he barely chose her at all. She had come to him and asked for the chance to work with him, and he had accepted without much enthusiasm. After all he needed a new assistant, and people did seem to speak highly of her. He certainly didn't regret his decision, but he just wished she would show a bit less enthusiasm sometimes and occasionally make some mistakes.

Anyway that didn't matter now; finally their work was done and they could do something they were both enthusiastic about.

"I have to say I'm a little tired," she replied. "Those last two glass bottles really were a challenge."

This sounded like a joke, another thing that Samorus disliked about this girl. Once you reach the age of around 140 years old you start to realise that jokes really aren't very funny; and it's probably best to try to ignore them. He therefore just coughed and continued with what he was about to say.

"Well I hope you're not too tired to learn a bit more magic," he continued. "Because I brought something special along with me this morning."

Petra smiled. "You know I'm never too tired for a magic lesson," she said.

Seven hours of putting potions into bottles and she was still smiling. It just wasn't normal. The main thing though was that she was just as enthusiastic when it came to real magic, which is why he had decided to take her on in the first place. He now got up again and started walking over to a cupboard on the other side of the room.

"It's been nearly a year since you started working for me now, and we've actually done a fair amount of magic together. I know I seem miserable a lot of the time but that's not your fault, even though you do talk a lot."

Petra didn't react, she was used to these kind of comments by now.

"Sometimes I just wish things were different; I wish magic could be taken more seriously as I know there's more to it than what we already know. The way I see it, the possibilities are endless; we've just been stuck in front of a brick wall for a seriously long time, that's all."

Petra nodded. The part about the brick wall was certainly true. She was well aware of the history of magic. It was something they still taught at school despite numerous claims that it should be dropped from the curriculum in favour of more useful subjects, such as Goblin and Ogre relations or contemporary Elvish literature.

The fact was that nobody knew when the word 'magic' was first used, but the first magicians were certainly Humans. They used to practice magic professionally as far back as the fourth age. These magicians would amaze and entertain the peasant folk through trickery and showmanship; making coins disappear and pretending to read peoples' thoughts.

Most people did not believe this was real magic, but nevertheless the magicians were very successful at it. In fact, the vast majority of coins that disappeared somehow always managed to reappear in the magicians' pockets.

It was not until the sixth age that the Pixies even showed an interest in magic. By this time almost everyone was convinced that there was no such thing; especially after the famous incident of Rohry the Magnificent back in year 83 of the sixth age, who had grown tired of making tiny coins disappear and instead claimed he could saw himself in half.

He turned out to be absolutely right, although most people had assumed that the result would be something slightly less realistic, and that he would still be alive at the end of it.

While magic had fallen into disrepute, the Pixies continued their research. Finally towards the very end of the seventh age, it took a genius by the name of Harpus Cordelle to make an important breakthrough. He was able to prove once and for all that magic did in fact exist; it was just that no magician was capable of doing it. That was a fact that still remained true today, and the main reason why magicians in the land of Humans still had to start every trick with the caveat "This is not magic but…"

"I heard a rumour that you were a direct descendant of Harpus Cordelle," said Petra.

She had wanted to ask him about this for weeks and now this finally seemed like the right time. Unfortunately she didn't quite get the reaction she was expecting, as Samorus just gave a sort of sarcastic laugh.

"Whoever told you that?" he asked.

"A friend of a friend. Well, actually he's not much of a friend. Just a friend of some guy I know," said Petra, feeling rather embarrassed and disappointed at the same time.

Samorus had now taken something out of the cupboard and was carrying it back to the table. It was a fairly large box, but covered with a black cloth. Clearly he was quite excited by it, and now Petra was too.

"I wish I were related to Harpus," continued the old Pixie. "In my eyes he was the first real wizard. And I bet he never had to spend seven hours a day making pointless potions."

Petra couldn't be bothered to argue with this statement; it was the end of the working day and right now she didn't care two pins about her day job. Besides she was too intrigued by what was under the black cloth. She really had no idea what it could be, although she was fairly sure it wasn't any kind of potion. She knew that her boss wasn't one for drama, so she was surprised that he was making such a scene of this.

"But now is not the time for pointless potions," said Samorus. "You have shown me that you have at least some magic powers, something which very few young Pixies seem to have these days."

Petra beamed; this was about the nicest compliment he had ever given her.

"Would you say I'm your best student of magic?" she asked. She was of course his only student, and instantly regretted saying this. Her boss did not do laughter, and in fact the best outcome from saying such a comment would be for him to completely ignore it. Luckily this is usually what happened with all her comments; and this one was no exception. He simply continued in his stride.

"So far all our work has involved static objects; whether they be wooden planks, flasks or anything else we could find in this room," he continued.

Petra was now beginning to guess what might be under there, and was getting more and more excited.

"But now it's time to take things to the next level." His voice was getting louder now and sounding more dramatic. "And I really think you're ready."

With that, he withdrew the cloth with one quick movement; revealing the cage that it had been covering.

Petra just stared. She wasn't sure whether she was overwhelmed or underwhelmed, or some other form of whelming in between the two.

Chapter 3

The night had only just begun, yet Orthica was already bustling with life. As Lord Protector Higarth walked, all around him he could hear the sounds of metal on stone and the footsteps of soldiers. He could hear the even more deafening shouts of their captains who clearly liked the sound of their own voices a little too much.

The Lord Protector could barely hear himself think while all this was going on, let alone listen to what his companion was telling him. Of course he barely considered this Ogre a companion; he was after all just a glorified builder, and he was the one who had suggested doing this viewing so early in the night.

Lord Protector Higarth had barely slept all day. Yet he had woken up when the sun had barely gone down, ready for an hour-long walk to the very edge of the city. He did feel tired, but of course he didn't let that show on the outside. Being tired was a form of weakness. So Ogres did not allow themselves to get tired, especially not Lord Protectors of the entire Realm.

"We do not have far to go now my Lord Protector," said Smedley, who was clearly concerned that they had been walking in silence for too long and was desperately trying to think of something pointful to say.

Though obviously this was pretty much the opposite of pointful given that they could quite plainly both see the tower right in front of them.

They could in fact see it ever since they had started walking. This was Yerin tower; the second highest in the whole of the realm. The highest tower was located within the Arrad Castle, which was so tall that many of the peons claimed no Ogre had ever been to the top of it.

This obviously raised the question of how they managed to build it in the first place; which was a difficult question in itself as none of them knew how, when or why it was built. One theory was that dragons were involved, though dragons are generally quite clumsy creatures who can barely build a fire with their own mouths.

The prevailing theory was therefore that the tower at Arrad Castle had always existed and always will exist, which is quite a convenient theory for the peons as it means that they don't ever need to worry about it falling down. The peons were of course wrong, as the Lord Protector had been to the top many times; he had even had breakfast up there once.

However there was no doubt about the purpose of Yerin tower. It was the main watch tower of the entire wall, and what's more its gate provided one of only two entry points into Orthica. It had stood strong for over four hundred years; and gave the Ogres an unrivalled strategic advantage to any Human or Elf who dared to try to breach their walls.

But four hundred years is a long time, and eventually the tower had started to show signs of ageing. When the first stone slab had fallen from its second turret it had landed directly on top of a passing wolf outside the city. Ogres are not generally fond of wolves, so this had been hailed as an ingenious piece of defensive strategy.

Many thought it a huge advantage to have a tower which could actually fall on people. However when more slabs started to fall without crushing so much as a blade of grass they started to accept that this was not actually an intentional design.

That was why Lord Protector Higarth had commissioned Yerin tower to be fully refurbished, so that it would look as great and fearsome as it did all those years ago. Once again it would provide a signal to those dirty Humans and Elves that they will never set foot inside Orthica. After thirty long years it was finally nearing completion.

"I can't quite put my finger on it, but there is something about the tower that just doesn't seem right," said the Lord Protector. They had now reached its very base and were staring straight up, still barely able to see its top.

"Any other comments?" asked Smedley in a tone that sounded fairly polite, but would have been far less polite had he been talking to anyone who wasn't the Lord Protector of the Ogres. He was clearly slightly cheesed off that after thirty years of hard work the first comment he gets is that something isn't quite right.

"Don't get me wrong," replied Lord Protector Higarth. "It's certainly impressive, and would strike fear into anyone who might come within a hundred miles of it."

Not only was it tall but it must have been a hundred yards wide. At the base were two magnificent black metal gates, bordered by stone on each side. Yet the sheer height of the tower made those gates look like nothing more than caves at the foot of a mountain. He wasn't lying, it was certainly fearsome; the spikes at the top were a very nice touch. The spikes themselves must be as tall as trees, not to mention as black as the night's...

"Smedley... the tower is black isn't it?"

"Yes my Lord Protector. It is most certainly a colour very close to black," replied the Ogre.

This was not the correct response; and even as he said it he could sense his Lord Protector's mood turning.

"Close to black?" he snapped. "Explain yourself this instant. Or you might find yourself in a situation that is very close to execution."

Smedley trembled slightly, and took a quick pause before he responded.

"Two thirds of the tower is of the blackest stone from the heartlands of our realm, my Lord Protector," he began. "But the size of the tower was simply too great for our resources. We ran out of stone, so we had to source the remainder from outside."

"Outside?" bellowed Lord Protector Higarth, "You mean you had to get the stone from those wretched Goblins?"

"Yes my Lord Protector, the Goblins. They did give us a very good price for it, and said that the dark grey is a very popular colour right now. Fearsome even; I'm sure they used the word fearsome."

"I can't believe what I'm hearing. Yerin tower, pride of the whole realm of the Ogres; and half the stone in it comes from a Goblin mine," bellowed the Lord Protector, getting louder with every word he spoke.

"A third," replied Smedley, although this achieved nothing except a soul-piercing glare. "And it wasn't actually from..." he began, but stopped before reaching the end of his sentence.

"From what?"

Smedley realised he had dug himself a hole here, and there was simply no way out. Right now he wished it was more than just a metaphorical hole, and that he could cover the hole and spend the rest of his life in hibernation.

"Well we thought the stone came from a Goblin mine. Only it turned out they had acquired it by trade themselves a few years back," said Smedley, who unlike the Lord Protector seemed to be getting quieter with every word he spoke.

"So you mean it was ours all along then?" said Lord Protector Higarth.

"Well no. They actually traded with someone else."

"What? Surely not the Trolls? Those feral creatures wouldn't know a stone from a tree trunk."

"It wasn't the Trolls either my Lord Protector," said Smedley rather slowly, hoping he didn't have to spell it out any further.

"Do you mean to tell me," began the Lord Protector, "that the tower we have spent the last thirty years repairing – the tower that was built for the sole purpose of striking fear and despair into the hearts of Humans – actually contains stone that they sold to us?"

His anger was getting the better of him at this point, so he composed himself for a second.

"Do you mean to tell me that?" he repeated.

"Well yes, though they only indirectly sold it to us," said Smedley, unable to think of anything better to say. Lord Protector Higarth took a few deep breaths.

"My whole life, I have fought against those disgusting creatures. Humans are our sworn foes, the enemy of the East of the Known World. And now they are helping us defend ourselves against them? Why don't they just design our armour as well?"

"I would never ask for help from Humans," started Smedley, desperately trying to save the situation. "Ogres designed this tower, and Ogres built this tower," with the help of a fair few Goblin workers, but he thought it best not to mention that now. "Yes a few stones come from the realm of Humans, but that's it, just the stones. And besides, we won't tell anyone that."

"Well you certainly won't," replied the Lord Protector.

"You'll be too busy covering the top half of the tower in tar and soot until it looks as black as the deepest dungeons of Angol."

"The top one third," muttered Smedley as the Lord Protector stormed off the way he had come.

He was quite relieved; given what had just happened things could have gone a lot worse.

Lord Protector Higarth was walking with such pace that he was almost marching. He simply could not believe what he was hearing. That moronic fool of a builder, importing the stone for their own tower? It wasn't even Smedley he was really angry at; it was those cursed Goblins. Ogres and Goblins used to be great allies. Yes the Ogres were obviously taller, stronger, more intelligent and their skin tone was a slightly nicer shade of green, but they were both fiercely united in their hatred of Human kind.

Yet now these Goblins were freely communicating and trading with Humans; these Humans who still occupied part of the Goblin lands.

He was not marching back to Arrad Castle. Instead he was heading straight for the sacred ground further to the South of Orthica.

He just needed to be somewhere quiet, and far away from any builders. More than anything else he needed time to think, and also to consult with the Gods. Well actually, more than anything he needed to have a nap; it was still far too early in the night for this kind of thing.

But after his nap, he would do some serious thinking. His mind was all over the place at the moment; and he didn't know what to do. But he knew that something must be done, something serious. And that something involved more than just covering a three hundred foot tower in soot and tar.

Besides, there wasn't a great deal of tar in Orthica; they would probably have to buy it from someone else.

Chapter 4

The main square in Peria was crowded with people as the middle of the day approached; the point at which the sun was at its highest in the sky, which presumably had some sort of meaningful significance.

Swarms of Humans had gathered in their capital to pay a long and drawn out tribute to their fallen soldiers, as was the custom after every major battle. Man, woman and child, peasant and knight were all standing together.

Well of course they were not quite together, the knights were entirely separate from the peasants who stood further behind. The knights and noblemen believed that all Humans were united across their realm, but obviously that didn't mean they had to stand shoulder to shoulder with peasants. That really would be taking things a bit far.

The centre of the square was empty except for the Lord of the People, a few high-ranking officials and a brass band of about twenty musicians. The band had now been playing for a good ten minutes, and seemed to be enjoying their music more than most of their audience. The crowds stood on all sides of the square watching, and the longer the music went on the more the nobles started to envy the peasants, most of whom were too far away from the square to hear it.

At last the music drew to a close. The musicians made their way from the square to join the rest of the crowd. As they did so the audience held their applause, some out of respect for the fallen soldiers and others out of disrespect for the musicians.

There was a brief pause before the Lord of the People slowly stood up to begin his address. He was surrounded on all sides, but he remained facing the side with the knights and noblemen, who were generally just nicer to look at and less foul smelling.

"My fellow Lords and Ladies, men and women from across this great realm of ours..." he began. "I thank you all for coming."

This was the standard introduction. In truth there were very few of his fellow Lords even there; the Lord of War and the Lord of Peace were away with the King, the Lord of Science was in an important meeting and the Lord of Health was off sick. This only left the Lord of Gold and the Lord of Religion, who were both sitting in the front row; one of only a few rows of seats while everyone else stood behind them.

Accompanying the two Lords were their wives and families, and of course the Queen and the royal children. They were all dressed in black as a mark of respect, and also wearing diamond earrings and necklaces, as a mark of the fact that they wanted to look nice.

"I wish I could address you all in better circumstances, but alas we live in dark times," he continued, before adding the words "Metaphorically speaking," as he caught the glare of the sun shining directly into his face.

"I am sure you all know by now, that our war with the Trolls has not been going well. Trolls are incredibly dangerous people. They know no laws, they know no rules, they don't even know basic table manners. A few days ago our soldiers fought bravely in Carlom, but alas many made the ultimate sacrifice in order to keep us safe. Today we honour those people."

There was a faint clap from someone in the crowd, who clearly didn't know whether or not they were supposed to start clapping but did so anyway despite the risk of embarrassing themselves.

Luckily more followed, and soon the whole crowd was in raucous applause across the square. This lasted for several minutes. Finally as it was dying down the Lord of the People again spoke.

"The Kingdom of Humans is like a brotherhood, and sisterhood. We value every man, woman and child in our realm as we are all one and the same under the eyes of the Gods."

The Lord of the People was there to represent the masses. His main role was to understand the concerns of the peasant folk, or at least to appear as if he understood their concerns. The peasant folk tended to speak with funny accents; so it was difficult enough to even have a proper conversation with one, let alone understand their concerns. That was why he preferred a more indirect approach.

He did have an open inbox near Lords' Castle, where anybody could voice a concern or make a request in writing whenever they chose.

While this was, of course, a brilliant idea, the slight problem was that so few of the peasants were able to read and write that he barely received any such requests. He did once receive a letter asking for a better literacy programme across the kingdom, but unfortunately he couldn't read the writing so nothing was done about it.

In general the lack of requests was seen as a good thing. It may be that the peasants could not read or write, or it may be that they are just so happy that they had nothing to complain about. If this were true then the Lord of the People must be doing his job rather well.

"I shall now read out the names of our fallen heroes."

There was a very slight murmur from the crowd at the prospect of standing there waiting as the Lord read out the names of about a thousand people. Everyone in the crowd was of course deeply empathetic of the fallen soldiers, but standing there waiting for all of their names really was taking things a bit far. One of the Lord's assistants got up and handed him a long roll of paper. He picked this up in a spectacularly dramatic fashion and began to read aloud.

"Achren, Hemley."

"Ackerman, Roland."

"Acton, Herman," he began. The crowd were providing a faint round of applause in the background while this was going on. Although he was reading the names reasonably quickly this was still going to take a long time, so they needed to pace themselves with this applause or risk getting some serious cramp in their hands.

"Aeron, Jonas."

"Aeron, Marlon."

"Affleck, Bruno."

Many in the crowd were not applauding at all, but simply stood there with their heads bowed low. This was to show their great respect, and so no-one would notice if they started dozing off.

One such man was Ridley; a tall and stocky man standing deep in the heart of the crowd. He had a reddish brown beard which he rarely trimmed, giving the appearance of someone who didn't even care about how they looked. Or rather it gave the appearance of someone who wanted to look like they didn't even care about how they looked. It didn't matter, as people barely even looked at him anyway. This included his wife, who mainly liked him for who he was as a person. He had a big heart, and of course a well-paid job as an Archer in the royal guard.

He was one of the best; at least he claimed to be even if it was difficult to tell for sure. For starters he wasn't dead, so he must have been better than most. He also did practice a lot, because he loved his job and also because it was mandatory to do so.

"It's not right, is it?" he muttered under his breath, just loud enough so that his wife could hear him.

"What?" said his wife; just loud enough so that the whole town could hear her.

"I said, it's just not right, Hari" said Ridley slightly louder, so that his wife actually could hear him this time. "All this, the whole plan was flawed from the start. These people are away fighting a war they are never going to win. And for what?"

"Allen, Jacque. Alliter, Rudger. Allith, Clint," continued the Lord of the People to faint levels of applause.

"You mustn't say things like that," replied his wife, slightly shorter than him but almost as stocky.

"There are dragons out there in the East; at least two of them. Each one can take on a thousand people. How are we supposed to compete with that?"

His wife paused for a second.

"Two thousand people?" she said sarcastically. Ridley just raised his eyebrows and continued.

"I'm being serious here. The King continues this pointless war, sending people off to fight even though he knows we're going to lose. And what's the point of it anyway? Have you ever even known a Troll to come and attack our lands? They don't want it; they're happy enough where they are."

"I don't think a Troll has ever been described as happy in his life," said Hari rather unhelpfully.

In fairness, Trolls were not generally happy people. All Humans knew they were angry at something, but nobody could ever find out what. Unfortunately they were so angry at whatever it was they were angry about, that no man was ever able to find out without being drawn into a fight.

The Lord of Peace had once suggested that perhaps fearsome anger and war cries were just a troll's way of greeting new people; and that we should therefore just respect their culture.

Although then the Lord of Science had pointed out that perhaps the Humans should honour their greeting by giving the same greeting back in return. This greeting was received by an even more handsome greeting from the Trolls, and now after countless years and numerous bloody battles, all Humans agreed that the Trolls' culture had been thoroughly well respected.

The mild clapping was still continuing; though a fair few people in the crowd could clearly hear them talking and did not seem too pleased about it. Ridley was sure he had heard the words 'disrespect' and 'back in my day' at least once by now.

"Aningdon, Donnel. Anise, Gorman. Aniston, Rory."

Ridley lowered his voice.

"Something has to be done," he said bitterly. "I don't know what, but I do know that I don't trust this King of ours. Or any of his advisers."

"Enough," said his wife, in a loud enough voice that Ridley was put off saying any more. People were looking round now and she was sure at least some had heard this conversation.

Clearly someone had. As Ridley turned his head he could just make out a hooded figure standing about twenty yards away from him. Surely he was too far away to have heard it properly, yet he was staring directly at them. In fact he wasn't quite standing still. He was moving. His movement was slow and subtle as he negotiated his way through the crowds. But he was definitely getting nearer.

Ridley was shaking like a Goblin in sunlight. Goblins don't like sunlight; they find it bad for their complexion. Although as Ridley stood there he wondered how bad this could really be. Had King Wyndham suddenly decided to return from his journey to the land of the Elves just so he could stand in the crowd in disguise? No, this wasn't the King, but whoever it was he was heading straight towards them.

"Aphin, Ruddy. Apletch, Heath. Apleton, Tobias."

Ridley's heart was racing. So was his wife's, as she desperately tried to avert her eyes and pretend she hadn't noticed. She started clapping along as though she had just realised the ceremony had started.

But suddenly the figure just continued straight past them into the crowd, barely touching Ridley on his way through. They both took a few deep breaths and then turned to face each other.

"So as I was saying," said Ridley, but then stopped and smiled.

His wife didn't smile but shook her head gently. That was enough excitement for one day. Now it was time to stand there and enjoy the savage monotony of the remainder of the ceremony, hopefully without any more hooded figures.

As he was thinking this, he reached a hand into his pocket. It wasn't empty. He pulled out a piece of paper with a few scribbles on. They were letters, and luckily Ridley could tell what they said. He had been taught basic writing skills in the forces. This was in case he ever had to communicate in silence, write a surrender message or play a word game to pass the time.

This was no word game, it was only a few simple words written in block capitals. It simply said:

MEET IN THE TAWNEY TAVERN AT MIDNIGHT TOMORROW. COME ALONE.
DON'T LET ANYONE SEE YOU.
SERIOUSLY.
IT'S IMPORTANT.

Chapter 5

King Wyndham had been riding for days. Nearly twelve days to be precise, but to him it felt more like twenty. The journey North towards the Elven city of Lanthyn had been fairly easy and without trouble, though this had also made it as dull as dishwater.

The benefit of a long journey is that you have the chance to discuss and debate important issues along the way. Unfortunately the King's only two noble companions were the Lord of Peace and the Lord of War, so the discussion was usually centred around which of them had the more important job. The Lord of Peace would usually win this debate, as the Lord of War would eventually accept defeat in the interest of keeping things peaceful.

These arguments aside, the three of them were all in agreement as to what they needed to do while in Lanthyn. Their fortress at Carlom needed more support, so they were to press the Elves for more soldiers as hard as they could.

King Wyndham knew that this was going to be about as easy as putting on a hat upside down. Which was hard. He once lost a bet trying to do it. And a hat. But nevertheless this strategy had to be worth a try.

If it did not work then there really was nothing for it; if they could not manage to hold Carlom on their own they would have to discuss abandoning their fortress.

The King stroked his short, white, beard and wondered just what was going on throughout the Known World. Of course he knew fairly well what was going on in the land of the Trolls; who were presumably getting angry at everyone else and then getting angry at each other when no-one was around.

They were tall and red-skinned, with teeth like Lothian daggers only less shiny and expensive looking. More to the point, they were vile and ugly creatures; and the King had always thought that was part of the reason why they were always fighting. If he had looked like one of them, he would be pretty angry himself.

Relations with the Goblins were going quite well. In fact it had been nearly two ages since the battle at Orlian Hill, which is still widely regarded as the most successful battle in the history of the Known World.

It took two hundred Humans to keep nearly six thousand Goblin soldiers at bay. There was only one door into the fortress at Orlian Hill, and there were no window holes in the entire tower. It made it very expensive to run the place with the constant need for torches even in broad daylight; and with only a tiny chimney in the roof for ventilation it was always too full of smoke to see anyway.

How that building could have passed a fire safety test the Gods only knew; but all that aside it made it an almost impenetrable fortress. Ever since the battle, the Humans had been able to hold onto their land at Orlian Hill without a soldier suffering from anything more than a few hurt feelings. And of course the odd rather nasty cough.

Although the Humans would seldom go as far as to call the Goblins 'friends', it had been a long time since they were ever considered dangerous. Besides King Wyndham knew the Goblin King quite well, and did not see him as a threat.

It was the Ogres that worried the King, as it always had been. The Humans had no settlements near the Ogre realm; and they found it very hard to keep track of what the Ogres were up to. They were always up to something and it usually wasn't something very nice.

The King didn't like to use the word evil; as he was sure there were some Ogres out there that were perfectly reasonable people and did not wish to get into any kind of fight. But he had never met one, and he wasn't sure he ever would. There were certainly some dark signs coming from the East. On the road North the King had caught a glimpse of Yerin tower in the distance which looked taller and more fearsome than he remembered, if not quite as dark.

A few days past he had also seen a swarm of black crows circling them up above, which may have been a warning sign from the Gods that treacherous times were ahead. Or maybe they had just found some food nearby. Obviously the Lord of Religion was not around to confirm this either way.

The King and his company rode on. They were a small

company of only forty people. This was a short visit to the Elven Kingdom, so King Wyndham had ordered only the essential people to join them. Aside from him and his two Lords he had fifteen guardsmen, his translator, a doctor, the royal butler, the royal hairdresser, the royal shoe polisher and another fifteen support staff. They had the two standard bearers, who were both also fairly good at polishing shoes.

"It cannot be much further now until we reach the outskirts of the city," said the Lord of Peace, riding next to the King.

He had said this a number of times before today, and it was starting to drive King Wyndham ever so slightly mad. In fact the King had just now been considering renaming his title to 'Lord of Stating the Obvious', although this would need approval from the other Lords and could take considerable time and effort.

"I believe we may already be in the outskirts of the city," said the Lord of War, who had just ridden up to join them. It was true that they were now coming across fewer trees and could see some buildings springing up. Elvish houses were very similar to human houses these days, except they all tended to be made from white stone and there was of course no wood to be seen.

The Elves considered the trees to be very sacred, and would do nothing to harm them in any way. This meant they would only ever use wood if a tree had reached its natural end; even then only after the tree had been properly blessed. No Human had ever witnessed such a blessing, mainly for fear of cracking up with laughter halfway through which would presumably cause great offence.

A fair few Humans had, in ages gone by, made substantial sums of money selling wood from their own realm to the Elves; claiming it had of course all died from natural causes. This practice was eventually stopped though once the Elves realised just how adept Humans are at lying, which meant that now wood was very hard to find anywhere in the Elf realm.

"It depends how you define outskirts," said King Wyndham, not knowing why he was bothering to partake in this conversation. "I have to say though that this is starting to look familiar, and I expect that very soon we will have someone come to greet us."

"That is a good point Sire and I'm sure you're right," said the Lord of Peace. "I find it quite surprising that we have not had anyone come to greet us so far."

"I fear it is not a good sign," replied the King.

"We can't know that for sure without the Lord of Religion here Sire," said his Lord of Peace, "although if you like I could make an educated guess. I do know that the signs from the Gods tend to take either a physical or a biological form, so the fact that in this case there is something without taking any kind of form probably suggests it isn't from the Gods…"

"I wasn't suggesting it was a religious sign," snapped the King. "I merely meant that it is not a good indication of things to come."

"I quite agree," said the Lord of War. "They will have heard by now in Lanthyn of the battle against the Trolls, and of course they know of our coming. These are dark times, and they must know that we are not here to bring them a barrel of Pixie dust."

"I do wish you would stop mentioning Pixie dust," said the Lord of Peace in reply. "You know full well the problems that stuff has caused in the past, and you don't want to offend any passing Elves who may hear you."

Pixie dust was once thought to contain magical powers. Humans, Elves and Pixies alike all found that when they inhaled it they were capable of seeing and doing things that they couldn't before.

It gave them great energy, made new images appear before them and made them become more at one with the world. Unfortunately people soon began to realise that these new thoughts and images were not actually real. This first came to light after the famous battle with the Ogres at Lothia back in the 16th year of the eighth age, when the Pixies reportedly won a glorious victory despite being vastly outnumbered.

It later came to light that this had all been in the heads of the Pixie soldiers after becoming over-acquainted with the dust supplies in the main army barracks. In fact not only had none of them killed any Ogres, but no Ogre had ever even set foot in Lothia. The battle still went down in history as an enormous success, given that the Pixies had not sustained a single casualty except for a great many sore heads the next morning.

The substance was later banned across the western lands, and the Pixies have never been quite as successful in any battles since.

"I think perhaps it is best to exercise caution," said King Wyndham, "and we should not talk at all on this road unless it is absolutely necessary."

Although he did think this, he mainly just wanted his two Lords to stop talking for the sake of his own sanity.

"It won't be necessary anymore," said the Lord of War.

They had now come to the edge of a clearing where they all abruptly stopped in their tracks. There in front of them, no more than a stone's throw away, stood the gates of Lanthyn.

It was a feast for the eyes, even for the King who had been here many times before. Two white stone arches came together atop a magnificent white wall, which extended across the horizon onto the steep, rocky mountains on both sides of the city. Which were also white.

"Lanthyn," exclaimed the Lord of Peace, already saying something completely unnecessary and disregarding what the King had said moments earlier.

"Still no sign of aid. Still no sign of any welcome at all," said the King. "But no matter; we should ride on to the city with no more delay."

And no more pointless conversation, he thought to himself.

Chapter 6

It was a bitterly cold night. The chilling wind howled as it made its way through the city of Peria. As Ridley walked he was imagining himself as a dragon, able to breathe fire and warm his whole body up in an instant.

Or at the very least he was imagining himself as a man who had thought to bring a second scarf with him before he left the house.

It was nearly a full moon, and more to the point it was nearly midnight. What could that note possibly have been about? Not for the first time, Ridley wondered what in the Known World he was doing actually coming here on his own. And also why in the Known World would they be so unspecific on the details.

Midnight tomorrow could have meant tonight, but technically it could have also meant last night. He was now fairly sure it didn't, having spent a good half hour waiting around outside Tawney Tavern the night before just in case. He was also fairly sure that anyone who might have seen him would now think he was either a burglar, a sleepwalker or just a raging alcoholic.

He approached the tavern. His dimly lit torch could barely reveal the sign on the front of the house, but this was certainly it.

He tried the door. It was locked, just like last night. He knocked. No answer. He waited a few seconds considering what to do next. Maybe there was some sort of secret knock. If there was, nobody had told it to him. Maybe the letter had contained some clue.

He pulled it out and held it up to catch the moonlight. This was pointless. He already knew what the letter said and sure enough there were no instructions on the back for how to do a super-secret door knock. He shrugged and just tried again, this time doing one long knock followed by two short ones. Then he jumped slightly, as the door started to open.

Ridley was slightly taken aback as he did not recognise the

face of the man behind the door. He was a young man with short fair hair and a very serious look on his face. Clearly he was not just here for a drink.

"Ah, you made it," said the man, who evidently knew who he was anyway. "Anyone follow you here?"

"No" replied Ridley firmly.

"You seem awfully sure of that answer," said the man hesitantly.

"Yes, that's because nobody followed me here!" he retorted, rather impatient now at having to wait out in the cold while someone half his age gave him the third degree.

"Very well," said the man, opening the door the rest of the way. "Welcome to our meeting place. We are all so glad you could come."

Ridley stepped into the hallway as the young man closed the door behind him. He had been to this tavern many times, though never before in this much darkness. Only a few candles were lit; just enough to show the faces of the other people in the room. There were three of them, including the man at the door.

In the corner sat an old looking bloke with long, dark hair; who had a face that seemed to suggest he was permanently squinting at something. He barely acknowledged Ridley's presence, and Ridley did the same thing in return.

The last man in the room however he did recognise, even if he did not know him personally. He knew that short but wispy white hair, he had seen it many times before. But what in the Known World was he doing here?

"My Lord?" said Ridley, not knowing what else to say. He wondered whether he should bow, but that seemed inappropriate given the circumstances. So instead he just gave a sort of nod, which even in the dark room probably looked ridiculous.

"That won't be necessary here my good man," said the Lord of Science calmly. He was wearing a long dark cloak with the hood down. This must have been the same cloak that had so terrified Ridley just yesterday.

"In this room you can call me Wilfred. And please no more of that silly bowing," he continued, with a reassuring smile on his face.

"But..." Ridley stammered, trying to take in everything he

was seeing and hearing here. "But what are you doing here? And what am I doing here? And where can I get one of those cloaks?"

"Relax," said the Lord of Science, apparently now also known as Wilfred. "All these questions will be answered. But first let me introduce you to the others."

Wilfred gestured towards the old looking man in the corner, who had not stopped staring at Ridley since he had arrived.

"This is Terry. He owns this fine establishment as I'm sure you know."

"Well actually I don't think I've ever seen him before," Ridley replied, then turned directly to face the old man so as not to appear rude. "I'm delighted to meet you though Terry; I can't think why I have never noticed you serving drinks before."

"I don't do much of the serving these days," he replied, evidently not as delighted at their meeting as Ridley was.

Wilfred just gave a short chuckle and continued, turning to the man who had made such a fuss of letting him into the tavern in the first place.

"And lastly, this is Fulton."

"Great to meet you," said Fulton. "And my apologies for being so difficult at the door. You can never be too careful these days; that's why I thought it necessary to introduce a secret knock."

"Yes, although usually when you have a secret knock it's helpful to at least tell the knock to the person who you want to come in," replied Ridley.

"Yes well there was no way of telling you discretely beforehand. And as I say you can never be too careful," he said in reply.

"Surely it's a bit worrying that I was able to guess the secret knock so easily?" said Ridley.

"Well actually you didn't get it quite right, but I thought I should let you in anyway."

"Right," said Ridley, before deciding this was not a conversation worth continuing. Instead he just turned his head back towards Wilfred and began to start a far more important conversation.

"And what is the purpose of this? Why have you invited

me into your society?"

"I don't think society is quite the right word," replied Wilfred.

"We are a brotherhood," butted in Fulton, who had done a remarkable job of getting on Ridley's nerves despite only knowing him for less than five minutes. "The brotherhood of men."

"We are not the brotherhood of men! That sounds, well that just sounds awful," said Wilfred solemnly, clearly finding this man nearly as annoying as Ridley did.

"Quite right," attested Terry, who still had the same squinting look on his face and had barely taken his eyes off Ridley since he had come in. "I prefer to think of us as the forward thinking cooperative."

"Well that's the most boring name I've ever heard," replied Fulton. In fairness Ridley at least agreed with him on that. "How about the justice squad?"

"I'm not even going to dignify that suggestion with a response," said Terry, who paused for a moment before adding, "It makes it sound like we're a group of terrorists."

"And what are you then?" butted in Ridley.

"We are nothing," said Wilfred. "At least we're not any kind of squadron or brotherhood."

Fulton looked a little disappointed as he said this; almost like a young boy who had just been told he wasn't ready to practice fighting with a real sword.

"But we are here for a purpose," the Lord continued. He took a deep breath, and then began again.

"The story of mankind can be summed up in one word. War. Another age goes by, another terrible conflict. Finally our forefathers got to a state of peace with the Goblins; and at least a sort of mutually assured non-destruction with the Ogres; but somehow this war with the Trolls still rages on."

Ridley nodded. He looked round at the other two. Fulton was nodding just as much, while Terry just kept his head perfectly still as if to say 'I agree so much I don't even have to nod'.

"And it could all be solved so easily if our beloved King would simply abandon the fortress at Carlom. Send all our soldiers back home and let the Trolls keep the stupid place. It may have belonged to Humans since the sixth age, but it's just not worth fighting over."

More nodding. Even Terry's head seemed to be moving up and down a little.

"But the King will do whatever it takes to keep that place. So will all his trusted Lords. The Elves, the Pixies and even the Goblin King seem to be on his side on this. Something has to be done."

Ridley nodded again, almost making himself feel dizzy. This man was saying everything he had been thinking all this time. Finally he had found some people who didn't just agree with him, but were ready to take action. Bold action. Decisive action. He knew what this 'something' was. Keeping his voice low, he began to speak.

"So what you're saying is…" he began, "we need to overthrow the Monarchy. Remove King Wyndham, get rid of his lords and noblemen and bring in real people to make the decisions. Peaceful people. People who can end this war!"

He hadn't been looking around the room as he was saying these words. If he had done, he would have noticed three rather shocked faces. A fairly awkward silence followed. Then, to Ridley's relief, the Lord of Science started laughing.

"Well that's certainly original," he retorted. "My dear boy, are you seriously suggesting we destroy our entire system of government, and remove our own leader? Who would replace him?"

Ridley was now feeling mixed emotions of disappointment and embarrassment. Rather than looking back at Wilfred he chose to stare down at his own shoes.

"Well I just…thought. I don't know. We could all decide together who we wanted as the next leader. Let all the people decide, rather than just the King."

Now all three of the others laughed.

"I can only imagine who the peasants would choose to lead them. Probably another peasant," said Wilfred.

Ridley kept his eyes firmly fixed on his shoes.

"Peasants choosing a peasant to make all our decisions. We'd become an Ogre colony before you could put a crown on his head," said Terry, displaying something fairly close to a smile.

That was enough for Ridley. He had moved on from embarrassment and his disappointment was turning into frustration. Surely he hadn't been through all this for nothing.

"Well enlighten me then," he said, looking firmly back at Wilfred. "What's the answer? What's the magic fix to ensure peace across the Known World? What do you think we should do?"

"The only thing we can do," replied the Lord of Science. "The only way to stop this war. We have to kill the Goblin King."

Chapter 7

"Keep your hands steady," said Samorus. He was watching Petra work her magic, or at least try to. Petra was standing upright, with one hand in front of the other. She hadn't moved for minutes now, her eyes fixed upon the rodent in front of her. It had been two weeks since Samorus had let her start practicing on a real animal; but she was just as excited as she had been on that very first day.

The cage door was wide open in front of her. The rat stood perfectly still on the table, unable to move. Paralysed by Petra's magic powers.

Unless it was just humouring her.

"Concentrate. Focus. Think about nothing else," her mentor continued.

The rat was still staring straight into her eyes, with a look that would have been fearsome if it wasn't for its bright red nose and light blue fur. Transfiguration was a skill that Petra was already beginning to master. It had taken her nearly two weeks to get the rat this colour, but it had all been worth it. She knew she had magic powers, and the proof was right there in front of her. If nothing else, in years to come when judgement day arrives and the Gods ask her what she had done with her life, she could point them to this bright blue rat and know she had made a difference.

But Petra was convinced she could go further. Any wizard can change an animal's colour or shape, and some can even change its size. Telekinesis however was a much more difficult skill, one that many wizards were simply never able to master. But she believed she had what it takes; she could do what the others couldn't.

She definitely could. Definitely.

Probably.

The cage door wasn't budging, but it would. No matter how long it took.

"Eyes on the animal at all times. Don't let yourself get distracted," said Samorus.

Helpful, thought Petra, wondering how many more ways he had of telling her to focus. A lot of time could probably be saved if people could just stop saying all but one of them. In fact, surely that was true for so many…

"Stop!" yelled Samorus loudly, as the rat bolted from the cage and jumped down from the table like a lemming that was trying to show off in front of its friends. Luckily the door to the laboratory was shut so the rat could not get far, but that just meant it started darting about the place in a frenzy, as if hoping that if it ran quickly enough it would turn back to its normal colour.

"Oh Gods!" cried Petra, trying to follow the bright blue blur that was making its way around the room.

The squeaking was the worst part; instead of changing its colour she began to wish she had spent the last couple of weeks doing something to its voice box. Maybe just muting it, or fixing it so it would sing a soulful melody with absolutely no high squeaky notes.

"Stay calm, just let it tire itself out," said Samorus, who ironically still did not appear to be particularly calm himself.

The rat seemed to be circling the room, clearly with no idea where it was supposed to go.

At that moment it suddenly stopped, and Petra looked up to see Samorus standing directly in front of it, his right hand outstretched just a few feet away from the creature. It was paralysed, looking right at him.

Silence followed. Petra just stared, considering whether to break the tension by sarcastically telling him to focus and not lose concentration. If ever there was a time for jokes with Samorus, this wasn't it. And there never was a time for jokes with Samorus, so this definitely wasn't it.

She gasped. This rat was perfectly still, but she was sure she could see air gradually appearing below it. Her mentor was making this thing move. It was a slow process, but there was now no doubt about it. Forget colouring things in, this was real magic.

The animal seemed to be floating now, making its way back towards its cage on the table. Petra could see the intense look on Samorus's face. Barely breathing. Not even blinking.

Minutes passed. Eventually the wise old wizard had returned the rat to the cage. He then flicked the door shut, without moving from his standing position. Finally he relaxed and turned back to Petra, who immediately started clapping.

Samorus smiled, pretending he didn't enjoy it.

"It's taken me the best part of my life to master that," he said.

"Oh it shows," replied Petra, not really knowing what else to say.

She was hoping to keep the attention on his wonderful magic, rather than her silly mistake which had caused all this trouble.

"Hmmm. Just don't lose focus next time you're practising," said Samorus after a pause, in a tone that somehow managed to be smug, patronising and condescending all at the same time.

"Sorry," said Petra, and to be fair she really was. All this hard work, but it was just so difficult. "I can do better. I know I can."

"It's ok," replied her mentor.

He wasn't one for empathy, but even he could sense she was a little upset right now.

"To tell you the truth, I've been amazed by your progress so far. Many Pixies are capable of magic, but very few can take it beyond a few transfiguration tricks. I believe you are one of those few."

Petra began to smile.

"Or at least, there's a chance that you might be," he added, as if to make sure he wasn't making her feel too happy. Just happy enough.

"I'll take it," she replied. She then paused for a moment. "Can I ask you something Samorus?"

Samorus? Apparently they were on first name terms now. No need for Pixies to respect their elders; he was only 140 for crying out loud.

"Of course," he replied, "and please, call me Sir."

"Yes, sorry," said Petra. "But thanks. Do you really believe that the opportunities in magic are endless? Sometimes I just look up at the stars, gaze into nothingness, and wonder if I'm wrong. What if the Gods only gave us Pixies a few magic powers to keep us entertained? What if there never will be a wizard who can use magic on people, who can make themselves fly or disappear? What if the Humans and the

Elves are right? What if..."

She stopped. No particular reason, she just realised she had run out of 'what if' questions and should probably just let him answer.

"What if, all those things?" she ended, rather more quietly than she had begun.

Samorus just shook his head. He had already been nice to her once today, and didn't see any need to do it again.

"I'm not the Oracle," he replied. "And I'm not a God, so I don't have the answers. All I know is that magic is real, and there is so much more to this world than any of us can possibly imagine. People used to think transfiguration was impossible, until Harpus Cordelle first turned a leaf pink all those years ago. Now half the forest is covered in pink; proof of what the Pixies can do."

Petra began to smile. She loved it whenever her mentor started talking like this.

"People used to think that telekinesis was impossible, until a certain Doctor Mahuzi managed to make his wand levitate without touching it; proving that wands were useful for something even if they weren't actually magic."

None of this was new to Petra, she knew all about the 'magic wands' some of the Pixies in the north used to make; selling them to Humans and Elves claiming they would only work if they believed they could work. Many of them believed very hard, but unfortunately not hard enough. Eventually most of them just believed even harder that they had been tricked by the Pixies; and after that the business of magic wands soon ground to a halt.

"People used to think," continued Samorus, "that magic could never be done on animals. That is, until Lionell Rinah first stopped a squirrel in its tracks and gave it a novelty blue tail. Now the forests are full of blue tailed squirrels, presumably confused as to why they look so funny."

"I get what you're trying to say," said Petra, feeling much more cheered by this point. "Anything can happen, so we should never give up."

"Yes," said Samorus, "and that our forests now look ridiculous."

Petra laughed, even though presumably this wasn't meant to be a joke.

"My point is that people, most people in fact, think we are wasting our time with this magic. They think that we'll never be able to use transfiguration on people, to turn the King of the Humans into a frog, or to turn the High Elf into a statue."

"Or the Lord Protector of the Ogres into a pleasant person," butted in Petra, which the old wizard ignored completely.

"And maybe we can't do any of those things. And maybe there are no new forms of magic to discover. But I'm just waiting to meet the first Pixie who can create fire quicker than any dragon, who can make things disappear, who can fly higher than a…well a dragon again."

"Me too," said Petra, and with that Samorus made for the door.

He was done for the night, and couldn't help thinking that despite being one of the greatest living wizards, the only things he had ever been able to make disappear were his money, his hair and his career prospects.

Petra began to follow him out of the door, but just stopped on her way to take one last look at the cage. The blue creature with a red nose was glaring back at her, almost as if it was thinking 'You'll never have what it takes, you'll never reach his level'. Although it was probably actually thinking 'Please change me back, for the love of the Gods please change me back.'

Either way, Petra just smiled and turned back to the door.

"We'll see," she said out loud, even though no-one was there to hear it.

Chapter 8

The torches were still alight on all sides of Yurgen Hall. It took over two hundred at any one time to keep the place properly lit; such was the size of the place. Of course it had windows, but they are not very useful during the night-time. And since Ogres do not tend to rise until the sun has well and truly set, they tended to serve no purpose at all.

Any problems with the light simply meant more torches were needed. This meant, unfortunately, that they tended to need a lot. Torches were, in fact, one of the basic necessities for any Ogre, and in tough times the Lord Protector would frequently stress the importance for everyone to have access to basic food, water and torches.

Many of the older and wiser Ogres would still hark on about the great torch shortages of the thirteenth age, when thousands were without torches for years on end. While people were still allowed to discuss this at great length, the phrase 'dark times indeed' had been universally banned across the realm on the grounds that it was no longer funny.

At this moment in time there were more torches in Yurgen Hall than necessary, since the banquet was over and only six Ogres remained at the table. Lord Protector Higarth sat at the head, with his five Generals on either side. The rest of the seats at the long and vast table had all been vacated.

"We do now have a full report on the latest battle between the Humans and the Trolls," said General Gorac. "My spies at Carlom send their apologies..."

"Sincere apologies," butted in General Litmus.

"Send their sincere apologies, that they could not get this to us sooner," continued Gorac. "They have confirmed that the Trolls were victorious, and continue to push the Humans back behind the walls of their fortress."

"Excellent," said Lord Protector Higarth. "How many dead?"

"Over a thousand Humans. Compared to about two hundred Trolls."

"Good. Good riddance to the lot of them," replied Higarth, taking a sip from his goblet of red wine as he did so.

"You mean good riddance to all the Humans, I assume my Lord? We should keep on record as showing our sympathy for the Trolls in the loss of so many of their own," said General Lang.

"Record? What record? Are you taking minutes of this meeting General?" he replied.

"Well, no but..."

"Are any of you taking minutes?" said the Lord Protector.

A few of the Generals shook their heads while the others just sat in silence.

"Very well," Higarth continued. "Since no-one is writing down my every word, I suggest I can say whatever I like, Lang. Do you agree?"

"Yes, Lord Protector," he replied.

"Good. Well as I was saying, this is excellent news. Surely it is only a matter of time now before the Humans have to abandon Carlom entirely."

"Oh I agree, Lord Protector," said General Chandimer, in such a sucking up tone that he may as well have been polishing the Lord Protector's boots as he was saying it.

"How many people do they still have there? Soldiers I mean, forget the women and children," said the Lord Protector.

"Well actually some of the soldiers are women, my Lord. This is the 14th age after all, they are very liberal with that sort of thing now," butted in General Litmus.

"Hmmm," Higarth replied, "they're just getting desperate; they need all the soldiers they can get."

Gorac waited for the faint and almost entirely forced chuckle amongst the Generals to die down before continuing. Litmus had clearly considered replying to this, presumably pointing out that some people could find it offensive, but in the end decided to keep his trap shut for once.

"I don't have an exact figure on the number of soldiers," said Gorac, "Unfortunately the fortress at Carlom is still fairly strong; none of my spies have been able to infiltrate it."

"Yes but do they have an estimate?" replied Higarth, getting slightly frustrated while continuing to nurse his glass of wine.

Gorac paused for a moment. "Six thousand," he said.

"Did you just pluck that figure out of thin air?" the Lord Protector replied.

"No, my Lord," said Gorac firmly, "this comes directly from the spies themselves." *Who probably plucked it out of thin air*, he thought to himself.

"Still seems like a lot to me," began General Hurgen, who had kept quiet for most of the meeting so far. "And I gather, having read through the report that they still have plentiful supplies."

"Indeed," continued Gorac, "thanks to the Goblins."

There were clear frowns appearing on all the Generals' faces as he said this. They were the most senior Ogres in the realm; even the youngest of them, General Chandimer, was still in his early fifties. And all of them knew their history better than they knew the backs of their hands. For any old fashioned and educated Ogre, the concept of Goblins even trading with the Humans was hard enough to stomach, but actually helping them fight a war was on a different level entirely.

"I think we have to accept," said General Hurgen, "that the Humans are not simply going to pack their bags and leave. If anything they will probably send even more troops. Six thousand could soon become ten thousand, or eleven."

"Yes," added General Gorac, wishing people would stop quoting his six thousand figure.

Lord Protector Higarth finished the last of his wine and instantly poured himself another glass. "So what you're saying is, that something must be done. If the Humans pull back from Carlom, they lose their last remaining settlement in the East."

"That would certainly be a sight to behold," said General Chandimer, quite unnecessarily.

"Right. So what are we going to do about it?" Higarth replied.

There was a short moment of silence, before General Lang began to speak. "Surely we have to at least discuss sending our own troops to fight alongside the Trolls," he said.

"We are not discussing that," replied Hurgen firmly.

"What is it with you and fighting, Lang?" added Litmus, "anyone would think you were half Troll."

"Well I'm not," he retorted, stating the obvious since it was a genetic impossibility for anyone to be half Troll. "But the fact of the matter is, that if we send our own troops in support we could have this blasted conflict over and done with in a matter of days. The Humans would be forced to retreat, and King Wyndham would be as devastated as a dragon who had just been told he had no wings, couldn't breathe fire and should probably have a go at being a snake instead."

"That may be so," replied Hurgen, "but what you're suggesting is we declare war on the Humans."

"And why shouldn't we?" said Lang in response, "they are at war with the Trolls, and last time I checked weren't they our faithful allies?"

Litmus coughed. "They are not faithful, and allies is a bit of an overstatement. When did they last offer us support on anything?"

"We are not the ones who need it," Lang replied, getting rather worked up by this point.

"We are NOT going to war with the Humans," said Gorac forcefully, briefly forgetting who was in charge, and then immediately turning his head towards the Lord Protector as if to say 'Assuming that's ok with you?'

Higarth sighed. He had to accept that his General was right on this. Sending troops to fight with the Trolls was a declaration of war. They couldn't afford a war with the Humans right now. Someday, definitely. After all the only true way to achieve world peace would be to kill every one of those filthy people so a war was no longer possible.

But not right now. They were not strong enough yet; their weapons were not up to scratch.

"He's right," the Lord Protector replied. "We cannot send any troops to Carlom. We are not ready for a war with the Humans."

Gorac nodded, and turned to Lang with a textbook 'I told you so' expression on his face. Lang's face on the other hand was doing the Ogre equivalent of blushing; his dark green skin was showing a distinctive red hue, turning it to a somewhat unattractive brownish colour.

"So you're saying we do nothing?" he replied to Higarth, "We let the Humans hold onto land that isn't theirs by right. We let them keep thinking they're the Known World's strongest power."

"I didn't say that," snapped the Lord Protector. "I simply said that declaring war was not an option right now."

He stared down at his wine glass, gently tilting it from side to side.

"Well what other options do we have?" replied Lang, "Send Ogres to Carlom in secret and sneak Pixie dust into the Humans' water supply?"

"Don't be ridiculous," said Higarth, who then stopped for a second as if to contemplate whether that would actually work. "No, that's not an option," he said finally.

"What if we don't declare war on the Humans," piped in General Litmus. "But we do threaten to, if they don't retreat from Carlom?"

Gorac turned his head to face him. "That still risks open war with the Humans. It's a chance we couldn't afford to take."

"You've all got to think about the big picture," said Higarth, which made the Generals all turn back to look at him. "What if I told you there was a way of defeating the Humans at Carlom without killing a single person?"

Blank faces stared back at him.

"Well, there isn't," he continued. "But there is a way of doing it by only killing one."

Hurgen leant forward from his chair and nodded, thinking he knew where the Lord Protector was going. Chandimer also nodded, though he had no idea where the Lord Protector was going.

"The Goblins and the Humans have been far too close for far too long. If we end their lovey-dovey relationship, the Humans just might find they won't be able to survive on their own."

Gorac murmured in agreement.

"And I'm not just talking about Carlom," added the Lord Protector, before smiling but then stopping short of doing an evil laugh.

"So what you're saying is..." began Hurgen.

"What I'm saying, Hurgen, is that we kill the Goblin King."

The Generals all paused, as if none of them wanted to be the first to respond. It was Litmus who finally did.

"So instead of risking war with the Humans, we're

prepared to risk a war with the Goblins?"

"There is no risk," replied Higarth calmly, "Not really. We have the finest assassins in the land, I believe we can do this without any trace of our involvement."

"Here, here," said Gorac, although secretly wondering if the assassination of the Goblin leader was about as 'risk free' as painting a bulls-eye on your chest and turning up at an archer's house claiming you had just spent the night with his wife. However, he convinced himself that this was still the best plan they had.

"This doesn't leave these four walls, although I'm assuming that goes without saying," continued Higarth.

"Lucky no-one was keeping minutes," said Litmus, before quickly deciding to say something more serious, "But yes, no-one else needs to know."

"If we're going to do this," interrupted Lang, "then it has to be an inside job. I think we need to get Prince Grumio on board."

Higarth smiled. "Oh he's already on board," he replied.

"You've spoken to him about this?" said Lang.

"No," replied the Lord Protector, "I meant that in a metaphorical sense. But he will be on board soon enough."

Prince Grumio was the Goblin King's eldest son and heir to the throne. For 46 years he had waited for the King to pop his clogs. When you wait for something for that long the phrase 'it's only a matter of time' begins to lose all meaning; and phrases like 'it's only a matter of chopping the guy's head off' start to sound much more appealing.

"So we're all in agreement?" continued Lord Protector Higarth.

"Well there are still so many questions," replied Hurgen. "How do we do it? When? What if someone finds out?"

Higarth answered without even looking at him. "Poison, the Dernbach festival, no-one's going to find out."

Hurgen paused, not expecting quite such a forceful response. "I see. And by poison you mean…"

"Tepnik water," replied Higarth. "The most dangerous substance in the Known World."

"And by the Dernbach festival you mean…"

"Any time during it, or before. We'll be among the Goblins for days, it's the perfect opportunity."

"Days?" said Chandimer.

"I mean nights," he replied.

"I see," answered Hurgen.

"And by no-one's going to find out..." started Litmus.

"I mean no-one's going to find out!" snapped the Lord Protector.

His five Generals all smiled, none of them saying a word. Hurgen shrugged. He lifted up his wine glass and held it out in front of him. The others all followed, as did the Lord Protector.

"Here's to the end of a truly awful king," he said.

"To the end of a truly awful king," they all replied.

Chapter 9

Ridley's mind was racing. It had been racing ever since that night in the pub, even though days had now passed. Somehow his mind continued to race, no matter how much time dragged on. Apparently it was involved in some sort of endurance event which showed no sign of ending.

He breathed in the cold night air as he walked briskly down the cobbled streets of East Peria. He needed time to think, and these men had given it to him. But a few days just wasn't enough. Was this really the right thing to do? It couldn't possibly be, could it? He wanted the war to end more than anyone, but couldn't they just turn up outside the palace with a bunch of protest signs, or send a crate of white flags to the soldiers in Carlom with a message saying 'Take the hint'?

And if they had to kill someone, couldn't it be their own King? Admittedly that probably wouldn't stop the war, but was killing the Goblin King any better? It was unthinkable; though not really, since it was pretty much all he had thought about.

And even if he agreed to it, how was he going to get there safely? Could he just turn up with a bow and arrow and ask the guards to have a quick word with their King?

And then what? Leave the room politely and explain to them that his finger slipped, and accidentally took off the King's face? He couldn't think any more; if his mind raced any faster it would probably be taken to one side and questioned about its use of performance enhancing potions.

He began to feel the cold wind brush against his cheeks, which at least provided a welcome distraction from all these thoughts. As he finally approached the Tawney Tavern he still had no idea what he was going to say to these people. Surely the word 'no' had to be there somewhere. But what if this really was the right thing to do? What if he would go down in history as a great hero? What if he could get them to pay him more money?

He pulled up outside the door. He knocked three times in

quick succession. He waited. No response. Breathing slightly faster now, he knocked again.

Still nothing. Maybe he was early. Maybe the others hadn't arrived yet. Or what if they'd been rumbled? What if two of the King's guards were inside with their feet up, just waiting for him to walk in, sit down and be arrested. Was this even a crime though? After all, he wouldn't actually be killing a Human... Yes was the answer; obviously it was still a crime.

At that moment the door opened slightly, and he was relieved to see a friendly face. Fulton had one of those faces that always made it look like he was up to something, even when he wasn't. Admittedly this was only the second time he had met him, and both times he had been up to something.

"You did a different knock last time," he said. Apparently a 'hello' wasn't necessary.

"Does it matter?" Ridley replied.

"Of course it matters. How are we supposed to know it's you?" said Fulton.

Ridley was in no mood for this. "Well next time I'll just shout 'it's Ridley' at the top of my voice, just to give you a clue."

He forced the door open wider and walked past Fulton into the dimly lit tavern.

"Evening Terry," he said to the old man, who was once again sitting down in the corner of the room. Ridley wondered whether he ever actually left this place. Perhaps he didn't want anything to do with this plan, but just couldn't be bothered to leave when the others had started talking about it.

"Evening," he replied. "Drink?"

Ridley was slightly taken aback by this. He wasn't expecting Terry to say a word to him, let alone two. And one of them was offering him a drink.

"Ale, thanks" he said. He wasn't sure he wanted one, but after all he was in a tavern at midnight; he could hardly ask for a glass of milk.

As Terry got up to go to the bar, Ridley walked to the other side of the room. He sat down next to the only other man in the tavern, who was busy playing with his pipe and so far hadn't seemed to acknowledge Ridley's presence.

"You know that stuff's supposed to be bad for you?" he said.

Wilfred laughed. "Yes thank you for that," he replied, "I do know. As Lord of Science you do tend to keep abreast of these things."

Fulton chuckled. He had also sat down near the two of them.

"And you have to take these scientific studies seriously," he continued, taking another puff. "Before you choose to ignore them."

Terry came back from the bar with a tall, frothy glass which he handed to Ridley.

"Now then," continued the Lord of Science, "let's get straight to the point. Do you have an answer for us?"

Fulton and Terry both leaned forward in their chairs.

"No," replied Ridley. "I mean, no I don't have an answer yet."

They sat back again.

"I just still have too many questions. I mean, is this really the right thing to do?"

"Yes," said Fulton. "Next question?"

"Look, we've been through this," said Wilfred firmly. "We have to be realistic. This is the only way we can guarantee to bring about peace."

"Yes…" said Ridley, "although we do have a Lord of Peace, who seems to think differently."

"The Lord of Peace should be called the Lord of Doing Nothing," Wilfred replied. "For thirteen generations we've had a Lord of Peace advising the King. That's more than three ages. And in all that time, the longest we've gone without a war is seven years."

"It's a joke," butted in Fulton, "it's like having a farmer who doesn't know how to farm."

"Or a soldier who doesn't know how to fight," said Ridley.

"Well there are plenty of those," said Wilfred, "generally we call them Elves."

Fulton laughed.

Ridley still wasn't satisfied. "But we're achieving peace by killing someone. How can that be right? If we go through with this, are we any better than Ogres?"

He paused for a second. "In fact, I wouldn't be surprised if they were planning on killing the guy themselves."

"I think you're clutching at straws," continued the Lord of

Science. "And of course we're better than Ogres; we don't spend all night shouting, drinking and fighting amongst ourselves; and all day lying in our own filth."

"You've clearly never been south of the river," said Ridley.

"This is not something I want to do," continued the Lord, ignoring him completely. "It's something we have to do. It's necessary."

"You could be a hero, Ridley," said Fulton.

"And we're paying you," said Terry, "let's not forget that."

Ridley paused for a moment. "Suppose I say yes. Just suppose. How could I possibly do this without getting caught?"

"We've been through this," Wilfred sighed.

"You'll be wearing a hood," butted in Fulton. "They won't recognise you".

"They won't recognise me because they are Goblins; they don't know who I am," Ridley replied.

"They won't recognise you," continued Wilfred more loudly, "because they won't know you're there."

"Tell me again," said Ridley, unconvinced.

The Lord of Science tapped his pipe on the table to remove some of the excess ash. Nothing happened, so he tried again harder. This time it was too hard, and caused the pipe to crack.

"Rats," he said. Although it did have the positive effect of creating a small pile of ash on the table. He brushed the remains of the pipe to one side and pushed the ashes together into a little mound.

"The Dernbach festival happens at the same time every year, when the night is at its longest and the day is at its shortest," he continued. "And as every peasant boy knows, it lasts for 5 nights, one for each of their Gods."

Ridley nodded. He wondered how many peasant boys actually did know this. Since most of them couldn't read or write, it seemed unlikely they were too familiar with the literature on contemporary Goblin culture.

"When the sun has set on the fifth night, every Goblin gathers in the Citadel to hear the King's speech. The place is well and truly lit up; it really is something."

"You've been?" said Ridley.

"Oh yes," replied the lord, "Yes indeed. It's a beautiful

occasion. Or at least it would be if you weren't surrounded by hundreds of hideous Goblins."

Fulton and Ridley both chuckled.

"Anyway, they call it a citadel, so you would expect that it's shaped like a tower." He looked down again at the mound of ash on the table.

"But in fact, it's quite the opposite," he proceeded to press down on the top of the mound with his finger until a groove began to form. "It's more like a bucket."

The others leaned forward to try to make out this small pile of ash with a hole in the middle, apparently now shaped like a bucket.

"The Goblin King," continued the lord, "stands in the very middle, while his audience gathers around him on all sides. Essentially he is talking up to them."

"So all I need to do…" started Ridley.

"All you need to do, my friend," continued the Lord, "is stand on the edge, look down, and fire."

"And run," added Fulton. "Run like a unicorn on pixie dust!"

"It's not that easy," said Ridley. "How big is the Citadel? How far will I have to shoot?"

"Oh I don't know, how am I supposed to know how far away something is?" said the Lord of Science. "Just get as close as you have to."

"Right," said Ridley. This plan had clearly been meticulously thought through.

"Anything else bothering you?" said the Lord.

"Well yes," he replied, "no matter how hidden I am at the edge of the bucket… er, Citadel, surely the Goblins are going to start noticing when a bunch of arrows start shooting out of nowhere?"

"Yes well you know the solution to that," said the Lord, "it's obvious. You only get one shot."

"Ah," said Ridley, wondering whether this could possibly get any worse. "Any more brilliant advice? Apart from don't miss…"

"Don't m… oh well you know it already," replied the Lord of Science.

A long silence followed. Ridley just sat there staring at the pile of ash on the table, wondering whether he was crazy, bonkers or just plain mad to even be considering this.

"You're the best archer in the land," said Fulton.

"Flattery won't work," he replied.

"Well then, maybe you're too scared," said Fulton.

"Reverse psychology won't work either," replied Ridley.

"Hmmm…" said Fulton.

"We'll pay you double," said the Lord of Science. "One hundred and twenty silvers."

"It's not about the money," he replied.

Another silence followed.

"Double," Terry echoed gruffly.

"All right," conceded Ridley finally, "All right, I'll do it."

"Excellent," beamed the Lord of Science. "Terry, go get our man his money. Half now, and half for his return."

Terry got up and left the room, a smile almost appearing on his face.

"We don't have much time," continued the Lord. "The Dernbach festival is a little over two weeks away. If I were you, I would set off first thing tomorrow. I'll get you your map in a minute, the route is all planned."

"Thanks," said Ridley, expecting a piece of paper with a circle drawn on it, and possibly an arrow saying 'this way'.

"Oh and Terry has already prepared more than enough provisions for both of you."

Ridley stopped. "Both of us?"

"Of course," said Wilfred, "you didn't expect to be going on your own?"

He turned his head to Fulton, who was beaming like a child who had just been told he was getting a pet unicorn for his birthday; which could also sing and do his chores.

"This is going to be fun," said Fulton.

Ridley declined to comment.

Chapter 10

Lanthyn really was an interesting place. It was the oldest city in the whole of the Elf realm. Or at least it probably was, nobody knew for sure. But it definitely was the biggest; in fact more Elves lived in this one city than in the second and third biggest combined. And that was surely interesting.

Unfortunately one person who didn't find it so interesting was King Wyndham, who had been here far too many times before. At least five, possibly more; that was far too many.

He was a little tired of the Great Marble Hall of Archrem, and even the Wishing River of Juliana was losing its appeal. Last time he went there he had wished that just one of his previous wishes would come true. As far as he was aware, none of them had.

At least the Elves were now being welcoming hosts, even if they hadn't greeted them when they first arrived. They were probably busy doing something else. Probably praying to their Gods. That was all they ever did.

The feast had been rather good the previous evening, even despite the lack of meat. Of course the Elves were all vegetarians, but they knew he was visiting; would it have been so much effort to whip up a few steaks for him and his fellow Humans? On reflection it probably would, given they wouldn't have any in the whole of their realm. But still.

He stared out of the window. The view from his room in the Rhodri Tower was certainly something; he felt like he could see the whole of Lanthyn below him. An Elf city was very different to the ones in his own realm. Buildings were so spread out, and everywhere was covered in trees.

It almost felt peaceful, and for a brief moment the King forgot how tired he was of this place and just let his mind wander. And then the Lord of Peace came in and startled him.

"Sire," he said, "I believe it is time to go."

He was right. Enough of this nonsense. Time to do what they came here to do. They needed the Elves to help them fight in Carlom, it was as simple as that. And they weren't going to get it by staring at trees out of the window.

"Very well," he said, putting on his coat before heading to the door.

"I understand they are waiting for us in the Main Hall," said the Lord of Peace, telling him something he already knew.

The Lord of War met them at the end of the corridor, and after exchanging a few pleasantries they continued down the steps towards the Hall.

The Rhodri Tower was the highest building in the city, one of the few that actually rose above the trees. While it was very kind of the Elves to give the King a room on the ninth floor, it did mean getting up from, and down to, the ground floor was a bit of an effort.

As he walked down the stairs King Wyndham did begin to wonder whether this was more of a punishment than a nice gesture, or some cunning plan by the Elves to tire him out before the discussions even began.

They reached the ground floor where two young Elves were waiting for them, both in silver armour with spears in their hands.

"Your Grace," said the one on the left, "step this way."

They followed these two guards into the Main Hall. Despite the name it wasn't particularly big, and apart from a couple of paintings it was also quite bare. If the King had his way he would probably rename it the Mediocre Meeting Room instead, but suggesting this would presumably offend them.

The stone table in the middle of the room was no more impressive. It was clearly very old and damaged despite apparent attempts to make it look new. They should have just removed the table years ago and let it fall apart in peace; it would have been the kinder thing to do.

There were marble halls and golden statues in Lanthyn, and yet they were holding the meeting in this miserable little place.

"Greetings Elders," said the King, "such a pleasure to be back in this wonderful hall."

"Indeed, most excellent," added the Lord of Peace.

"Thank you. The pleasure is all ours, King Wyndham," said Elder Norith.

He and the other three elders had all risen from their seats to welcome the visitors. The King then took his place at one head of the table, with his two Lords sitting either side of him. The seats unfortunately were no better than the table, if indeed you could call them seats.

Lumps of rock might have been a better name, or stone devices designed to cause immeasurable pain to anyone who dared try to sit on them. The three Humans were all doing their best to pretend they were sitting comfortably.

As the elders sat back down; just one empty 'seat' remained at the other head of the table.

"And where is the High Elf?" asked King Wyndham.

"He shan't be long," said Elder Lewell, "he sends his apologies for his tardiness, but he has had some urgent business to attend to."

"Not a problem at all," replied the King, wondering what business could possibly be more important than a meeting with the King of the Humans. Maybe someone had accidentally killed an animal, or chopped down a tree.

"He also wished to apologise again for leaving the feast so early last night," added Elder Dawes.

"Quite all right," said King Wyndham.

The High Elf had been very distant last night and didn't seem to want to talk about anything besides the weather; it had actually been a relief when he said he had to leave.

At that moment the door opened and two Elf guards appeared, alongside a shorter, older and rather fatter Elf. His hair had long since given up on turning grey and gone for a soft white colour instead. Combined with his pale face and pure white robes it was difficult to know where his hair ended and the rest of him began.

King Wyndham thought it was lucky that it didn't often snow in Lanthyn, since if he fell in the snow they would probably never find him again.

The Lord of Peace wondered how the Elf had lived in the Known World for over 200 years and yet had never managed to get a sun tan.

The Lord of War wondered how someone who was 5 foot tall could possibly be called the 'High Elf'.

"Your Highness," said King Wyndham.

"Your Grace, please be seated," replied the High Elf, as the

King and his Humans were rising to their feet.

"Thank you," replied the King, more grateful than anything else at having the chance to get up from his wretched seat if only for a moment.

"I must apologise for my tardiness," began the High Elf as he made his way to his seat at the head of the table, "I should explain myself. Unfortunately circumstances arose which were beyond my control."

"Please, that's quite all right," replied King Wyndham, wondering in what realm that possibly constituted an explanation.

The High Elf smiled. "Thank you, King Wyndham," he said, "I knew you would understand. Despite your wonderful cities and fabulous history, I think it is your kind and forgiving nature that I admire most of all about the race of Humans."

A nice compliment, thought the King. A little too nice in fact. It was the kind of compliment a gaoler might give his superior before explaining that he had accidentally left the cell doors open last night and all the prisoners had escaped. And then adding the good news that they had at least significantly reduced the prison's running costs.

There was only one thing for it, he had to retaliate. He was not going be out-complimented by this Elf.

"You flatter us, High Elf Roulen," he began. "Your kind words epitomise the wisdom and benevolence of the Elves. The relationship between our two great realms is something I treasure more than anything else in the Known World."

"Here, here," added the Lord of Peace, before receiving a look from the King which suggested he should probably stay silent for the rest of the meeting.

"Indeed," replied the High Elf. "It is a testament to Humans and Elves alike that this relationship remains so strong to this day, despite the many difficult times we have faced, and despite our differences."

"Our differences are nothing compared to what we share," replied the King. "We share a common purpose, a common understanding that during these difficult times we must look out for each other."

The Elders could probably all see where this was going by now.

"Indeed, we both share the common purpose of achieving peace across the Known World," said the High Elf.

The Lord of Peace nodded.

"We all want peace," continued the King. "But we both know that when war is forced upon us, all we can do is fight."

"Any Human or Elf can wield a sword. But when the time comes, only the strongest can hold a white flag," replied the Elf.

"Hmmm," said the King, wondering whether the High Elf was even strong enough to hold a spoon. "The wisest people know when to hold the white flag. And when not to."

How profound, thought the Lord of War.

"And right now, there isn't a white flag in sight around Carlom for one simple reason. Our land has been attacked, and we will not surrender."

"I fully understand," said the High Elf, in a tone that almost sounded sincere.

Carlom was over a hundred miles from the rest of the realm of Humans, and the King knew very well what the Elves thought about it. 'Just let the Trolls have it' he was probably thinking to himself.

"Thank you," replied the King, "it is tremendously reassuring to know that we have the support of the Elves during these dark times."

"Indeed, our thoughts are with you and your people," replied the High Elf.

"Yes, well I thank you for those thoughts," said the King, not knowing what else to say. "But that is not the only support we are after."

"Quite," added the High Elf, "our prayers are with you too. May you have the support of every one of the Gods who protects our realm."

"I am eternally grateful," said the King, doing his very best not to sound at all sarcastic. He knew they were both thinking the same thing, and was tired of tiptoeing around it.

"What we need are soldiers," he began. "At the last battle we lost a thousand soldiers."

"Over a thousand," added the Lord of War, please that he was at least able to contribute to the conversation, "we simply didn't have enough. There was a dragon."

"Our forces are depleted, and morale is as low as it's ever been. Roulen," said the King, hoping the personal touch would somehow make the difference, "we need your help."

The Elders exchanged glances with each other, before turning to the High Elf. His face did not move, and remained looking directly into the King's eyes.

"Our thoughts and prayers are with you," he said, "but our soldiers remain here with us. Sincere apologies," he added, "but this is not our fight."

"I see," said the King, doing his best to remain calm despite the anger boiling up inside him.

Right now he wanted to do nothing more than to get hold of a white flag and shove it down the High Elf's throat. He composed himself.

"How interesting it is to finally know what this relationship really means. The Humans protect the Elves, and the Elves sit back and watch them."

He got up from his chair without even looking the High Elf in the eye, and made for the door. As he reached it he stopped and turned his head back to the Elf.

"The time will come, Roulen, when the Ogres or the Trolls attack your own lands again. And when they do, we'll be thinking of you while they burn your cities to the ground."

His two Lords got up and followed their King.

"Thank you for your hospitality," added the Lord of Peace before leaving.

Chapter 11

The Pixies were a proud race of people. They may not have been the biggest or the strongest race; in fact they were the smallest and almost certainly the weakest.

Many often wondered how the Pixies had survived so long. Some claimed it was down to their fighting spirit, which it obviously wasn't because none of them really liked fighting. Others said it was just hard work and determination, which it obviously wasn't because the Ogres and Trolls had always seemed just as determined to kill them.

No, the answer was surely down to their intelligence. Lady Vernipula had once famously stated that mind will always overcome muscle, and claimed that one Pixie could defeat ten Ogres in open battle simply by using his brain. No-one had yet volunteered to test this theory.

Samorus was well aware of his own intelligence. With a brain apparently big enough to defeat ten Ogres and 140 years to his name, he was fairly confident that when he had an opinion about something he was probably right. And Petra was now as determined as ever to show him that he was right about her. If only she could get this stupid rat to move. Even an inch. An inch would be fantastic.

They stood once again in the potions chamber, where Samorus seemed to spend half his life these days. Truth be told it wasn't a bad job; healing potion was still in high demand and he could usually sell it for 6 silver pieces per barrel. That was more than enough to pay for the upkeep of his laboratory, and the storage space above. The best part of course was that he sold it to the same merchants every week, so he rarely had to talk to anyone new.

"Keep your hand held out firmly," he was saying to his glamorous assistant, "I can see it shaking."

Petra glanced at her right hand. It was indeed shaking. She tried to maintain focus, closing her eyes briefly before looking back at the hand. Still shaking. She tried instead to keep her eyes directly focused on the hand, willing it with all her mind to stop. Still shaking. She then tried to use reverse psychology, telling the hand to shake even faster and hope that it stopped. It shook faster, obviously, because hands aren't capable of independent thought so aren't generally swayed by reverse psychology.

"Look, there's no need to rush this," said Samorus firmly, "we can always just come back another day."

It was a Friday night, and she was choosing to spend it playing with a rat in an underground laboratory. Of course so was he, but he was an Old Pixie. He didn't have the energy to go to the local tavern, dancing establishment or whatever it was the young kids liked to do these days.

"I'm ok," Petra replied, "Honest."

"Well I'm not opening the cage door until that hand stops shaking."

Petra looked back at her right hand. It was shaking like a Troll soldier who had just told his superior that he wanted to quit the army and take up knitting instead.

"Alright," conceded Petra, "let's just give it a few minutes."

She sat down on her usual stool and stared at the wall in front of her. Maybe if she stopped looking at the rat it would calm her nerves. Although she didn't really feel nervous; maybe she was just tired. Or maybe she had just lost all her magical ability and was instead doomed to be a potions assistant for the rest of her life. To be fair, at least she was working with healing potion so it would probably be a long life. If the potion worked. Which it didn't.

That depressing thought was enough to get Petra back on her feet and raring to go once more. She was ready to give this another try.

"I can do this. I'm ready," she said.

"Good. Let's do it," replied the old Pixie.

Petra took her position a few yards away from the cage. Her fiery green eyes focused intently on the creature that lay within it. The rat's fur was bright blue, and its nose red, but its eyes remained as dark as an Ogre's cave at midnight during a severe torch shortage.

As she stood she began to slowly lift her right arm up in front of her. The chamber was completely silent. Samorus was saying nothing; probably a good sign. Either he had nothing to criticise right now, which was encouraging; or he had left the room, which would be even more encouraging. Maybe she was so focused she hadn't even noticed him leave. That would be impressive.

"You're holding your breath," said her mentor, who apparently was still in the room, "You must remember to breathe."

Petra started to breathe heavily. "Open the cage door," she said to Samorus, "I'm ready."

"You're not ready," he replied. "If I open the door now that thing will run straight out and onto the floor again. Have patience."

Patience. That was a word she was tired of hearing. Half of Samorus's teaching seemed to consist of saying the word 'patience' over and over again. It was no wonder it had taken him so long to become a wizard. He was so patient he would probably wait for an animal to grow up, die and get reincarnated as another animal before he started to practice magic on it.

For once, Petra was tired of hearing it. She had been working for this old Pixie for years now. She knew Samorus was a great wizard, but that didn't mean he was always right.

"I said I'm ready" Petra snapped, without taking her eyes off the rat.

Her mentor didn't reply for a moment. He clearly wasn't expecting this.

"Excuse me?" he said.

"Just open it," she said almost instantly.

"I'll tell you what," replied her mentor, "if you're just going to ignore what I'm telling you, then maybe you don't need me at all. You can open the door yourself."

Petra glanced at him in surprise, and then turned back to the rat realising she probably should have stayed focused.

"What's the problem?" continued Samorus, "just use your magic."

She could almost feel the sarcasm; it stung like a stinging nettle. A really stingy one.

She couldn't do this. Opening a cage door while keeping the rat still at the same time? That was madness. Only a real professional could do something like that.

Nevertheless she focused. She held out her left hand

alongside her right. Her eyes moved rapidly between the cage door and the animal inside. Then she focussed some more. And then some more. Then a little bit less. And then a lot more.

Still nothing. The rat started to squeak. It wasn't even looking at her any more.

Her head sank.

"Pity," said Samorus, "even I didn't expect you to give up so quickly."

She didn't look at him.

"I think we're done for the night," he added. "It's my fault really, I sometimes forget how young you are."

Well that wasn't at all patronising. Petra still kept her head down, but her heart started beating faster.

"You're just not ready to be a real wizard," continued the old Pixie who probably should have shut the hell up by now.

Petra took a deep breath. It wasn't enough, so she took another. Her head rose and her eyes once again met those of the caged creature in front of her.

"I am a real wizard!" she retorted.

Samorus just chuckled. Great, now was the time he found his sense of humour. Well Petra hadn't found hers, but her sense of anger was definitely growing.

"I think it's time we took a break from magic. For the time being, maybe you should just stick with potions and test tubes."

Her blood started to boil. She felt anger like she had never felt before. Almost rage. Almost fury. Something was burning inside her. And not just in a metaphorical sense.

At that very moment she felt a white flame appear from her right hand. Before she knew what was happening it flew in front of her like a rocket, straight at the cage she was staring at.

It was all over in a flash. In a heartbeat. In another really short metaphor. The cage was in pieces, shrapnel all over the floor and table. And the inhabitant of the cage was no more. The rat that was once a distastefully light blue colour was now looking somewhat blacker. And somewhat less alive. It had gone from a beast to a pile of ash in seconds.

Petra was breathing fast. What in all the Gods' names had just happened? Was she dreaming? She must be dreaming.

She looked across at Samorus, who stood motionless. His jaw was wide open. He too was wondering whether he was dreaming, or whether he had accidentally put Pixie dust instead of sugar in his tea this morning.

At last he spoke. "Did you just..."

"I think so," she replied, still getting her breath back.

"But how did..."

"I don't know," she said. She looked at the palm of her right hand. It looked perfectly normal; it didn't even feel warm.

"That wasn't a trick. Please tell me that wasn't a trick," said Samorus. He already knew the answer; how could she possibly have faked something like this?

Petra smiled, and shook her head. "Please," she said in a deservedly smug tone, "I'm not a magician. I'm a wizard."

"You're not just a wizard," replied her mentor, who still seemed to be in a state of shock, "you've just done something no-one has ever done before in the history of magic!"

Petra's smile grew even wider. "What does it mean?" she asked.

"What it means, Petra, is that infernication is possible."

"Infernication?"

"Yes infernication, you know, making fire using nothing but magic," replied her mentor.

Petra paused. "It's not a great name..." she said.

"Who cares? We'll work on the name. The point is, it's possible, and you're the only person in the Known World who can do it!"

Petra looked back at the bundle of ash and metal in front of her.

"Cool," she said. "But what do I do now?"

"Well if you're wondering whether to use your powers for good or evil, I'd suggest using them for good," replied Samorus.

Petra laughed. She really didn't know what else to do.

"But seriously," she continued, "I mean, surely I've got to be careful. What if I set fire to a building? Or a church?"

"Well a church is a building," said Samorus, apparently focussing on the unimportant part of the issue. "But do you think you're able to do that?"

Petra shrugged. "Who knows?"

Samorus thought for a moment. "Yes, of course you're right," he began. "We do need to be careful. We need to harness this talent, make sure you've got it fully under control. Make sure you never do anything outside this room until we know you're ready."

Petra nodded, although she rolled her eyes a little. Once again it was back to patience. Patience and more patience. But this time he was certainly right.

"And we need to be discrete. I'm guessing we don't want anyone else finding out."

Samorus frowned. The enormity of the situation suddenly struck him. What if the Goblins found out? They would probably try to capture her to learn her powers. And what about the Ogres? They would want her dead. So would the Trolls. The Humans might protect her, or they might just want to use her as a weapon. And the Elves? They would probably worship her as a god, provided she didn't set fire to any trees.

"No," he said solemnly, "No, I need time to think. For the moment, only you and I can know about this."

Chapter 12

Ridley turned back to his travelling companion, who had just stopped in his tracks. It had been about four days now since they had started their journey, and this was quite possibly the first time Fulton was actually behind him.

He was young, keen and constantly smiling. It was almost as if he thought they were going on holiday, rather than on a murderous mission to assassinate a Goblin.

"What's up?" he called back to Fulton, who now seemed to have an uncharacteristic frown on his face.

Ridley on the other hand was in fairly high spirits. The sun was shining, and the walk had so far been surprisingly pleasant. The South East of the realm was full of green fields and vibrant woodlands. And what's more they were making good time. They were now approaching the Turner River; the river which marked the end of the realm of Humans.

"Don't tell me you're scared of a little river?" said Ridley, wondering whether that was the reason his companion had stopped.

"I didn't say I was scared," replied Fulton.

"Because we could always go round it," he added.

"Really?" said Fulton.

"No," Ridley retorted, "it's a river."

Fulton didn't respond, but started walking once again.

"I'm not scared of the river. I'm just taking it all in," he said as he passed Ridley by. "The truth is, I've never been to the realm of the Pixies before. I've never even been outside the realm of Humans."

Ridley hadn't really appreciated this. To Fulton, this really was an adventure. Admittedly it was still one that would probably get them both killed, but at least he could say he had seen the world before he died. And maybe that made it all worth it. Except it obviously didn't.

He smiled. "You know why they call it the Turner river, don't you?"

"Why?" asked Fulton, genuinely curious.

"Because as soon as you get to the other side, you want to turn around and go home."

Fulton paused for a minute. "That's not funny."

"Not true either," replied Ridley. "It was actually named after its discoverer. Gordon Turner."

"Well that makes more sense," said Fulton. "And I bet when he discovered it, he didn't turn around and go home."

"Nope. He drowned in it."

Fulton glared at him.

"Great explorer. Not such a great swimmer," he continued.

Fulton didn't respond; he decided instead to change the subject. "You're not a fan of the Pixies, are you?" he said.

"Nah they're fine," replied Ridley. "In fact, some of my best friends are Pixies," he added, slightly hesitantly.

This wasn't particularly true; there were hardly any Pixies in Peria for a start. And Ridley didn't really have many friends anyway. But still, he didn't have a problem with them, even if they were annoyingly short and a rather pointless race.

They approached a small wooden hut at the bank of the river. It had no door, and was only just about large enough for the old man who sat inside it. He had a bleary-eyed look on his face, and almost all of the hairs on his head had long since packed their bags and left him.

"Two silvers to cross," he said, barely looking either of them in the eye.

Ridley reached into his pouch and handed him the money.

"Per person," added the old man, who had clearly lost his passion for this job and whose only satisfaction was overcharging people as they tried to cross the river.

Ridley grudgingly handed the man another two silver coins, prompting him to get out of the hut and make his way to one of the boats which were tied up on the river bank.

Boat probably isn't the right word; it was more of a raft. Or a few pieces of wood which had been cobbled together and somehow managed to float. Ridley and Fulton both looked at each other and then joined the man on the 'boat'. Somehow despite three full grown Humans and two rather heavy wolfskin bags, it did stay afloat.

"So where are you both from?" asked the old man as he pushed the boat off the bank and started to paddle with something that vaguely resembled an oar.

"Stonem," said Ridley, without hesitating.

"We're merchants," added Fulton, pre-empting the next question. "We're on our way to Nuberim. The markets are always heaving in the Goblin realm at this time of year."

Ridley nodded. In an ideal world he would have been the one doing the talking. Although actually in an ideal world everyone would be at peace and he wouldn't be on his way to kill a King. In fact in an ideal world he would be a King, riding around on a unicorn while young ladies cheered him from below.

But this wasn't an ideal world, and Fulton was actually doing fairly well. It had taken them long enough to agree on a suitable cover story; he had spent hours trying to convince Fulton not to pretend to be a magician or travelling lute player.

In the end, his young companion had finally accepted that he couldn't do magic or play the lute, which were quite important factors in such cover stories.

"I thought you might be merchants," said the old man, who seemed surprisingly adept at rowing the boat even though he must have been in his late fifties. "I could tell by the size of those bags you're carrying."

"Quite," said Ridley, staring across the river.

It was peaceful; as far as he could tell they were the only ones crossing at this time. And since he had paid four silvers for this he was at least going to enjoy the view.

"What's in 'em? If you don't mind me asking," said the old man, who presumably had a name but neither of them wanted to ask what it was.

"Spices, mostly," answered Ridley mechanically.

"Yes, spices," added Fulton, evidently enjoying his new acting role. "Chives, wicka, tarragon, all sorts really. Things you can't get down in the Goblin realm. The prices of these things shoot up around the time of the Dernbach festival."

Ridley nodded again, slightly concerned that this was more improvising than acting. He clearly knew the script, but was starting to add to it. Not that there was any real danger of the old man checking the bags, and finding nothing but food and other supplies. And of course a bow and arrow buried among it.

"Aye, sounds nice," he answered. The raft was making steady progress, and must have now been past the halfway point of the river. "I don't suppose you have anything to spare?"

Fulton looked down at his bag. "Well I can have a quick look."

"No," interrupted Ridley quickly, before taking a breath. "I'm afraid not, good man. We need to save every ounce we have."

The old man nodded. "No problem, friends," he said, as he continued to row at a steady pace.

"I'm assuming we're not the only merchants who have come by this way in the last few weeks?" asked Fulton to his new friend.

"I daresay," replied the man. "Although most of them travel in larger groups. And have their own boats, or cargo equipment."

Fulton thought for a few seconds, realising he probably shouldn't elaborate any further on their story.

"Yes, well we're very independent," he replied, "and we find it easiest to only carry one bag each. The lighter we travel, the faster we travel," he added, quite pleased with himself.

The old man seemed content with this, and that was the end of the conversation. For the remainder of the journey they sat in silence.

As they approached the other side of the river, Fulton began to feel that sense of excitement once more. The grass on this side looked just as green, and the trees were probably just as tall. But this was Pixie land, and he was far from home now. It meant the adventure had well and truly begun.

Ridley was still feeling this too, but in the back of his mind another thought started to work its way in. From now on, it was only going to get harder. Every day brought them closer to the Goblin capital. Every day the grass would start to feel less green, and the air less clear. Every day, the risk of getting caught would grow higher.

The boat hit the bank of the river with a thud. Two men stood waiting, and held it steady as the passengers disembarked. The old man handed Ridley and Fulton their luggage and let the two new passengers join him on the boat.

He then immediately pushed against the bank and set off in the other direction.

"Many thanks," called out Ridley, acknowledging the other two men as he did so, and wondering why they didn't have to pay the two silvers each.

"Best of luck in the Goblin realm," the old man called back as he paddled away.

"Thank you," replied Ridley, muttering "We're going to need it," under his breath afterwards.

They both marched on from the river with their bags hoisted firmly on their backs, and Ridley's pocket four silver coins lighter.

It was Ridley who finally broke the silence. "The price of these things shoots up around the time of the Dernbach festival?"

Fulton smiled. "Well, it's probably true," he said.

"Hmmm" replied Ridley. "Although next time someone asks if they can have any of your imaginary spices, you should probably say no."

He laughed. "What makes you think I couldn't make some magically appear?"

Chapter 13

It wasn't so much what the Goblin King had said, it was how he said it. Or rather it wasn't how he said it, because he said it in quite a nice way. But it had still made Prince Grumio upset. It was more what he didn't say.

His father's exact words were, 'I have no doubts about your ability to rule my Kingdom one day'. Maybe it was the 'one day' which did it; it made it seem like he had to wait another eternity to become king. His father had got to wear the crown at 17 years of age; and yet here he was, a 46 year old prince who hadn't even come close.

Of all the injustices in the Known World, this was probably somewhere towards the bottom of the list, but to the prince it was most certainly up there. At least the peons didn't have any expectations of becoming king, so they could just get on with their lives; the lower classes just didn't realise how lucky they were sometimes.

Still, as he sat face to face with the Lord Protector of the Ogres he had to think carefully about his response. When someone asks if they can kill your father, you don't just say 'okay then'.

Of course he was in favour of the idea in principle. The king had grown old and senile; yes he seemed perfectly healthy, but his mind was certainly going. Why else would he be so receptive to the Humans? Why else would he offer them his support at the expense of the Trolls? Grumio always knew it was a dangerous strategy, but his father would never listen.

He had to go. For the sake of the realm, he had to go.

It was a kindness really; he was sure that once they met each other again in the afterlife, his father would understand.

"He won't suffer, will he?" asked Prince Grumio. "I know Tepnik water is a lethal substance, but is it a quick and painless death?"

Lord Protector Higarth thought for a moment. It was just the two of them sitting in the Hallow Chamber at Rubin

Kraw. It was the Lord Protector's favourite room in the whole of the city. Dimly lit, and decorated with the skulls of former Ogre Generals, it was a rather fitting place for a meeting like this.

"I can guarantee, my prince, that your father will feel no more pain than absolutely necessary," he began. "It can take several days to take effect, but I'm sure you understand that this is a requirement. It simply cannot be traced back to us. If a group of Ogres arrived at Nuberim and suddenly the King finds he's missing a head it might look a bit suspicious."

"Well yes," said Prince Grumio.

"I knew you would understand," added Higarth.

At that point they heard a loud knock on the door, followed by the phrase "My Lord Protector, General Lang has arrived."

"Send him in," replied Higarth.

The door opened slowly, and in walked the general accompanied by a female Ogre. She was half the size of General Lang, but looked just as intimidating. People in the west would often claim that the only way to tell the difference between a male and female Ogre was by whether they had hair. The males didn't have any, while the females tended to have long and white locks. This one was no exception, so unless an Ogre male had cut off someone's hair and fashioned it into a rather fetching toupee, it was safe to assume that this was probably a female.

"My Prince," began General Lang, "and my Lord Protector," he nodded to both of them, and received similar acknowledgements in return. "Allow me to introduce you to Margha, one of the finest chemists in the East."

Higarth gave him a short but piercing glare.

"And indeed the West!" added the General, realising his Lord Protector didn't much like the implication that the Humans and Pixies had better chemists than they did.

"Indeed," said Lord Protector Higarth, "and does she have what we require?"

The three of them all turned to Margha, who slowly reached into her pocket and brought out a small glass vial, about the size of a finger. She held the vial out to the Lord Protector, who began to find the woman a little creepy. She hadn't said a word, and what's more her eyes hadn't even blinked yet. They were so pale; almost as white as her hair.

He snatched the vial from her and held it up to the light. The liquid inside looked as clear as crystal; it could have been pure water. There were no clues that this was actually one of the most deadly poisons in the Known World. In fact, legend had it that was how the inventor of the substance met his untimely end. Poor old Tepnik; he had done too good a job at inventing something which looked and smelt almost identical to water. If he hadn't done such a great job, he probably wouldn't have accidentally drunk a cupful of the stuff.

Prince Grumio just stared at the Lord Protector. He couldn't believe how arrogant the Ogres were sometimes; there were four guards outside this room, and they had walked straight past them carrying a vial of poison.

The Lord Protector turned his head to his Goblin friend, offering him the Tepnik water as he did so.

"You want me to take it?" he asked, quite taken aback.

"Yes of course, why do you think we brought it here?" replied Higarth.

"Well, I…" the prince stammered, "I thought you just wanted to show it to me, to prove it was the real thing. Although I still can't tell if it is."

"Then drink it," muttered Lang under his breath.

"It's real," answered Lord Protector Higarth.

The prince didn't respond.

"Look," continued the Lord Protector, "we're not asking you to do anything with it yet. Just hold onto it until we arrive at Nuberim."

Prince Grumio still didn't seem overly pleased at the prospect of carrying a jar of poison around with him for a week.

"Just keep it safe," continued the Lord Protector in a low voice. "You must understand that we can't risk bringing it with us when we enter the Goblin Kingdom."

The prince gave a slight nod. How nice of the Ogres to let him take all the risk instead.

"But what makes you think I can?" he replied.

Higarth was ready for this. "No matter what your father says, he doesn't trust us. Ogres and Goblins may have a great history, but they are still very different people. You are his son. Can't you see, it has to be you?"

The prince looked around the room, as if hoping that General Lang or the chemist would suddenly say something to make Higarth change his mind about the whole idea of killing the King; perhaps just decide to think mean thoughts about him instead.

Nobody said a word. Prince Grumio had to accept that they were probably right.

His father had to die. And he had to be the one to kill him.

He grabbed the vial and put it straight into his pocket, without saying another word.

The Lord Protector grinned. "All you need to do is hide it until the night we arrive. The first night of the Dernbach festival."

"So we do it at the feast?" asked Prince Grumio, trembling slightly, and putting on a purposefully low voice to try and make it sound like he wasn't trembling slightly.

"Exactly. At the feast. You will be one side of the king, and I will be the other. As you well know, there will be a prayer before every course. As we bow our heads, you slip the vial into his water goblet. One small movement is all it takes."

He made it sound so simple. Even though there were about a million things that could go wrong.

"It really is so simple," continued Higarth, "nothing could go wrong."

Well that was reassuring. "But what if it does?" said the prince. "What if someone notices me doing it?"

"You drop it," replied the Lord Protector instantly, "if the vial breaks, the Tepnik water will spill. It looks and smells exactly like regular water, and no-one will know the difference."

Prince Grumio then proceeded to highlight the obvious flaw in this argument.

"Yes, but it might look a bit suspicious if I say I was carrying a small glass vial full of regular water, and just wanted to top up my father's drink?"

"Say it's alcohol then," said the Lord Protector, who seemed to have an answer for everything. "Say you just wanted to liven up the party a bit. It is the Dernbach festival, who could blame you?"

The prince still couldn't believe how calm the leader of the

Ogres seemed to be about this. Anyone would think he was planning a dinner rather than an assassination. Grumio on the other hand felt as if he was going to pass out at any minute. The small vial of Tepnik water was practically weightless, but right now it felt like a lump of lead in his pocket.

"Okay then" he said, his heart pumping fast.

The Lord Protector then grinned even wider than before, showing off every one of his hideously yellow teeth. "When the dust has settled my friend, you will be a King. And together, we can rule this Known World of ours."

Prince Grumio let out a smile of his own after hearing these words.

"One kingdom at a time," he said in reply.

The Lord Protector laughed, as Prince Grumio turned and made his way to the door.

"And I'm sure this goes without saying. But if anyone asks, we had a constructive meeting today. All we were doing was making plans for our arrival at the Dernbach festival."

"No word of a lie," said the prince in return.

Chapter 14

"It's perfectly safe," snapped King Wyndham.

"Yes your highness," replied Robsun, one of his Royal Guard, "but it might be safer if I went with you."

"I don't want it to be safer. I just want to go for a walk in peace," replied the King.

"But your Grace, I must protect you at all times. It is my number one duty," he stammered.

The King rolled his eyes. It had been two days now since they had left Lanthyn. The Lord of War had ridden East to Carlom; he was needed to support the soldiers in the war against the Trolls. And the Lord of Peace had gone back South to Peria; he wasn't needed there, the King just didn't want him around anymore.

King Wyndham however, was riding North. He was losing a war, and his Elf friends had forsaken him. He needed advice. He needed wisdom. He needed to see the Oracle.

He also needed five minutes of peace, which his annoyingly faithful guards didn't seem to allow.

"Listen," began the King, "your number one duty is to keep me safe."

"Yes…" said Robsun, hesitantly.

"But you also have to obey orders without question?"

"Well yes," he replied.

"So in that case I order you to leave me in peace," said the King.

"Ah, but that's a number two duty. I can't obey an order if it violates the first."

King Wyndham paused for a moment. This kid had probably had the Royal Guards' code memorised since he was two years old.

"If you don't leave me alone I'll kill myself," he said.

The guard thought for a minute. Then left him alone.

King Wyndham strolled away with a wry smile on his face. The Elf realm was full of vibrant woodlands, but now they had reached a clearing with nothing but green grass in sight. The air was clear; there wasn't a cloud in the sky. Anyone could have mistaken it for a summer's day if it wasn't so ridiculously cold. But the King didn't mind; he was just glad to have a few moments of peace. Finally alone with his thoughts.

He thought about the war. Then he tried not to think about the war, which meant he just thought about it even more. Then he wondered how long he could manage to go without thinking about the war, which didn't turn out to be very long. Then he managed to distract himself briefly by thinking about chickens. And then back to the war.

And then he stopped, as two different things had suddenly caught his attention. One was a white rabbit, scurrying along the grass in front of him in some sort of rush. And the other was the sound of footsteps. Footsteps. If this was one of his Royal Guard he swore to the Gods he would tell them where to go.

As he turned his head though his frown vanished. It wasn't a guard at all. It wasn't even an adult. It was a child.

He must have been a young Elf, barely ten years of age. His hair was jet white and his eyes a pale blue. He stopped in his tracks and looked at the King with an air of both intrigue and bewilderment.

"Why are your ears so funny?" said the boy.

King Wyndham laughed. That was a new one. It was rather hard to comprehend the idea that the pointy ears of an Elf were normal, while his ears were apparently the odd ones.

"You're a Human, aren't you?" he continued, "You don't live here. Why are you here?"

The King wondered whether he should actually try and answer any of these questions. He chose not to, but instead asked one of his own.

"What's your name?" he asked the boy.

"Fimbel," he replied.

"Well you're right," began the King, "I don't live here. I live further South in the realm of Humans."

"So…you are a Human then," said the boy.

"Well yes," he replied, "but there's more to me than that. You see Flimbel, I also happen to be the King of the whole realm; the leader of all the Humans."

He stopped, waiting for a gasp or a 'wow' or at least some form of astonishment. Instead the boy just nodded. He didn't even correct the King for getting his name wrong.

"King Wyndham? Yes I've heard of you."

Well that was something at least...

"So why did you come to our realm?"

The King thought for a minute. "I don't even know any more. I came because I wanted something, but unfortunately I didn't get it."

"Well you can't always get what you want," said the boy. "Maybe you should try praying for it."

King Wyndham chuckled. "You Elves all sound the same."

"Not all of us," he replied, "my father can speak Elvish. He sounds very different when he speaks Elvish."

"Isn't that nice," said the King.

Hardly anyone in the Known World knew how to speak the language any more. Half the time when someone claimed to know, they would just make a load of random noises and pretend they were speaking Elvish. Since no-one knew any different, they usually got away with it. And nobody wanted to challenge them just in case it actually was Elvish, and they came across as stupid.

"So what is it you want?" continued the boy. "Maybe I can help."

The King sighed, not really knowing where to start. "I want the world to stop fighting," he began. "I want the Trolls to leave alone what is rightfully ours. I want to be able to sleep at night without worrying that every Ogre in the East wants me dead. I want to know that my people trust me, and believe what I believe. And I want to know that our Elvish allies are behind us, in times of peace and in times of war."

He turned back to the boy. "Can you help me, Flibble? Can you help with any of that?"

The boy paused. "Exercise," he said at last. "That will help you sleep."

King Wyndham laughed again. "Thanks," he said, "any other advice?"

He shook his head. "I think you need the Gods to help you with the rest. Although," he frowned as he was speaking, "You don't worship the real Gods, do you? You worship something weird instead."

"Yes, well," replied the King, not really in the mood to teach the boy a lesson in world religion. "Our Gods are different from yours, but that doesn't mean they are wrong."

"But how are they different?" asked the Elf.

"Well, for starters we only worship five."

"Five?" replied the boy, finally astonished at something he had said. "Only five?"

The Elves worshipped 46 different Gods, or at least they did the last time King Wyndham had checked. For all he knew they could have knocked up a couple more by now.

"Yes, only five," he replied. The boy still looked slightly shocked. "It's not a competition," added the King.

Admittedly if they did hold a competition for who had the most Gods, the Elves would win rather comfortably.

"Yes, but five? I mean, that's not even one for every day of the week."

"Hmmm." The King had never looked at it that way before. "It's what we believe. Every Human in the realm worships the same five Gods. The God of Birth, the God of Death, the God of Re-birth, the God of Re-death and the God of Re-resurrection."

"Right," said the boy. "Well…"

King Wyndham stopped him before he could start listing every one of their Gods. He didn't have all day, and besides he had heard them all before. His favourite was probably Elgaret; the God of Standing Still. It was rather impressive that they actually worshipped someone whose power was to stand there and do absolutely nothing.

Of course his statue in Lanthyn received a lot of attention. This was partly because some Elves still believed the rumour that it wasn't a statue at all, but the God himself; his powers were just so good that no-one ever noticed the difference.

Then of course there were Tarterya and Sulder, the Gods of Happiness and Sadness. Why they needed two different Gods for this was beyond the King's comprehension. The High Elf had once explained that sadness was an important part of life. Until we know sadness we can never be truly happy. He found this a rather depressing thought, and immediately went to pray to the God of Happiness to try and make himself feel better.

"Have you ever seen the Oracle, Flibble?" asked the King, changing the subject slightly.

The boy's eyes widened. "The Oracle? No, I haven't. Not really."

"Not really?"

"Well, no then," replied the boy, "although I did see a painting of her once."

The King smiled.

"Have you seen her?" he asked, his eyes widening still further. In fact, any wider and he would probably need a second face.

"Yes," replied King Wyndham. "Although not for over twenty years."

"Wow," exclaimed the young Elf, "What's she like? Does she look like the painting?"

"The painting you saw of her, which I've never seen?" asked the King. "Sure, why not?"

The boy nodded. "And what did she tell you?"

The King turned his head to face the trees on the north side of the clearing. He could just about make out the snow-capped mountains in the background.

"She told me that one day, I would be King of all Humans."

"Amazing," said the boy.

"Yes," replied the King. "I don't know how she did it. Although the fact that I was a prince at the time probably helped."

The young Elf nodded. "Is that where you're going now, Wyndham? Is that why you're so far away from your own realm?"

The King nodded, wondering when was the last time that someone had called him by his own name, rather than 'sire' or 'your grace'. It was partly refreshing, but mostly quite annoying. Still, he didn't see the need to correct the kid.

"And what do you hope she will tell you this time?" he asked.

King Wyndham turned back towards the boy.

"I'm hoping she'll say that we can win this war. But she might say that we have no chance, and should lay down our swords. Either way is fine. I don't need sugar coating, I just need answers."

"And what if she doesn't give you any?"

"Then the next time you see a painting of her, there's every chance it will have a foot shaped hole through it."

Chapter 15

There was something about being a Human in a land full of Pixies that sounded quite appealing. Wherever you went, you could be fairly sure that you would be the tallest person there. Everyone would look up to you, and marvel at the giant that stood before them.

You could probably amaze them with your slightly superior strength, or play that game where you hold something they want just above their heads, then lifting it slightly whenever they come close to reaching it. Hours of fun.

That was why the phrase 'like a Human in a land full of Pixies' was often used to imply they were in a great situation; a leader amongst followers. Unfortunately the reality was often quite different, since the novelty would soon wear off and the Human would begin to realise they were too tall for the place and didn't really fit in anywhere.

The whole land was designed for people who were four feet tall; and Humans would generally either have to crawl, duck their heads or do a fairly impressive limbo in order to get into any of their buildings. And that was why the phrase 'like a Human in a land full of Pixies' became increasingly used to describe someone who couldn't stand up straight.

After three days of trudging through the Pixie lands, Ridley and Fulton both thought the novelty had well and truly worn off. What Ridley would have given to spend the night in an inn with normal sized beds. At least Fulton was a few inches shorter; his feet probably didn't even touch the floor that much when he slept.

As they began another long day of walking through these sort-of magical lands, Ridley wondered how the Pixies could still be so unprepared to accommodate Humans. It was the 14th age, surely they could build a few Human-sized beds somewhere. He was fairly sure that there were plenty of places in Peria that could easily accommodate Pixies; although admittedly they were probably all just designed for children.

He then wondered whether Pixies were so different from children. They were short, often behaved oddly and were still slightly obsessed with silly things like potions and magic. Then he thought that was a bit harsh, and he should probably stop thinking it.

They had been travelling through Madesco since the night before last, and despite the annoyingly small buildings it was a rather splendid city. It was the capital of the whole realm, although it was hard to really know where it began and where it ended.

This was mainly because it was so widely dispersed, with so many gardens and fields between buildings. You could probably walk for hours without seeing so much as a stone. People would sometimes say you could never truly leave Madesco; even if you didn't see a building for days you were probably still in the city.

They were wrong, but didn't tend to accept it unless they happened to wander so far that they reached the Goblin realm. And at that point they would be too busy hiding in fear from hideous green creatures that they didn't really care about cartographical terminology anymore.

"I still think we could do more to make the most of this place," said Fulton, as he gazed across the wide path they had now found themselves on.

There were a few buildings either side, but the two Humans were walking right in the middle. There was probably some sort of protocol about which side to walk on, but nobody had said anything so far. Perhaps they were too afraid to do so since these Humans were so tall and intimidating. Or perhaps they just didn't want to cause a fuss. In fairness, there didn't seem to be anyone else on the path as far as Fulton could see. Despite the city being rather a maze, he was fairly sure they were coming to the outskirts of it now.

"Making the most of this place?" replied Ridley after a slight pause. "You seem to keep forgetting that we're not here as tourists. We are in fact on a rather important mission, and don't have time to take in all the sights of the Pixie realm." Not that there were any sights Ridley was particularly keen to take in.

"That's not what I meant," said Fulton. "I mean we should take advantage of what the Pixies can offer us. Supplies;

things we're going to need when we get to the Goblin realm."

"We've got plenty," said Ridley straight back, "bread, meat, even vegetables. And I've got about as much water as I can carry in my baggage without falling flat on my back."

"Well yes," said Fulton. He had to acknowledge that they had been fairly good at stocking up whenever they had stopped for the night. "But I'm not just talking about food and water. We're in Pixie land, a realm full of magic and wonder. Just think what other useful things these folk may be able to provide."

Ridley sighed. It was times like this that he wondered whether Fulton really was 22 years old, or just a child standing on a pair of stilts. The boy probably still believed in fairies, and they had almost certainly been wiped out years ago.

"And what magic and wonderful supplies were you thinking of, exactly?" he asked. "Perhaps we could buy a couple of wands, which might well come in handy in case we run out of arrows and need something to poke the Goblins with?"

Fulton looked slightly taken aback, clearly unprepared for such a high level of sarcasm.

"Or how about a vial of invisibility dust? I hear that was all the rage back in the 12th age. Of course the fact that it only seemed to work at night, when it was pitch dark anyway was a fairly odd coincidence."

At last Fulton butted in. "I wasn't thinking about magic wands or invisibility dust. I know that some of these Pixie inventions haven't stacked up, but you can't just dismiss everything they have."

"Hmmm," replied Ridley, "and what did you have in mind?"

"What about healing potion?" he said.

Ridley let out a noise which was sort of a cross between a grunt and a laugh. It sounded a bit weird so he coughed a couple of times to try and pretend he had done it by accident. He then recovered and spoke.

"What about healing potion? You mean the stuff that people used to claim would magically cure you from any ailments you suffered?"

"Well, yes…" replied Fulton.

"And have you ever seen it work?" asked Ridley, who then continued before his companion had a chance to answer. "For hundreds of years that stuff has been around. And the only things that have got any healthier are a few Pixies' bank balances."

"That's not true," said Fulton. "My mother used to give it to us when I was a child. She used to swear by it, she said no matter what happened, you were never in danger as long as you've got a jar of healing potion."

"Right, and does she still say that?"

"Well no, she's dead now."

"I'm so sorry," replied Ridley, deciding not to draw this out any further.

He noticed Fulton had slowed his pace, so he did the same until they both came to a halt in the middle of the path.

He looked down at his companion, who was clearly a little upset. Although despite this, he somehow still seemed to be smiling slightly.

"Listen," he reached out his arm to touch Fulton's shoulder, then decided this was too much and withdrew it fairly quickly. "I didn't mean to cause any offence."

"It's okay," said Fulton, "you weren't to know."

Ridley paused for a moment. "I tell you what," he began, "if we come across a shop that sells the stuff, we'll stop by and pick some up."

He was happy enough to say this, after all they were now in the outskirts of the city. The chances of them suddenly coming across a healing potion store seemed rather unlikely, and they probably wouldn't even know one if they came across it.

Fulton smiled. "We don't have to do that."

"Honestly, it's okay," replied Ridley.

"Well in that case, great! Because we passed one a few minutes ago."

Fulton then abruptly turned and started heading towards a small stone building on the left hand side of the path. At least, Ridley thought it was made of stone, but it was so far away that it was hard to tell.

How in the Known World Fulton knew this place had healing potion, only the Gods knew. He probably didn't; more than likely he was just bored and wanted to take a detour. Ridley rolled his eyes and ran to catch up with him.

As they drew closer the only thing Ridley could tell was that it definitely was made of stone, but it was also covered in green plants which seemed to be taking over the walls. The place looked abandoned, or if anyone did live here they clearly didn't make much of an effort to maintain it.

He looked up at the roof, although he barely actually needed to raise his neck given this was only a bungalow, and a Pixie bungalow at that. As he did so, he saw three wooden sticks, all nailed down at the base and joined together at the top. As if someone had tried to write the letter 'M' if an exciting new way, but it probably didn't catch on.

"That's it," said Fulton, and Ridley noticed that he was also looking at the same symbol. "That's an apothecary sign, it means they must have medicines here."

Ridley nodded, while at the same time furrowing his brow. He wondered how he had seen this from so far away, and more to the point, how Fulton knew what it meant.

He laughed. "It's called reading, you really should try it sometime," he said, as he noticed the blank face staring at him.

Ridley rolled his eyes once more. He knew how to read, of course he did. It was part of basic training in the army; vitally important in case your commanding officer lost his voice from shouting so much that he had to write everything down.

But he clearly hadn't had the education of his companion. Fulton was probably able to read and write before he was even old enough to drink. It did make Ridley wonder whether he had been thinking about this all wrong. While his companion was doubtlessly lacking in the brain department, maybe he did possess some useful knowledge which could help them in their quest. Who knows, he could even end up saving them both.

"Maybe they'll have some invisibility dust too!"

Or maybe he would be the reason they both died horribly.

Fulton knocked on the door. No answer. He knocked again. They both waited in silence.

"Maybe it's not an apothecary symbol at all. Maybe it actually means 'please don't knock, I'm sleeping'," muttered Ridley.

Fulton paused for a moment, crouched down and pressed

his ear to the front door.

"Or maybe it means, 'this place is falling to pieces, and nobody has lived here for years'."

He then stopped, as it was clear that Fulton wasn't listening to him. Instead, he seemed to be listening very intently to something else.

"There are people inside all right, I can hear them."

He then put his eye to the keyhole.

Ridley hesitated. "Maybe we should just go," he said.

Fulton turned back with another trademark smile on his face. "Don't tell me you're scared?"

"No, of course I'm not scared," he replied.

He genuinely wasn't, but obviously the more you tell people you're not scared, the more you sound scared. It's a bit like being drunk or crazy; the more you say you're not, the more you are.

"It's just a few harmless Pixies," said Fulton.

"Exactly!" snapped Ridley, "and they might be slightly startled when they see a scary Human staring through the keyhole of what is probably just some nice person's home."

Fulton accepted he had a point, and moved away from the door. Instead he knocked again, but this time louder.

"Hello?" he said, a little too loudly. "We're not here to scare you, we just want to buy some of your products."

Ridley shook his head.

"What?" said Fulton, "surely it's worth a try?"

"Maybe you should confirm you're not going to murder them and steal their stuff too, that would put their minds at ease."

"Yes well at least I'm trying! In fact," said Fulton, looking through the keyhole once more, "I think they heard me."

Chapter 16

"The merchants are probably just early," said Samorus as he made his way to the front door.

"Don't they always come at nine o'clock?" asked Petra, trotting behind him.

"Well what time is it now?" he said, stopping a few yards before the door.

"Thursday."

"Hmmm. So they are four days early."

"That is pretty early. Maybe it's someone else?"

Petra's eyes widened. Nobody else ever seemed to visit this place. A stranger knocking at the door was about the most exciting thing that happened here. Apart from discovering that she had magic powers the like of which no-one had ever seen before. She could make living creatures spontaneously burst into flames with a flick of her hand. That was pretty exciting. But apart from that, this was the most exciting thing that ever happened here.

Samorus turned back to her. "Who else?"

"Could be a friend of yours?"

A short silence followed.

"Or a member of your family?"

Another silence. In fairness, the old Pixie never talked about himself, surely there was a chance he still had some family members somewhere? Judging by his expression, she guessed probably not.

The knocking continued. Whoever it was seemed rather keen for them to open the door. Either that, or they just really enjoyed knocking.

"What if they're dangerous? What if they're Ogres or Goblins, come to hurt us?" rasped Samorus, who seemed to be changing his expression every few seconds.

"The basement is full of healing potion, I'd like to see them try!" replied Petra, although this probably wasn't the time for jokes.

The old Pixie didn't look back, but walked past the door

and picked up a small wooden stick. His walking stick. He
never used the thing; Petra wasn't sure why he even had it.
And then it came to her; he was planning on using it as a
weapon, just in case. Just in case whoever was at the door
was an axe-wielding maniac, who would somehow be
overpowered if an old Pixie hit him with a walking stick.

Another knock. Surely they would give up if he didn't
answer soon.

Samorus slowly put his hand on the door handle and turned
it. Then for some reason he pulled the door wide open with a
sudden jolt, as if to shock whoever was behind the door.

Admittedly they did look slightly shocked; although also
probably slightly relieved that they didn't have to continue
knocking. Petra's eyes widened as she stared at the door. It
wasn't Ogres or Goblins. It was two Humans. One tall, dark
and rugged; the other a little shorter, blonder and somewhat
younger. Both towered above the door, slightly crouching so
they could see inside.

"Yes?" said Samorus rather aggressively.

Evidently he wasn't at all reassured by the fact that they
weren't Ogres or Goblins; his hand still clasped his walking
stick as if it were ready to spring into action any second.

"Hi," said the young looking Human, with a nervous smile
on his face. "We just wanted to see if you had
any...um...healing potion?"

"Who wants to know?" replied the old Pixie.

"We do," the young Human looked at his companion and
then back to Samorus. "We're merchants, spices mostly. Our
business is our own."

"But you just told me your business," replied the Pixie.
"What you didn't tell me are your names."

There was an awkward silence as the two Humans looked
at each other.

"Our names are our own," said the young Human, before
being interrupted by his companion.

"Enough of this," he said. "We have money. All we want is
a small jar of healing potion and we'll be on our way."

Petra still stood there, staring. She had seen Humans before
of course. Closer to the centre of Madesco there were often a
fair few wandering around, showing off their superior height
and ability to grow unnecessarily long beards. But these two

were different. Her gaze was drawn to the young one in particular; there was something about his bowed head and nervous stammer that made him seem quite endearing. A couple of times his eyes had met hers directly, and somehow she felt unable to look away.

Samorus didn't seem any calmer than before.

"So you're two Humans, who have their own names but won't reveal what they are. You're merchants who deal in spices, apparently with the exception of healing potion. And you've come all the way to a small house on the edge of Madesco just to buy a small jar of the stuff?"

The dark haired Human remained unmoved. "Look, can you help us or not?" he said.

"Hmmm. Well aside from the fact that I already have my own buyers, who generally want more than a small jar; I wouldn't sell to someone I don't trust."

"You should have just made up names," butted in Petra, without thinking. A silence followed, and the other three all turned their heads towards her; as if they hadn't noticed she was there until now. And since everyone was now staring at her in a more than uncomfortable way, she thought she should probably continue to speak.

"It's easily done, just say the first thing that comes to your heads. That way it doesn't look suspicious."

They were still all staring at her, so she carried on, trying to think of something else to say.

"Or you could have just given your real names. We're perfectly harmless, and I believe that you are too. Even if my friend doesn't."

That was surely the first time she had ever referred to Samorus as a friend, but what else was she supposed to call him? Her boss? The guy who's teaching her magic?

"I'm Petra, by the way. And you can believe that's my real name if you want."

As she said this she looked directly at the young blonde Human, and a smile began to appear across her face.

Thankfully the Human smiled back at her.

"I'm Fulton, and this is Ridley." He turned to his companion. "Sorry, you don't mind me giving your name, do you?"

His companion rolled his eyes.

"Well there you have it," he said, turning back to Samorus. "Anything else you need to know before we can do this trade? How about our favourite colours? Our hopes and dreams? The names of our first childhood pets?"

"Blinky," said Fulton, "he was a little white rabbit, could never keep his eyes open."

Samorus gestured for the two Humans to come in, apparently at least a little reassured that they probably weren't Ogres, Trolls or axe-wielding maniacs. Although the expression on his face didn't seem to have changed.

"Take a seat," said the old Pixie, and they both duly obliged, sitting at the rather small wooden table on one side of the room.

It was small by Pixie standards; for the Humans it probably looked like a foot stool. They didn't seem to mind though, Petra guessed they were just glad they could sit down rather than having to keep ducking their heads.

"We keep all our produce in the basement," said Samorus. "I'll just be a minute."

He made his way towards the stairs. Petra, not knowing what else to do, nervously joined the Humans at the table. She smiled at both of them in turn, receiving a cheery smile back from Fulton and a sort of miserable forced smile from Ridley. She then turned back to Fulton.

"So where are you two heading? Is that something I'm allowed to ask?"

"It's okay," he replied. "We're actually going to the Goblin realm. To Nuberim."

"Oh wow!" said Petra, "That's exciting. Is that for the Dernbach festival?"

"Yes, it's a great place for traders like us; always buzzing with people, with money in their pockets."

"It sounds amazing. How many times have you been before?" she asked.

"Ah, well never," said Fulton, "it's just what I've heard."

Petra nodded. "I've never been either, I've never even been to the Goblin realm."

"You should definitely go sometime," replied Fulton. "In fact, why don't... actually never mind."

He was glad he was able to stop himself from suggesting she came with them. His acting was so good that for a moment he forgot they weren't actually going there to trade at all. And he would probably struggle to keep up the pretence when it came to shooting an arrow at the Goblin King. Most traders didn't do that sort of thing.

"What?" said Petra.

"No really, never mind."

There was a short silence, and Petra decided she should probably change the subject.

"So you told us your first childhood pet, but you never said your favourite colour," she said, smiling.

Fulton chuckled. "Green," he said, "definitely green."

"You mean a dark green, like an Ogre? Or more of a Goblin coloured pale green?"

"More of a bright green actually," he replied, looking directly at her eyes.

Petra grinned. She didn't know what to say. Did the Human really almost invite her to come along with them to the Goblin realm? He had stopped himself, but she was sure that was what he was about to say.

"So have you always worked in potions?" said Fulton.

"Since I came of age, yes," she replied. "Although that was only a year ago. I also do a bit of magic now and again."

She thought it was okay to say that. A lot of Pixies could do magic; as long as she didn't reveal the true extent of her powers it was surely fine.

"Magic, really?" replied Fulton, looking genuinely impressed. Samorus appeared again having climbed back up the stairs, with a small jar in his hand.

"So you two are wizards as well as potion makers?" Fulton said to the old Pixie.

He stopped in his tracks, dropping the jar of healing potion which smashed on the floor. He then looked down at the broken jar; and without saying a word turned round and went back down the stairs. Though he did give a cold glance to Petra as he did so.

Petra then hurriedly got to her feet, grabbed a broom from the closet and began to clean up the mess.

"Well just a little magic, now and again," she said, trying to cover herself. "Samorus is the real wizard, I'm only just starting to learn really."

"Well it's still impressive," replied Fulton, "what kind of

tricks can you do?"

Petra swept the remains of the glass into a bucket before she answered. Or at least sort of answered.

"Um, well…" she said, sort of answering.

"Feel free to show us if it's too difficult to describe," said Fulton, beaming, apparently thinking this would help.

She looked down at her feet, her rich dark hair more or less covering her face.

"I'm not very good," she said. "It's not really something you can just show people."

"Ah yes, I've heard that said before," piped in Ridley, who seemed to have taken no interest in the conversation until now. "Magic only works when no-one is there to witness it, isn't that the general idea?"

"Ignore my friend, he can be a bit cynical sometimes," said Fulton. "But don't worry, you don't have to do any tricks for us."

"Maybe next time," she said, smiling back at Fulton.

Samorus returned once again, with another jar of healing potion as if the previous incident hadn't happened. He walked straight over to Ridley, who got up from his chair, hitting his head on the ceiling and then ducking down in one swift movement as if it were all deliberate.

"How much is that going to cost us?" he asked, realising he probably should have asked this at the very beginning.

"Three silvers," said Samorus.

"Is that negotiable?" replied Ridley.

"No. Never, not a chance" said the old Pixie. "Oh well all right, two silvers. No more, no less."

"Fine," said Ridley, as he parted with the two coins.

"Thank you," replied Samorus, giving the jar to Ridley in return.

"I never realised it was so cheap," said Fulton, once again showing his general enthusiasm regardless of the situation.

"Indeed," said Ridley, "It was either this or throw the coins down a wishing well, after all."

The others laughed as Ridley wondered which of these would have actually been the better investment.

"Well anyway, thank you for being so hospitable but I'm afraid we really can't stay any longer," he continued.

"Yes, you're right," added Fulton, "long road ahead of us."

He got up with a jolt, and just like his companion also hit his head on the ceiling. Unfortunately the jolt made him drop his satchel, which opened slightly and spilt a few of its contents on the floor.

Fulton and Ridley both stared at the bag in silence. It looked like they were okay; just a few clothes had fallen out and a couple of apples rolled along the floor.

"Sorry, let me get gather those up," said Fulton.

"Wait," said Samorus, who was now looking intently at the bag himself. "What kind of a spice merchant carries a quiver full of arrows?"

Chapter 17

People would often say that silence is golden. If that were actually true then the quality of it must still vary rather a lot; from the perfectly polished 24 carat silence one might encounter on a warm summer's day by the sea, to a nasty slab of 9 carat silence that might result from forgetting your wife's birthday. Which was on the same day as your anniversary, which also coincided with that friend's fishing trip you really wanted to go on.

In a small hovel on the outskirts of Madesco, two Humans and two Pixies were experiencing a silence that was closer to a sharp piece of hideously fake gold you might have the misfortune to cut your foot on during a barefoot stroll.

When he realised what had just happened, Ridley didn't think twice about pulling out the dagger he kept concealed in his breeches. He pointed the sharp end directly at Samorus. The old Pixie, in turn, held his walking stick with both hands in front of him, as if ready to spring into action at the drop of a needle.

They were at a stalemate. Ridley could stab this Pixie to death, but he risked getting an unpleasant knock with a stick if he did so. Samorus could give this Human a nasty bang on the knees, but he risked being stabbed to death if he did so.

Fulton and Petra were both frozen to the spot. Unable to move. Unable to speak.

At last, the silence could continue no longer.

"You're risking your life, old timer," said Ridley, maintaining his stare.

"Tell me who you really are!" cried Samorus, ignoring this completely.

Fulton found his voice once again.

"Put the weapon down Ridley! They are two harmless Pixies. Whatever they know, or think they know about us, it couldn't possibly matter!"

"It matters," replied Ridley. "It matters a lot. I'm already putting my life on the line for my realm."

"And a hundred and twenty silvers," added Fulton under his breath.

"And it's enough of a risk as it is without leaving a trail of clues behind us!" continued Ridley furiously.

"What clues?" replied Fulton, desperately trying to remain calm. "All they know is that we're carrying a bow and arrows."

"And that's all they'll ever know!" growled Ridley, lifting his blade above his head.

"STOP" cried Petra.

The blade came crashing down, but never reached its intended target. A flash of white light appeared, and struck the metal head on. Before Ridley knew what had happened he dropped the remains of the weapon, which landed on the ground with a thud.

Ridley had never meant to hurt the old Pixie; all he meant to do was slice his silly walking stick in two. But he didn't even get to do that, since the damn thing had burst into flames. Wait... daggers don't burst into flames? What just happened?

A 14 carat silence followed as he and Fulton turned to the apparent source of this flame. Samorus started to breathe heavily but also did the same, albeit looking slightly less astonished.

Petra put her hands behind her back and did her best to look as nonchalant as possible. Three pairs of eyes were now staring at her. She thought about whistling, but then thought better of it.

"Well I did tell you to stop," was all she could think of to say.

Ridley said nothing. He was still in shock.

"Did you just..." started Fulton.

No one interrupted him, he just didn't know what to say next.

"Did you just...make fire?" he added finally.

Petra looked at him and nodded. "I did a bit, yes. Sorry," she said.

His eyes widened. "But what? How? So you're...a wizard?"

"Well..." said Petra.

Samorus sighed. "No," he said. "I'm a wizard. This little

girl is something much, much more."

"What do you mean?" said Fulton.

"I mean she has talent that I have never seen before. That no-one has ever seen before. She can do things I didn't even know were possible."

"But how? Since when? How long have you known?" Now it was Ridley's turn to ask a load of annoying questions.

Samorus moved to pick up the remains of Ridley's dagger, which was nothing more than a mound on the floor.

"Not long. Not long at all." He turned to Petra. "It just sort of happened one day."

Fulton's eyes looked like they were going to pop out of his head.

"Have you thought about what you could do with this? All the amazing things you could achieve?"

Petra smiled at him. "Like what?" she said.

"Well…" Fulton hadn't actually got that far. "You could keep peoples' homes warm in winter?"

She laughed. "Or create light during the darkest nights. Torches for all to see."

"You could burn whole cities to the ground!" he continued. The others looked at him. "Not that you would… necessarily want to," he added.

Samorus nodded.

"Exactly," he said, "this is something very dangerous. We have to be really careful."

Ridley thought for a second. "Nobody else knows about this, do they?" he said.

The old Pixie shook his head. "No, and we have to keep it that way. At least until we can figure out what we're going to do about this."

"You want my advice?" said Ridley, who then proceeded to give them his advice despite the fact that neither of them responded. "I think you should go somewhere safe and secure. Go to the White Castle, it can only be two days from here."

"You mean Lady Vernipula?"

"She'll know what to do," continued Ridley. "After all, it's either that or sit here and wait for someone else to walk by and discover your secret. Someone taller, greener, and even keener to burn cities to the ground than my friend here."

Fulton smiled. They had come across an amazing girl with

magic powers. And Ridley had just referred to him as a friend. This really was the best day.

"You may be right," replied Samorus.

"I think he is," said Petra.

"Me too," added Fulton.

Samorus frowned. "But we can't just pack up and leave. What about all this healing potion? We have two more barrels to prepare before Monday."

"Just fill them up with water, no-one will know the difference," muttered Ridley.

"Get Petra to set fire to them and pretend they never existed," said Fulton.

Petra smiled. "Or we could just wait until they're finished, and then leave?" she said.

"Yes I think probably that one," replied Samorus, not dignifying the two men with as much as a glance. "It should only take us a couple of days and we can leave them for collection."

"And then onto the White Castle," said Petra. "I don't suppose..." she looked back at Fulton. "I don't suppose you two would be able to join us?"

Fulton looked hopefully at Ridley as if to say, 'I know we can't go, but can we? Can we just go, even though we can't?'

To his surprise Ridley didn't answer straight away; he seemed to genuinely be considering this. And then he said no.

"I'm afraid there's no chance of that," he began. "We have some rather important business to attend to. In fact, we really can't stay here any longer."

And with that he hoisted up his luggage and gestured to Fulton to do the same.

"But I wish you the best of luck," he added as he made for the door.

"Just a minute," interrupted Samorus. "You know our secret, now surely you can tell us yours. Where are you really going?"

"We're merch..." started Fulton, but didn't even bother getting to the end of the sentence.

"What do you think about the Goblins?" butted in Ridley. "And the war between the Humans and the Ogres?"

Samorus shrugged. "I don't really follow that stuff to be honest. I just make potions."

"Very well," said Ridley with a sigh. "We actually are off to Nuberim, but not to sell spices. We're going to kill the Goblin king," he added, before opening the door and walking out without saying another word.

"Nice meeting you," said Fulton to Petra as he then swiftly followed, leaving the two Pixies wide eyed and open mouthed, trying to take in everything that had just happened.

The two Humans marched on in silence, both also trying to take in everything that had just happened. It wasn't until they had got a hundred yards from the hut that they heard a soft voice behind them.

"Wait!"

They both turned round to see the young Pixie trotting after them.

Ridley stopped in his tracks, wondering what in the Known World was going to happen now. What if this girl didn't want the Goblin king dead, and was going to try and stop them. What if she intended to set them both on fire or turn them into frogs? Not that she could do the latter as far as he was aware, but the former was presumably bad enough.

Fulton wasn't worried, mainly because he hadn't even considered this. As he started walking back towards Petra he was too preoccupied wondering whether she used some sort of magic to make her hair that colour; surely it wasn't naturally such a deep black.

They both stopped as they caught up with each other.

"I thought the Goblin King was good?" she began, grinning as she spoke. "I thought he was the one of the friendliest kings they have ever had."

Fulton was quite taken aback. He didn't know what she was about to say, but he certainly didn't expect this. If he had done, he probably would have said that although the Goblin King has had a good relationship with the Humans, he is still part of the reason they are at war. And better to have a cold relationship if it finally brings about peace across the Known World.

He didn't say this. Instead all he could manage was "Umm well…"

"It doesn't matter," replied Petra. "I didn't come after you to talk about politics."

Fulton was still flustered, and this time decided not to say anything at all.

"And I'm not here to ask if I can come with you," continued Petra.

"So why are you here?" asked Fulton, finding his voice at last.

She paused. "I don't know," she started. "I guess I wanted to tell you to take care, and make sure you come back in one piece."

He smiled. "And the same to you," he said.

"And...I also wanted to say that I hope I can see you again. Sometime."

Fulton began to blush. "You will. I promise I'll be back, and that our paths will cross again."

He bent down and kissed her on the cheek.

"Goodbye," she said, as she turned and began to run back the way she had come.

"Goodbye," whispered Fulton as he watched her slowly disappearing towards the hut.

He then turned back to his companion, who was clearly doing the opposite of smiling. Fulton didn't look directly at Ridley as he caught up with him once more.

Once again, he was trying to take in what had just happened. And wondering why he had just made a promise to her that he was almost certainly unable to keep. If they did manage to make it back from Nuberim, how in the Known World was he supposed to find this girl? Just spend all day looking for bonfires and hope for the best?

They continued on their way. Ridley eventually broke the silence.

"You know she's half your height?" he said.

"Two thirds," replied Fulton. "At least two thirds. I'd say it's more like three quarters actually. Besides," he added, "she's a wizard, she could always make herself taller if she needed to."

"Or burn your legs off," replied Ridley sarcastically.

The two men looked at the road ahead. They both knew that the best part of the journey was now behind them. In two days' time they would reach the Goblin realm, and a few days after that they would have just one chance to change the Known World forever. And hopefully do so without anyone burning anybody else's legs off.

Chapter 18

"You can say what you like about Goblins, but they don't half know how to build a wall," muttered General Lang to the Lord Protector.

Higarth nodded. There wasn't a great deal about Goblins that impressed him, but he had to admit that the main gates at Nuberim did look rather spectacular. Two great stone arches towered above them, with long metal pillars extending all the way to the ground. And on either side, the grey stone walls which continued all the way around the city.

They had clearly been refurbished since the last time the Lord Protector had come here. Evidently no expense was spared.

He did wonder why they went to all this trouble. It would have made sense if this were the only entrance to the city. In actual fact there were many; 138 the last time the Ogres had checked. Tunnels and caves extended well below the ground, and surfaced on all sides of these walls.

Perhaps the Goblins just hoped that if they were ever at war, their attackers would at least have the courtesy to invade through the main entrance. Maybe they would be so in awe of the gates that none of them would notice the other 137 ways of getting in.

Or maybe the one Goblin with half a brain was off sick the day they made these decisions.

Of course courtesy was the only reason they now stood outside these gates. One problem with the gates being so spectacular was that they took forever to open. Higarth and his Ogres had been waiting here so long that they could have probably walked around the whole city by now, and then gone back the other way.

Finally the gates were just about fully parted, and they made their way swiftly into the city. Not that they needed to hurry; it would take another forever to close them again.

It was a small contingent that the Lord Protector had taken with him to the Goblins. He didn't see the need for any more than twenty; after all he wanted to make as little an impression as possible. He wanted the Ogres to be barely noticeable. He wanted people in the future to look back on this time and say 'do you remember the day when King Grieber was killed?' 'Were there any Ogres there?' 'I don't remember' 'Oh, they can't have been the ones who killed him then'. Or something like that.

The Lord Protector had brought three of his trusted Generals, whom he knew well and who knew every part of his plan. And a group of peons whom he barely knew and who presumably knew very little about anything. And that was it. He didn't bring any of his wives; not even that one he quite liked.

It wasn't long after they had entered the city that they encountered some familiar faces.

"My Lord Protector," bellowed the voice of King Grieber as he held out his embracing arms.

Higarth bowed his head, as usual doing whatever he could to avoid touching this Goblin. Ogres didn't really do hugs; they were a sign of sensitivity; and therefore a sign of weakness.

"My King," he replied, shuddering inside as he always did.

He had always hated having to recognise this Goblin as a King, when he was a foot shorter than him and about half as intelligent. 'My inferior creature' would have been much closer to the mark.

King Grieber then nodded back, and the Lord Protector began to exchange pleasantries with the King's Companions.

"My Queen," he said, bowing his head to her as he did so.

"Prince Grumio," he nodded again as he made his way down the line. "Prince Nutrec," he continued. "Nice to see you again," he defaulted to once he started forgetting their names.

His Generals followed suit, and for several minutes there was nothing but a series of Ogres and Goblins bowing to each other.

When it reached a point that everyone had just about acknowledged everyone else, the King turned to the Lord Protector.

"This way," he said, gesturing to a large hole in the ground only a few yards away.

A few Goblin guards led the way, every one of them bearing torches. The Goblin King and the Lord Protector followed, with the others trailing behind.

It's probably a bit unfair to call it a hole in the ground; it was actually a rather well designed set of stone steps which took them directly into one of the main underground tunnels.

"It seems like a while since you were last here," said King Grieber as they made their way down the steps.

"Too long," answered Higarth mechanically. "A lot seems to have changed."

"Thank you," replied the King, apparently finding a compliment in that somewhere. "Our builders have been doing a fine job."

"I'll say," said the Lord Protector. "Those gates are looking fierce, as big and strong as I have ever seen them."

They were too far down the steps to see the gates any more, but Higarth was fairly sure they were still wide open. Maybe by the time they leave in 5 days' time they'll have just about closed them again.

"Indeed," said the King. "It's a new material, you see. Recton stone, it's lighter than the stone we have in Nuberim, yet just as strong."

"Ah," said Higarth, "recton stone. So the Humans supplied it to you?"

"That's right," he replied. "Very reasonable too. I don't know how they do it, but they're able to supply us with all we need. It's made such an improvement to the city."

The Lord Protector made a noise in disagreement. A sort of grunt that sounded like a sneeze trying to get out.

"Well it certainly has made a difference to the gates," he said.

"Not just the gates," replied the King. "We use it everywhere. The walls, the floors, the stairs."

The Lord Protector looked down at the steps which he now realised had most likely come from the Humans too. He almost tripped but managed to stop himself, realising he didn't really have much of a choice but to continue his way down them.

It was all rather shocking, yet at the same time he wasn't at all surprised. He barely recognised the Goblins anymore; even 50 years ago they wouldn't have let a Human near their realm. Now they had practically let them design it.

Of course there was some recton stone in Yerin tower, but that was an accident. One which would never happen again if any of his Ogres still enjoyed having their heads attached to their bodies.

This was different. The Goblins were different. And it was all because of this sad excuse for a King.

They reached the bottom of the stairs, which opened out into a great tunnel, about fifty feet wide and at least twenty feet high. It was lit up on all sides and bustling with life. Some Goblins were working on the walls. Others stood talking by the sides; while most were simply walking one way or the other, not bothering to talk or acknowledge each other's presence.

They took a left turn and started walking down the tunnel. A space began to open up around them, presumably because people realised this was the King and they probably shouldn't get in his way. Some murmured "Good evening, my King," as they walked by.

"May the Gods be with you," he replied to a few of them.

Higarth soon began to recognise his surroundings. This tunnel led directly to Tygon Hollow, the King's main residence. It was sort of the Goblin equivalent of a palace, but also nothing like one in any way.

If an Ogre wanted to build a palace underground, they would probably dig a massive hole first and then start construction from scratch. Goblins preferred to do it in one step, digging away at the ground in such a way that rooms and passageways would form. Of course they would then add wood or stone, but only to stop it all from collapsing. Or for things like doors which you can't really make by digging.

An alchemist called Treborg the Great once claimed he had managed to dig a door in the ground; this was deemed impossible and it was generally agreed that he probably used magic, which was later deemed equally impossible, and the consensus then became that he had built it out of wood. People then began to question why he was called Treborg the Great in the first place, and by the time he died he was more widely known as Treborg the Distinctly Average.

Tygon Hollow, however, was anything but distinctly average. Similar to the gates of the city, the doors were unnecessarily big and looked newly refurbished. Guards were standing on both sides; great strong Goblins who were probably as big as some Ogres.

To the Lord Protector's relief, the doors seemed to open a lot quicker than those gates. As they did so, King Grieber turned to him again.

"The Guards will show you to your rooms once we're inside," he began. "The night is yet young, and we all have time to rest before the feast."

"Excellent, thank you," replied the Lord Protector. Of course he didn't need to rest, that was a sign of weakness. But he needed some time away from the Goblins.

"Something tells me we're all going to need our energy. Night one of the festival has only just begun," added the King.

The Lord Protector nodded. It was amazing how excited the Goblins always became about the Dernbach festival. Their Gods really meant a lot to them. What a shame everything they believed in was total rubbish.

As they entered Tygon Hollow the passage began to diverge in a number of places. It wasn't long before one of the guards gestured for Higarth to follow him, and for the Ogres and Goblins in the company to go their separate ways.

"I am sure everything will be to your satisfaction, but don't hesitate to send for me if otherwise," said the King as he turned away, going down another set of what looked like Human made steps.

"Thank you," replied the Lord Protector, moving towards this guard. His three Generals went the same way; the peons had already been led towards their separate quarters.

As Prince Grumio followed his father down the steps, he couldn't help but exchange a brief glance with the Lord Protector.

Higarth gave a slight nod. The prince's eyes seemed to say it all. They said 'I know what I'm about to do, and I'm scared. But I'll do it, because I'm also scared of you.'

Chapter 19

The Known World was a rather magical place. Of course very little magic ever actually happened, but it wasn't just about the magic. There were so many exciting creatures and always new things to discover.

So there was actually quite a lot still unknown about the Known World. Few people had ever ventured near the top of the Lonergan Mountains up North, where it was so cold that no living creature could survive there. Some claimed that yetis still dwelled in the higher most mountains, and since no living creature could survive in those mountains nobody could go up there and prove them wrong.

And of course there was the forest of Blackthearn, where the vegetation was so thick that it would completely block out the sunlight. There were apparently trees that were so big that they could swallow a Human whole, and still have room for dessert. Most people preferred the old fashioned types of trees which just stayed still and didn't try to eat anyone, so they tended to avoid this kind of forest.

But these gloriously unknown places were still part of the Known World. People at least knew they were there. They existed; and they could always visit them if they ever wanted to freeze to death or get eaten alive by vegetation.

What separated the Known World from the Unknown World was one thing. Water. There was a sea surrounding the whole of the Known World; and as far as anyone knew, no matter what direction you travelled in, there was nothing on the other side.

People had ventured out many times, heroically setting sail from the harbour hoping to be the first explorer ever to discover a new world. They would hoist up the ropes as hundreds of people cheered them on, waving goodbye with a smug smile on their faces. And then either disappear forever or more likely return a couple of days later, defeated, claiming they never wanted to discover a new world in the first place.

So people didn't generally even try any more, accepting that whatever was out there might forever remain unknown. But they couldn't help but stare out to sea sometimes, wondering what it could possibly be.

Some thought there was nothing; just water, water and more water. Others thought there were creatures in the water so vile and scary that no sailor could ever speak about them. One group of villagers thought that a land of paradise was waiting for them across the sea if only they believed hard enough. It still didn't seem to exist yet, but obviously that just meant they needed to believe harder.

And a rather large group of people had given up caring. King Wyndham was most certainly one of them. There was enough to worry about in the world which did exist without having to worry about a world which probably didn't.

It had been days since he had last heard from Carlom. The last message he received had said that everything was fine, which was a rather optimistic way of saying that everything was horrendous but it hadn't got any more horrendous since the last message. It had been weeks since the Trolls had last attacked. They were re-grouping, and his Humans were sitting in the fortress licking their wounds. His remaining soldiers were probably tired and weak, while the Trolls would only be getting stronger.

The King was beginning to question whether he should have come here at all; to the far North West of the Known World where messengers could barely reach him, where half the Elves could barely speak the common language, and where the sun barely bothered so show its face.

But he had to make the most of this opportunity. At least he kept convincing himself that he did. It had been over twenty years since he had last seen the Oracle, and now at last he had made it here again.

The Oracle lived in a stone house in the middle of absolutely nowhere. The King felt sorry for the two guards standing outside it, who presumably had a rather long commute from wherever they actually lived.

Both guards nodded as he and his company approached. They were expecting him. The King gestured to his own guards that he could go it alone from here. They wouldn't allow anyone else into the building anyway; it was too sacred.

Not that it looked very sacred from the outside. It was a dull grey colour, and only a couple of storeys high. Of course that wasn't what made it impressive. It was impressive because of its sheer age. It was far older than anyone could remember. Some said it was older than the world itself. But that was just silly.

One of the guards opened the door for the King; he walked straight through without saying a word. Despite how long it had been, this whole place was eerily familiar to him.

"Good morning," said a very unfamiliar voice, the second he had stepped through the door. A middle-aged Elf sat at a desk opposite him, looking pre-occupied with something despite her desk looking all but empty.

This was new. The last time he had come here he had seen the Oracle, and no-one else. He hadn't expected anyone to be here.

"Who are you?" he asked; a reasonable question under the circumstances.

"I hope you have had a safe journey," said the Elf, completely ignoring the question. "Here to see the Oracle?"

The King paused for a moment, wondering what she could possibly be expecting him to say to that.

"No, I came all this way just to say hi to those guards outside," he responded.

"Yes well there's no harm in asking," said the Elf, who seemed to be writing something on her desk and paying little attention to the King.

"Right, well is she ready to see me?" he asked.

"Not yet, your Grace," she replied. Apparently she recognised him, or was just making an educated guess because of the whopping great crown on his head. "First, I have to ask you a couple of questions."

Wyndham raised an eyebrow. "What questions? I don't have time for this."

Of course he had spent the best part of six days just to be here, and in truth he could probably spare a few more minutes. But this still seemed rather unnecessary.

"It'll only be a few minutes," continued the Elf. "Firstly, what's your full name?"

"Wyndham, King of all Men," he replied gruffly.

"Okay. And what is your profession?"

He paused. "King," he said at last.

The Elf continued to write on her parchment, without looking up at King Wyndham whom she had now established was a King by profession.

"And where is your usual place of residence?"

He was losing patience, but thought there was nothing he could do except continue.

"My main residence is in Peria, as you probably know."

"Yes, thank you," replied the Elf.

She probably didn't know, he thought to himself. *She had probably never even heard of it. She probably didn't even know there was a world outside of this building.*

"What do you do here when no-one's visiting? Which I'm assuming is almost all the time?" said the King.

"If you don't mind, your Grace, I'll ask the questions."

He did mind. But it wasn't worth saying anything. He just stood there, wondering why they hadn't even put a second chair in this room.

"Why haven't..."

She looked up from her paperwork.

"Never mind," he said.

"Well we're making progress," she continued. "How have you travelled here today?"

"I've ridden here mostly. And I have no idea what you're going to do with that information," replied the King.

"Thank you," said the Elf. "Now then. Is this the first time you've visited the Oracle?"

"No."

"I see. And how did you first hear about the Oracle?"

He shook his head. "I can't remember. It was a long time ago. Even longer than this conversation."

He wondered whether she would actually write that. Not that he was at all interested either way.

"Now then. What are you going to ask the Oracle?"

The King was slightly taken aback by this.

"That's one of the questions?" he asked.

"Yes. The last one, actually. There are some multiple choice options if that would help?"

"What are they?" he asked. He had no idea what he wanted to reveal to this Elf; surely any conversations with the Oracle were completely confidential.

"Are you seeking her advice; are you after information; do you want to see your future; or other?"

"A little of everything really," said the King.

"That's not one of the options."

"The first one, then!" he snapped.

"No need to shout, your Grace," replied the Elf. "After all, these questions are for your benefit. We're just trying to enhance our visitors' experience with the Oracle. We want to make sure they are as practical, useful and memorable as possible."

He glared back at the Elf.

"It would be useful if I actually got to see her," he said. "Is she ready to see me yet?"

"Not yet," she replied, still scribbling away on this paper. She then folded up the paper and put it in a box beside her desk.

"Now she's ready," replied the Elf.

Chapter 20

The King couldn't help but slow down as he climbed the stairs of the building. It was of course all falling apart, with gaping cracks creeping down the walls from the ceiling; other gaping cracks had given up on creeping and were instead running down the walls without a care in the world.

But there was a beauty to this building too. Despite looking like it could be brought down by a badly timed sneeze, it somehow still felt secure. It felt safe. It felt like if everything else in the Known World got destroyed by Trolls, this building would stay standing. Probably because from the outside, the Trolls would have assumed they had already destroyed it.

He approached the top step and almost came to a halt. The room was very dark, and seemed to be full of smoke. Or maybe it was steam; he had no trouble breathing it in. There were no windows. Aside from another multitude of cracks in the walls, the only light came from a dimly lit ball in the middle of the room.

The orbuculum.

King Wyndham knew it well of course; it must be the same one he had seen twenty years ago. After all, where were they going to get a replacement? It was covered by a thin cloth, but through the cloth and the smoke he could still make it out quite clearly.

He made his way towards the orb; it was only a few yards away. Anyone who gazed upon it would see nothing but a nice looking crystal ball. Except of course for the Oracle, who could see visions as clear as day.

She could stare into the glimmering light and see the wonders of the Known World. She could see the past; the wars, the poverty, the mistakes. She could see the present; the conflicts, the hardship, the miscalculations. And she could even see the future; the battles, the destitution, the blunders. She could see what no-one else in the Known World could. Or if not, she was very good at pretending she could.

"King Wyndham," bellowed a voice from the back of the room. The King was slightly taken aback. Apparently she had been in the room the whole time, hidden behind the smoke.

"I was just looking at it, I wasn't going to touch it," he said.

"I never said you were, don't worry," replied the Oracle. "After all, if you can't trust the King of Humans, who can you trust?"

"Quite right," said the King, stepping back from the orb as he did so just in case it looked suspicious.

The Oracle on the other hand stepped forward; her face appearing through the mist. She took a deep breath, and smiled at the King.

"Twenty years, King Wyndham," she said softly, "has it really been that long?"

"I believe so," he replied. "And yet, it seems only yesterday that I last set foot in this place."

It sounded rather clichéd but he couldn't think of anything else to say. To be fair it was sort of true. It wasn't just the building; the Oracle looked exactly the same as when he last saw her. It was amazing really; she must have been on this earth for well over a hundred years, yet didn't look any older than twenty-five. She was tall, fair-haired and had a generally reassuring look about her. It was the kind of look that made you feel like everything was okay, even when you knew it wasn't.

She smiled at the King. "I sense that you are troubled. I sense that all is far from perfect in the realm of Humans?"

"Well yes," said Wyndham. Not really much of a deduction; he was hardly going to trek all the way up to the far North West of the Known World just to tell her everything was fine.

"Are you here for guidance, King Wyndham, for knowledge, or simply for reassurance?" she said.

"You sound like your receptionist!" he replied. "Well, I don't know, but right now I think I need all three."

The Oracle's smile faded slightly, and she nodded. "Tell me everything," she said.

Now it was Wyndham's turn to take a breath. "Well, the war with the Trolls rages on," he started.

"Ah yes, the trouble in Carlom," she said. This wasn't surprising, everyone knew about the war.

"Indeed."

"Your soldiers are struggling; down to your last five thousand," she continued.

"True," replied the King. Not that impressive, she could have heard this from a messenger at some point.

"Morale is as low as it has ever been, not just in Carlom but back in the capital too."

"Well yes but…" How did she know that? "Wait, that's not true, is it?"

"Dear Wyndham," she replied, "you should not dwell on the negative mood of your people, or what they are all saying about you."

"I know that, I just… hang on, what are they saying about me?" he replied.

"It doesn't matter, my King. You should do what you believe is right, regardless of whether people are calling you a war-monger, a blood thirsty tyrant or a balding slob."

"Well I hardly think that last one has anything to do with…"

"King Wyndham, what does your heart tell you? Do you think you can win the war?"

The King looked down, then realised he obviously couldn't see his heart so just pretended he was thinking deeply instead. He sighed.

"The Elves won't help us. The Pixies can't. I have no more Humans that I can send to Carlom. There are ferocious dragons on that side of the world, and my soldiers don't have as much as a sparrow."

He looked up, and continued. "But yes, I still believe we can win this war. We're Humans, and we've fought against the odds before. And besides, the Goblins are still supporting us."

"Indeed they are, but for how long?"

She moved closer to the King, so she was now plainly visible. She wore a long white robe, with silver lace around the neck. Her pointed Elvish ears were both studded with diamonds. Apparently being an Oracle was fairly well paid these days.

"What are you saying?" he asked.

"In time, my King," replied the Oracle. "All will become clear. But first, you asked for guidance and I will give it to you. You're outnumbered, and facing a bitter foe which gets stronger every day. But you should listen to your heart and not the voices of your Humans."

"Thank you," said the King, "I think I understand what you're saying."

"Yes. Anything is possible if you believe it's possible," continued the Oracle. "But you should also be rational in your beliefs, and know when to stop believing."

The King looked slightly taken aback. "Actually I'm not sure I do understand what you're saying."

"I'm telling you not to give up, King Wyndham. Until the time is right."

"Generally I was always taught never to give up. To always try harder!" replied the King.

"Yes, never give up. Unless it's the right thing to do," continued the Oracle. "Consider for a moment, a young wolf cub. Finding its legs for the first time, it wanders, and comes across a great mountain in front of it."

King Wyndham began to wonder where this was going, but kept his mouth shut and listened patiently.

"The peak of the mountain is barely visible, the slope is steep, and the terrain is unforgiving. But the wolf cub believes it can climb to the very top. So it tries its very hardest; it runs, then it walks, then it gets so tired it can barely hobble. But it believes it can do it, and just doesn't give up. At last, the wolf cub makes it to the very peak, and it stands there tall and proud. It looks down on the Gods' creation and truly believes that anything is possible. It believes it can run, it believes it can climb; it even believes it can fly. So it makes its way to the edge of the peak, jumps off ready to spread its wings, and immediately falls to its death."

The King frowned. He didn't seem to like this story.

"Right," he replied. "So you should never stop believing, unless what you believe in is silly."

"Exactly," said the Oracle. "I think you are beginning to see."

"So I think the real question is; am I a wolf cub trying to climb from the bottom a mountain, or trying to fly off the top?"

The Oracle smiled. "You're a wise Human, King Wyndham," she replied. "You're well aware that you don't have wings."

The King nodded.

"Well then," said the Oracle, "I do hope my guidance will help. Now, you are also seeking knowledge. And knowledge I can provide you too."

She reached out her hand and pulled off the thin cloth which covered the orbuculum in front of them. The King held his breath and stared down at the dazzling ball in front of him; his mind racing at what this was about to show. He was about to find out his future; the future of the Known World.

Or the Oracle was about to make something up, but it was still exciting.

Chapter 21

The Lord Protector had no need to fear. It was all going to go like clockwork. Starters. Main Courses. Poison the Goblin King. Dessert.

Not that he was at all afraid of course; that was a sign of weakness. But all the same he hadn't let himself think about it any further. It was all meticulously planned, nothing could possibly go wrong.

He looked around the table and couldn't help smiling to himself. The Ogres had insisted on a small party for the feast; the smaller the number of people, the less likely that someone would notice what was going on.

There were only 10 of them in all sitting at the round table; the Lord Protector and his three generals, the King, Queen Afflech, their two sons Grumio and Nutrech, and two Goblin warlords whose names Higarth didn't even remember.

It was rather satisfying; half the people in the room were in on the plan. The other half would be bowing their heads in prayer as the deed is done, unaware that the King is being slowly poisoned to death, by none other than his eldest son.

Higarth cackled to himself.

"Lord Protector?" said the Goblin King. "I don't think the war in Carlom is particularly funny."

"What? Oh no, not at all," replied Higarth, realising he hadn't been listening to a thing the King had been saying.

"It's a very delicate matter; it's not like you can simply pick a side," continued King Grieber.

"Indeed," replied the Lord Protector. *Although we both know you already have picked a side*, he thought to himself. The filthy Human-loving Goblin.

The King turned to his son, sitting on his other side. "You've been awfully quiet so far tonight Grumio, is everything all right?"

He had a point; the Prince had barely said a word since the Ogres had arrived. He looked flushed, almost shaking. He even gave the Lord Protector a glance before replying, as if to check it was okay.

"Yes, fine thank you father," he replied at last. "Just feeling a little under the weather."

Higarth rolled his eyes. He should never have trusted a Goblin with something this important. The prince had the vial in his pocket; all he had to do was wait for the prayer and pour it into the King's drink. Surely even a Goblin could manage that. It was all meticulously planned.

The waiters began to place their starters in front of them. King Grieber of course got his first, followed by the Lord Protector.

Once everyone had been served they bowed their heads in prayer, while the King said a few words. Higarth kept his eyes half open the whole time, for no other reason than to check whether anyone else was also keeping their eyes half open. To his relief they weren't; all other heads remained firmly bowed.

"Right, let's begin," said King Grieber as he opened his eyes, and picked up his knife and fork with a flourish. The other guests all did the same. The starter wasn't half bad; smoked rabbit covered in red berries, and a couple of figs on the side. The portion size was a little small, but it didn't really bother Higarth. It would be a bit much to complain about the meal when you're also planning on killing the host.

"A triumph, thank you," said King Grieber as they removed his empty plate. Higarth shrugged; he was already getting sick of the King's positive attitude to everything. Although he took solace from the fact that he wouldn't have to put up with it for much longer. One more course, two more prayers and then all they had to do was wait. It was all meticulously planned.

They could of course have just done the deed during the first prayer, but they needed to let the dust settle first. Let the King have a few glasses of wine; let him relax; make sure he isn't fully alert when it happens. It was all part of the ingenious plan.

"More wine, your grace?"

"Oh no thank you, I'll stick with the water," replied the King.

"What?" said Higarth, a little too loudly. "You're just having the one glass tonight?" he added, steadying his voice.

"I think so, yes," replied the King. "We have five nights of celebrating ahead of us, I should probably take it easy tonight."

"Quite understandable," said the Lord Protector, thinking it better not to try and argue. It was hardly a big deal; only a very minor hiccough. Although Higarth did notice the Prince had taken a rather different approach. He was already half way through his second glass, and this probably wasn't a good thing. The best assassins tended not to get drunk before assassinating someone.

"Perhaps your son should follow your example," he said, gesturing to Grumio.

"Not at all," replied the King. "He's young, he should be enjoying every minute of this to the full," he added, grabbing a nearby bottle and filling the Prince's glass to the brim.

Higarth laughed unconvincingly and took a sip of his water.

The conversation moved on to the events planned over the next five days. The Lord Protector did little more than nodding and occasionally saying 'wow, that's impressive' as King Grieber went on about the multitude of shows, feasts and parties that were happening. Apparently there was even an indoor gunpowder display planned during the third night. Higarth was actually quite intrigued by this, because it sounded so ridiculous.

"Before the main course, I wonder if we should all change places," said the King, changing the conversation quite abruptly.

"Excuse me?" said Higarth, once again far louder than he should have been. "Why do you say that?"

"Oh well I was just thinking I haven't even spoken to everyone in your party yet; and I'm sure you would appreciate some time with my Warlords too. So it might be fun if we moved around a bit, don't you think?"

"But we can't!" butted in Prince Grumio. "I have to sit beside you so I can...so I can sit beside you," he said.

How subtle. The Lord Protector couldn't believe how close he had come to giving it all away. Luckily the Goblin King laughed and didn't seem to infer anything untoward.

"Dear boy, I know this is against tradition, but some traditions are only made to be broken," he said.

"Even so," said Higarth, "I wouldn't feel comfortable breaking this one. I'm more than happy staying where I am."

"Of course," replied the King. "I wouldn't dream of asking you to move, Lord Protector. I'll be the one to move."

He called to the other end of the table to one of his Warlords. "Sepping! We're swapping places, I've just decided."

The King was off his chair and on his way to the other side of the table before Higarth could utter another word.

Warlord Sepping looked as confused as everyone else, but duly obliged and moved round. As he took his new place in between the Prince and the Lord Protector. King Grieber also suggested a few more rearrangements so that everybody had someone new to talk to.

Lord Protector Higarth and Prince Grumio were still sitting in their original places, but with new companions either side of them. And more importantly, the King who they were about to poison was now sitting on the other side of the table.

They began to bring in the main courses. Higarth needed to think, but in the meantime had to make do with making small talk with this Warlord. Who was about as interesting as a retired tax collector. Prince Grumio meanwhile seemed to be dealing with the situation by taking a few more gulps from his wine glass.

"And now, please bow your heads again before we eat," bellowed the Goblin King from the other side of the table.

Once again, Higarth kept his eyes half open. He looked over the Warlord and noticed that Prince Grumio was now doing the same. They shared a meaningful glance before turning their heads away.

The Lord Protector then looked across at the King and made a fist under the table. The Goblin still had his head bowed and his eyes closed, whilst muttering some gibberish about being thankful and keeping courage during difficult times.

The Lord Protector had to admit everything wasn't quite going as smoothly as he expected. Although of course it had all been meticulously planned.

The King was sober, yet his assassin was getting drunker by the minute. And now their target was on the other side of the table, completely out of reach of either of them.

It was almost as if he knew.

Chapter 22

King Wyndham just kept staring at the crystal ball in front of him. His eyes were lost in the white smoke that danced around inside it, desperate to catch a glimpse of something more; a vision of the Known World which nobody but the Oracle could see.

Of course he didn't manage this, since nobody but the Oracle could see it. So he finally pulled his eyes away from the orbuculum and looked up at the Elf standing in front of him. She too had her eyes fixed on the crystal ball. Her face was motionless, but her pupils widened as she stood there. He noticed she was breathing deeply, her pale face even appeared a little flushed.

"What do you see?" said the King.

She didn't reply. She was so fixed on the orb that Wyndham wondered if she had even heard him speak. He looked down again, just in case. Still white smoke. Nothing but white smoke.

"What do you see?" repeated the King. "Can you see my future?"

"Not exactly," replied the Oracle at last, without taking her gaze off the orbuculum even for a second. "I see the future, but I don't see you."

King Wyndham stared back at her. "You mean… I'm dead?" he said at last.

"What? No. Well maybe, it's hard to say whether you're dead or not."

"That's comforting," replied the King.

The Oracle turned her stare away from the orb and returned the King's gaze.

"You don't understand. I didn't see you, because I didn't see any Human at all."

"You only saw Elves?" asked the King.

"No, no. I saw Goblins. I saw a sweet celebration turn sour. I saw the olive branch of peace crumble into dust. I saw a golden crown fall to the ground and break like glass."

Wyndham frowned. "Are you telling me you saw the death of the Goblin King?"

"Yes, well, there's no need to be so direct about it. There's an art to this, Wyndham, and you don't want to ruin the magic."

The King nodded whilst barely listening. "How does he die?" he said.

The Oracle sighed. "That is not clear. I saw his final breath. That is all."

Wyndham thought for a moment. His heart was beating fast. He had come here expecting the Oracle to predict the sun would come up tomorrow, or the sky would remain blue. This was new. Could she possibly be right about it?

If she was, the consequences could be catastrophic. In past times, the death of any Goblin would only be a good thing. But times had changed, and Grieber was a friend of Humans. His people were supporting them. Without him, the war with the Trolls was surely lost.

And what about the King's heir. Wyndham had never thought much of Prince Grumio. He had always been cold to him, and he had no confidence that the Prince would continue his father's work. What if he shunned the Humans, and took things back to the dark days where the two races would do nothing but fight? What if the death of the King meant the start of a global war the like of which the Known World had never seen?

King Wyndham shuddered. He then tried to get a hold of himself; surely now he was just being paranoid.

"I'm sorry," he said to the Oracle, realising he had probably been standing there blankly for a long time now. "If what you're saying is true, I just fear the consequences."

"Indeed, they could be catastrophic," said the Oracle, as if reading his mind.

"But is this definitely what you saw? Can you be sure it's true?"

The Elf smiled. "My dear King, I have not travelled to the future, nor will I ever be able to do so. I gain but a glimpse of it from this magical ball."

She looked down at the orb again before returning her gaze to the King.

"And what is the true future anyway?" she continued.

Wyndham gritted his teeth, preparing for an unnecessary lecture.

"If we know the future, but we have the power to change it, then the future may be different from the one we know."

The King paused for a moment. "So then we don't know it."

"Exactly," replied the Oracle.

"But then why am I even here? How can I even trust what this vision is saying?"

"Well, in this situation you have three choices," she said, as if she had expected this question. "You can ignore the vision and assume that it's wrong, try to change the future, or see it as inevitable and prepare for what is to come."

Wyndham nodded, though he didn't know what to think any more. How could he possibly try to change the future when he knew so little about it? If this vision was even true at all, he didn't know when it was going to happen, or how. What was he supposed to do to stop it?

"Wait," he said suddenly.

"Um, I'm not going anywhere," said the Oracle.

"Yes, I mean I just thought of something," replied the King. "What you said before; you said you saw a golden crown fall to the ground. And a sweet celebration turn sour."

She nodded.

The King's eyes widened. "What if that means the Dernbach festival? What if the Goblin King's going to be killed at some point in the next five days?"

"Well that would be most unfortunate," replied the Oracle, unhelpfully.

She had once again turned her gaze towards the orbuculum and was paying little attention to him. Wyndham took a deep breath. He needed time to think, to make sure he was seeing things clearly. But he also needed to act quickly.

"I think perhaps it's time for me to leave," he said. "Unless, there's something else you want to tell me?"

The Oracle still had her eyes fixed on the orbuculum. Either she was doing some sort of impression of a statue, or she was having another vision.

The King waited with bated breath. He didn't want to utter another word, in case it disturbed her during this crucial time.

Fortunately he didn't have to wait very long. The Oracle

closed her eyes for a moment; and then looked up at King Wyndham, with a satisfied expression on her face as if she had just finished a roast dinner and decided she would also go for a second dessert.

"Well?" said the King, not knowing what else to say.

"Very well indeed," replied the Oracle.

"What did you just see?"

She took a deep breath, almost as if she was preparing to translate what she saw into some strange, cryptic phrase.

"I saw a pair of magic hands on the smallest of all creatures," she began. "I saw them turn the darkness into flames."

King Wyndham thought for a moment. "You mean... nope, I've got nothing. Any chance you could give me more of a clue?"

The Oracle sighed. "I saw a magic Pixie," she said.

"Oh, great," replied the King. "That's hardly a revelation. Magic Pixies are everywhere, with a very special talent of convincing people that turning a plant blue without touching it somehow has a point to it."

"There's a point to this one, Wyndham," replied the Elf, calmly.

The King paused. Something told him this was all the information he was going to get. He felt like picking the Oracle up, turning her upside down and shaking her in a hope she would tell him everything he knew. Instead he just asked her a question that had been bugging him for some time.

"I've come all this way to be in the room with you right now. Why haven't you seen a single vision of me?"

"That's not how this works," she replied instantly. "I may be the one who can see these visions, but they only appeared because you're here."

"So that's what I'm saying," said the King. "Why do they have nothing to do with me?"

She smiled. "Because they do."

Wyndham frowned. Thoughts of a magic Pixie vanished from his head, as he once again started thinking about the Goblin King. Enough of this nonsense; if there was any chance that Grieber was in trouble then he had to do something. He had to leave. Now.

"I am truly grateful for everything you have told me," he

began. "But unless you have anything further for me to know, I'm afraid I must go."

The Oracle looked down at the orbuculum, which still gave a radiating glow through the smoke surrounding it. But she shook her head. Two visions in one visit was evidently above average, and he could see from her expression that there was no chance of a third.

"Let us hope, my King, that we do not have to wait another twenty years to meet again."

"Indeed," replied Wyndham as he made his way to the door.

"Wait," said the Oracle.

The King stopped in his tracks.

"You asked for three things. Guidance, I have given you; and knowledge, which you no doubt now have. But you also asked for reassurance."

"Yes?" said the King.

"It's going to be okay."

Wyndham turned back to the door and kept walking. "Thanks," he muttered as he left.

The stairs down to the ground seemed half as long as they had on the way up. The King took them two at a time, barely looking where he was going.

"King Wyndham?" said a voice as he reached the bottom. "I wonder if you could fill in this short feedback form regarding your visit to the Oracle today."

The King went straight for the exit, without even giving her a passing glance.

Robsun was waiting for him outside the building, with the rest of his company a little way behind. The young knight had his sword pointed to the ground and was leaning on it like a walking stick. It was probably far less comfortable than he was making it look.

"Send a message to Nuberim," barked the King as he saw his guard.

"Right. What should it say?"

"It doesn't matter, just send it!"

"Yes sire," replied Robsun, nervously.

"No, wait," said the King, stopping in his stride. "It's actually quite important what it says."

He looked up at the sky while he composed his thoughts.

"Tell the messenger that he sends word directly from the King of Humans. Tell them to take extra care, because King Grieber's life may be in danger. The Oracle has seen it."

The young guard nodded.

"And send two guards with him," continued Wyndham. "Offer their services, for protection until we know that the Goblin King is safe."

"Yes sire," said Robsun again. He waited a second to see if Wyndham had any more to say, and then darted off towards the rest of the King's company.

The King waited a few minutes before following. He was still trying to compose himself after everything that had happened.

And finally a pleasant thought came to his mind. After weeks of travelling through distant Elvish lands, he realised it was finally time to go back home to Peria. To return to the palace again. To see his wife and children. To get some decent food.

For the first time in a long time, he actually began to smile.

Chapter 23

It was a widely acknowledged fact that every civilisation needs a leader. Someone to stand up and make decisions so the rest of the people don't have to, and so they have someone to blame when everything goes wrong.

Deciding who should be the leader was always the more difficult question. Some people just accepted that their leader was born to do the job, and the best person to lead them would just be the son of the previous leader. The Humans seemed happy enough with this system; there was something comforting in assuming that the leader had already been chosen, so they never had to worry about this question. Unless of course the leader only had daughters, but that was not worth thinking about.

Others, like the Ogres, never seemed satisfied with this. Ever since the third age, and in particular the days of Turgor the Jaw-Droppingly Incompetent, they had decided that there were better leaders out there than those who were born into it.

Many of the Ogres questioned whether one leader was even enough. They experimented with having a council of 12 leaders; wise, strong and all equal in every single way. It worked perfectly until a few days later, when they realised they weren't all equal in every single way, and started to disagree with each other.

The main thing they disagreed about, of course, was who was actually in charge. One by one the counsellors were either killed or forced to resign, until only the biggest and strongest remained. He then decided to form a new council; the only difference being that everyone now knew who was in charge.

This tradition remained to this day. When one Lord Protector died, the next one was decided from his council of Generals. Some would concede defeat, others would fight until only one remained.

The Ogres took pride in this system, which is why they

found it so odd that some societies still insisted upon having a king. They found it even odder that one of these societies was the Goblins. Not only did they still have a king; they still had princes, a palace, and any number of crowns and unnecessary jewellery.

And this was probably why Lord Protector Higarth had no problem with the concept of assassinating the Goblin King. As he sat in the dining hall tucking into his main course, he was more concerned with how they were going to slip the poison into the King's drink now that he sat at the opposite side of the table.

King Grieber caught his eye, and smiled. Higarth smiled back, making a mental note to stop looking at the King so he didn't have to keep smiling. He noticed that Warlord Sepping, sitting to his left, seemed to have given up trying to converse with him; not surprising given he had barely looked in the Warlord's direction or muttered more than a one-word answer to whatever it was he was saying.

Queen Afflech, sat on the other side, seemed deeply engaged in a discussion with General Litmus; or, at least, both were doing a great job at pretending to be interested in what the other one was saying.

The Lord Protector surveyed the rest of the table. General Lang was sharing a laugh with the other Goblin Warlord. Having overheard the odd word Higarth gathered his name was Uoro. The names these Goblins came up with; maybe when he was born he let out a yawn and they just decided to name him after that.

King Grieber now sat next to his other son, Prince Nutrec. They both seemed to be happy enough, talking quietly to each other while they vigorously tucked into the plates of grilled mutton in front of them.

It was at that point that the Lord Protector noticed his other General, sitting on the left hand side of the King. He couldn't believe he hadn't thought of it until now; he had been sitting there thinking about ways of getting Grumio to the King's side of the table. And so far his best idea was for him to crawl underneath it, and if anyone asked to pretend he had accidentally dropped his fork and thrown it across the table. But he didn't need to do this; all he really needed to do was to get the vial to General Chandimer.

Higarth and the General made eye contact. This was still not going to be easy; he had to get Chandimer and Grumio out of the room together, so the prince could hand the Tepnik water to his General. And all this without saying a word.

He nodded to the General, hoping that was enough. It obviously wasn't, as Chandimer simply furrowed his brow. He waved his head towards the prince, and then back to the General. Still nothing. He then picked up his water glass, took a sip and pulled a face, then gestured towards King Grieber. Admittedly this probably looked odd if anyone else was watching, but it was fairly evident that nobody was.

General Chandimer's eyes widened and he nodded to his Lord Protector. The General then looked at Prince Grumio, which suggested to Higarth that he understood. He then watched as Chandimer made a gesture towards the door with his head, had a brief word with the Goblin King, then got up and walked towards the exit.

The Lord Protector took a deep breath. Now he just had to wait, and hope to the Gods that Prince Grumio followed him.

"Everything all right with your General?" Warlord Sepping asked, as he watched Chandimer leave the room.

"I'm sure he's fine," replied Higarth immediately. "Must just be a call of nature."

The Warlord nodded.

"In fact," continued Higarth, "I'm sure he's not the only one. I've seen Prince Grumio here get through three glasses of wine already, so I wouldn't be surprised if nature called for him soon too."

Sepping chuckled, while Higarth directed his gaze to the Prince, desperately hoping that he was able to take the hint. The Lord Protector couldn't have been any less subtle without standing up and announcing to the room that they were about to poison the King.

A moment passed. And then another.

"Do you know what," started Prince Grumio at last. "I think that time has indeed come."

The Lord Protector tried to mask his relief as the prince rose from his chair and walked in a less than straight line towards the door. There was nothing more Higarth could do now; it was entirely out of his hands. The two of them would make the trade, and when the next prayer came, Chandimer could do the deed.

He took a large bite out of his mutton joint and smiled. The meticulous plan hadn't been quite as meticulous as it should have been, but as long as it was meticulous enough to get the job done Higarth would still be happy.

"So how long have you served in the military?" he asked Sepping. He nodded enthusiastically as the Warlord replied, and began an enthralling conversation about the career of a Goblin soldier, by which Higarth was anything but enthralled.

It was enough though to keep the atmosphere light; and when his two partners in crime re-entered the dining hall nobody so much as battered an eyelid.

As desserts arrived and the party bowed their heads in prayer, six eyes remained as wide open as an unbuilt gate. The Lord Protector and the Prince could do nothing but stare as General Chandimer lifted the vial of Tepnik water from his side, removed the lid and poured the contents gently but swiftly into the Goblin King's glass. It was flawless. Masterful. And so very discreet.

The Ogre deserved a fine reward. A promotion. Of course he was only one rank below the Lord Protector. So not a promotion, but a reward nonetheless.

It's amazing how normal things seem even when the most abnormal thing has just happened. The Goblin King sat there quietly tucking into his smoked orange, seemingly unaware that with every sip of his water he took he was cutting his life expectancy. From a matter of years, it would soon only be a few nights. They say that what you don't know can't hurt you. They are idiots.

Lord Protector Higarth took another sip from his wine goblet, making steady progress through his third glass of the night. There was something that still puzzled him about this whole evening. He knew the King was an eccentric Goblin, but was that really the only reason he insisted on moving seats? And why had he refused to drink alcohol on one of the wildest nights of the year?

Of course if he knew about the plan to poison him, he had hidden it very well by drinking every last drop of the poison without a moment's thought. No, there was something else. Probably. With that, the Lord Protector finished the remainder of his glass in one and decided not to give it another thought.

As dinner drew to a close, the Goblin King rose from his seat and announced that the morning had just begun. No sooner had he spoken than a band came marching in. A team of buglers, pipers and two drummers filled the room and began to play at full volume. King Grieber grinned and remarked that now their stomachs had feasted it was time for a feast for their ears.

Lord Protector Higarth's ears were perfectly full, and certainly didn't need feeding with the odd combination of squeaks and vibrations that these Goblins apparently called music. But nevertheless he remained in the room and did his best to enjoy the evening. He laughed and joked with his fellow Ogres and Goblins as if nobody was assassinating anybody.

When the music finally came to an end, and his ears had feasted about enough to last them for several years without needing to hear another drumbeat, Higarth was more than ready to depart. He followed the King and Queen Afflech out of the dining hall and headed towards his chambers. The sun had probably been up for hours, and it was most certainly time for bed.

The Lord Protector slept peacefully. The Goblin King slept just as peacefully; the effects of the Tepnik water still yet to take hold in his system. General Chandimer slept reasonably peacefully, despite his mind buzzing at what he had achieved this morning.

Prince Grumio however apparently didn't sleep so peacefully. At least that was the Royal Guard's assumption, since he found him the next evening with a knife in his throat.

Chapter 24

"I probably will join the army, just not yet," said Fulton as he polished off the last of his plate of pig's liver. "When I'm ready, but I'm not really in a hurry. And there's no shame in being unemployed."

"Of course there is," replied Ridley. "If there was no shame in it, you wouldn't have to keep telling people there's no shame in it."

He laughed it off, and then continued softly.

"Something tells me I'll be ready when we return. After all, how many trainee soldiers can say they have assassinated a Goblin King?"

Ridley smiled but shook his head at the same time.

"We haven't assassinated anyone yet," he whispered. "And even if we do, you'll just be the one who watched me do it."

"Fair point," Fulton acknowledged, raising his voice once again. "But people would still be impressed."

Ridley looked round the room. It was fairly small, but still very lively. Underground, of course, but dimly lit with a few torches on the walls. Each table was taken up by Goblins merrily enjoying the ample food and reasonably priced drinks on offer. They were the only Humans in the room; not surprising really considering where they were. He did spot a couple of Ogres in the corner but quickly turned away; they were probably harmless, but best not to take any risks.

Ridley had to admit that for a Goblin hostel, this place wasn't half bad. He hadn't even expected to find sheltered accommodation this far to the East; it really was a sign that times were changing. They were in a small village called Dagmah, still a few days away from the capital.

He got the feeling that Humans seldom passed this way, and most Goblins here had probably never left the village. Admittedly they had been turned away from a few places, and even in the more welcoming areas they were getting some funny looks.

But many Goblins would smile at them, even ask how their

night was going. It did make Ridley feel a little bad that he was soon going to kill their King. For about the millionth time he questioned what in the Known World he was doing here. Was it really the right thing? Did the ends justify the means? The money. At least if nothing else, he was getting paid for it.

"I expect it's nearly daybreak," continued Fulton. "I have to say I'm exhausted."

"Yes. Straight to the room after this," replied Ridley.

It was their third day in the Goblin Realm, and they were adapting reasonably well. Goblins of course are nocturnal, so their sleeping patters were rather different to those of the two Humans. Ridley and Fulton probably didn't need to start sleeping during the day and staying awake all night, but they thought they should probably try. After all as the saying goes, 'When in Dagmah, do as the Dagmahrians do.'

Besides, they stood out enough already without walking around the empty streets during the day like sun-crazed fools.

"I still think we could have got separate rooms," said Fulton.

"We've been over this!" replied Ridley. "We're not in quiet little Pixie villages any more. I know this place seems perfectly friendly, but we're still in the Goblin realm. We have to stick together, and that means sharing a room in case an emergency happens."

Fulton brushed the hair away from his face. Days on the road had meant the light blonde curls had grown rather long, and looked slightly menacing; as if they had taken control of the top of his head. And they were now doing their best to take over his eyes too.

"I'm still not sure what kind of emergency you're thinking of," he replied. "You mean like if someone finds out about us, and comes to kill us in the night? So at least if we're sharing a room, they can kill us efficiently without the hassle of breaking in two different doors?"

"Yes, maybe that," replied Ridley impatiently. "Or maybe there would be a chance of the two of us overpowering them. Or one of us would hear them coming, alert the other and we could both escape. It may be unlikely, but if it makes us slightly safer I think it's probably worth doing!"

Fulton sat back in his chair.

"But isn't there a chance that people will see us and think we're, you know?"

"What?" replied Ridley.

"Well, you know? I mean it's not just sharing a double room, we are now eating together, it just looks a little…"

"Oh for the love of the Gods," said Ridley. "Here we are on the most life threatening mission to bring peace to the Known World, and you're worried that people will think we're a couple?"

"It just. It just looks a little odd, that's all," replied Fulton. "I mean, I wonder what Petra would think if she saw us like this."

Here we go. Any excuse to bring up the Pixie again. Ridley held his tongue, hoping that would be the end of the conversation. It wasn't.

"You know, I wonder if it's possible that Petra will actually come and join us at some point?" continued Fulton. "She must have made it to the White Castle by now. Maybe the Queen will tell her to come with us, to help us in our mission."

"Hmmm. Pretty unlikely," said Ridley. "For a start, she swore she wouldn't tell anyone about our mission."

"Ah yes," the young Human acknowledged. "And besides, even if she did come, how would she be able to find us?"

"She could just ask around for the two Humans who share a room?" replied Ridley.

Fulton laughed. He then took his last sip of his jar of ale, which had taken him less than twenty minutes to get through.

Ridley looked round the room again. He couldn't help but notice that the general buzz of conversation in the place had suddenly stopped.

His heart began to pound at what he saw. Last time he looked he could swear there were only a couple of Ogres in the place, but now it seemed to be full of them. If anything, they even outnumbered the Goblins.

"What is it?" said Fulton. He had his back to the room and couldn't see what was going on. But he could see Ridley; and the fear that had suddenly gripped him.

"I think," said Ridley, slowly. "I think that it's time for us to call it a night."

"You mean call it a day," said Fulton, unhelpfully. "We're

in the Goblin realm now."

"Yes," said Ridley, clearly not even listening. He was thinking hard; wondering what they could possibly do if something kicked off right now. There were at least ten of these Ogres, probably more like fifteen. As he looked again he caught one glaring directly at him. The Ogre's eyes were a fiery red, and he revealed a set of bright yellow teeth which looked sharp enough to chew through steel.

Ridley's teeth, by contrast, were struggling to chew through the last of the chopped beef in front of him. Clearly these Goblins didn't know the meaning of the term 'medium rare'; every ounce of flavour had been grilled out of this meat. But that wasn't important right now.

Very slowly, and shaking slightly, he began to rise from his chair. The Ogre did the same thing, and once again their eyes met across the room.

Ridley swallowed. Three more Ogres at nearby tables also rose to their feet; along with a couple of Goblins. The room had now fallen deathly silent.

Without knowing what to do, Ridley sat straight back down again. Unfortunately this time the Ogres didn't follow; all this achieved was to make them slightly puzzled.

He kept his head down, desperately hoping that if they did nothing, and said nothing, the Ogres would leave them alone.

They didn't. Ridley felt something small and wooden fly past his ear and hit the wall behind him with a crash. And then before he knew what hit him, something did hit him. Another Ogre had thrown his ale jar at him with great force, and this one hit Ridley square on the chin.

He flinched, but didn't let them see he was in pain. He rose from his chair once again.

"Look, we don't want any trouble," he yelled across the room.

"Oh really?" replied the red-eyed Ogre in a deep, piercing voice. "I suppose that's what the Trolls said when you raided their lands hundreds of years ago."

It was true that the Humans had historically been rather keen to take over as much of the Known World as they could, conquering villages and plundering vast lands to the East. But those days were long gone, and it seemed rather unfair to blame all that on Ridley. After all, he was only a soldier.

Ridley kept his eyes fixed on this Ogre. Fulton, not knowing what else to do, also rose to his feet and turned to face them. Both men now had their backs to the wall.

"We don't know what they said; we weren't alive hundreds of years ago!" said Fulton defiantly, as if hoping to outsmart the Ogres with hard logic.

The red-eyed Ogre ignored this completely and remained fixed on Ridley.

"What are you doing here anyway?" he continued. "I thought Humans were supposed to be afraid of the dark. As well as afraid of Goblins, Ogres and pretty much anything else."

"Don't forget Pixies," added an Ogre to his right, causing a few of them to chuckle.

"We're not afraid of any of those things, or of any of you," replied Fulton as he trembled with fear.

"Enough of this!" shouted the ring leader. A few gasps were audible around the room as he pulled out a dagger from his trouser pocket. Its blade shone as it caught the light of a nearby torch; it really looked closer to a sword than a dagger.

Ridley of course had nothing of the kind, since his bags were locked away in their bedroom. He did have his steak knife, which he initially reached for and then thought better of it.

The gang of Ogres and Goblins began to move forward, surrounding the two men on both sides. The other people in the room were all heading for the door, clearly not wanting to witness this.

"Wait," said Ridley suddenly. "What are you going to do, kill us? Surely this isn't a fair fight. I thought Ogres had a reputation for always giving their enemies a chance!"

"Nope," said the Ogre as he moved directly in front of Ridley. "Certainly not me. I have more of a reputation for bullying helpless people and cutting their brains out."

One of the others, almost as tall and quite a bit fatter grabbed Fulton by the neck and thrust him back against the wall.

Ridley didn't move, too preoccupied by the steel blade flashing in front of him.

"Stop!" cried a voice suddenly from across the room.

Chapter 25

Ridley caught his breath. He felt a sense of relief but also had no idea what was going on. Two Goblins had entered the room dressed from head to toe in chainmail. Both carried a broadsword at their waists.

They were guards. Or soldiers. Maybe even knights; Ridley was pretty sure the Goblins had those, even if they were called something else.

The group of Ogres and Goblins had heard the cry, and were now looking back at these two soldiers. Even the ring leader had ceased his plan to cut out Ridley's brain, at least for a few moments.

"Well then," began one of the soldiers as they both strode across the room. "It seems they were telling the truth outside. Planning on doing something with that knife were we?" he said, addressing the red-eyed monster in front of Ridley.

"It's a dagger," muttered the Ogre, who was beginning to look a lot less menacing.

"Yes of course it is," continued the soldier, with an air of self-importance. "And I think you had better hand it over, don't you?"

Ridley was amazed at how calm these two Goblins were, considering the Ogres still towered over them. Ogres are generally a good foot taller than Goblins, and these ones were no exception.

He looked across at Fulton. The Ogre that grabbed him by the neck had clearly now let him go. He was rubbing the sides of his throat as if to check it was all still there.

"Yes of course," said the fiery red-eyed Ogre, now turning to face the soldier. "Here you go."

Unfortunately he didn't hand it over in quite the way the soldier had intended. Instead, he plunged it straight into the Goblin's ribs.

As quick as a flash, his fellow soldier drew his sword and swung it at the Ogre. With one swift motion he took his head clean off.

The reaction from the rest of the gang was interesting. It turns out the real way to tell the difference between an Ogre and a Goblin, aside from the fact that they look so obviously different, is how they respond to a bar fight. The Goblins in the gang fled like fleas in a flea market, while the two remaining Ogres pounced on the soldier.

Ridley and Fulton stayed completely out of it. Apparently Humans react to a bar fight by standing at the back and trying to keep out of everyone's way.

There was only going to be one winner. A Goblin soldier with a broadsword and full suit of chainmail was always going to defeat two Ogres with no weapons and a few too many ales inside them.

It was effortless how the soldier held one at bay while pushing his blade through the heart of the other, before turning round to finish the job.

He then rushed to his companion, who was lying in the corner with his hand covering the wound to his ribs. The two men still just stared, not sure whether to thank him or to... yes actually they should probably thank him.

"Thank you," murdered Ridley. "Is there anything we can do for you?"

"Get out of here!" snapped the soldier in response.

"Yes, well we can certainly do that."

"And send for help. We need an apothecary in here as soon as possible."

"Right," said Ridley.

"Well we do have some healing potion if that helps..."

Ridley grabbed Fulton by the arm and pulled him away from the scene. The two Humans shot out of the door and alerted the people in the corridor outside. Then they kept on running. Then they remembered they had put all their stuff in their room, so they went back to get it. Then they started running again.

"Humans certainly are odd creatures," Ridley heard one of the Goblins mutter as they ran past.

"I've never encountered one before," said another. "Rather savage creatures really. And why did they share a bedroom?"

They went straight past the reception, up the winding stairs to the daylight outside. Without saying a word they trudged on down the street; exhausted but unable to stop.

"So what do we do now?" said Fulton at last in between breaths.

"We keep walking," muttered Ridley, his eyes fixed on the road ahead.

"And then what?" replied the young Human. "We're still days from Nuberim; we'll have to stop at some point."

"Don't you see? It's just going to get worse!" continued Ridley. "We're getting closer and closer to the Goblin capital. One wrong move and we'll get eaten for breakfast."

"Dinner," replied Fulton. "Since we're in the East it's still more like dinner time here."

Ridley stopped in his tracks and gave him a piercing glare. It was so piercing that it went right through him, and probably pierced a couple of the distant hovels they were passing.

"What's wrong with you? How can you remain calm?" Ridley was almost shouting, but still managed to do it in a low whisper so as not to draw attention to himself.

"I'm not joking. People may say that Humans are welcome here these days, but we're not. It's only the elite who say that, the ones who travel around the world; most of the Goblins in the heartlands want us dead and gone."

Just as he said that, he caught sight of a dishevelled looking creature approaching them. He was clearly an old Goblin, past his prime. It was well and truly daylight now, and this fellow should probably have gone to bed hours ago.

He exchanged a glare with Ridley; who was too tired to do anything but stand there and catch his breath.

"You two aren't from around here, are you?" he growled.

"What gave it away?" said Fulton, sarcastically. "Was it the fact that we look like Humans, and don't look anything like Goblins?"

The Goblin's expression didn't change, but his glare was now fixed on Fulton.

"You also smell different," he replied.

"Oh," said Fulton, guessing this probably wasn't a compliment but he didn't ask for clarification.

"You know some people don't take kindly to your sort around here," continued the Goblin.

Ridley moved his hand towards the dagger in his right pocket.

"I however am not one of them," he added. "Welcome, good sirs."

With that, he turned and continued on his way.

Fulton turned to Ridley, both of them looking slightly taken aback.

"Well that was a nice change!" said Fulton.

"Yes," admitted Ridley. "But it doesn't change anything. From now on we avoid all contact with Goblins whenever possible. No more taverns, no more stays in fancy inns. From now on we only travel during the day, and avoid the main footpaths."

Fulton nodded, reluctantly but knowing his companion was almost certainly right.

"And no sharing bedrooms," he said. "After all it draws attention."

"No bedrooms at all!" continued Ridley.

"Where are we supposed to sleep then?"

"We have to be careful. When night comes we'll find hiding places, and take it in turns to keep watch."

Another reluctant nod and with that the two men set off again, though walking a little slower than before. Ridley took them straight off the path, away from the hovels and signs of civilisation. Or what passes for civilisation in the Goblin realm. The land was damp and muddy. They were only a few hundred yards from the path and it felt like they were in marshland.

Fulton followed behind, trying to comprehend how it had come to this; how wandering into the middle of nowhere was somehow the safer option.

"What are you going to do when this is all over?" he asked Ridley, trying to take his mind off everything else.

Ridley paused. "If I'm still alive," he started. "I'll just go straight home to Hari, let her know I didn't die. And then spend all the reward money on booze and food. Mostly booze. In fact probably entirely booze."

"Where did you tell your wife you were going?"

"Carlom," said Ridley. "To fight in the war. Best cover story I could think of really."

"I suppose so," replied Fulton. He then had another thought, something which hadn't occurred to him until now.

"And what did you tell your sergeant? Presumably not the same thing?"

"Well no, obviously. I just told him I was taking my leave for the year. Going on holiday."

"Ah yes. Couldn't have picked a better holiday destination myself," replied Fulton, as his foot got stuck in the marshy ground and he had to wedge himself free; the sudden jolt causing mud to spray over his face.

Chapter 26

"Well let's face it, we never expected the plan to go that badly wrong," said General Litmus.

"The plan did not go wrong!" snapped his Lord Protector.

It had been hours since the Prince had been found dead, and this was the first time the Ogres had managed to get a room to themselves. They didn't have long; the Goblins would probably start to get suspicious if they weren't already.

"Well it didn't exactly go right," replied Litmus, defiantly. "Instead of poisoning the King, Grumio stabs himself in the throat. Not only does he kill the wrong person, he uses the wrong bloody method to do it!"

Higarth shook his head.

"We still poisoned the King. Chandimer did it. The plan went perfectly, we just didn't foresee this little hiccough."

"You mean the prince killing himself?"

"And what makes you think he killed himself?" replied the Lord Protector, as he began pacing up and down the room. "I just don't see it. Suicide is considered one of the highest sins under the Goblin religion."

"I think killing your father is quite high on the list too?" added General Lang.

"Yes, maybe!" barked Higarth. "But let's just suppose for a minute that it wasn't suicide."

"Well in that case the Goblin guard must have killed him. Plain and simple," said General Lang.

"And what makes you so sure of that?" said Higarth.

"There was one soldier guarding the prince's room all day. Just one. If anyone had tried to get in, he would have known it. If someone killed Grumio then either the guard did, or he willingly let someone do it."

"They could have sneaked past him?" said Chandimer. "What if it was someone really small?"

Lang glared at his fellow General.

"Or invisibility powder?" suggested Litmus.

"Don't be ridiculous," said the Lord Protector. "There were torches everywhere. And invisibility powder only works when it's pitch black."

General Lang took a deep breath. "Well what are you suggesting, Lord Protector?" he said.

Higarth closed his eyes for a couple of seconds. Not that he was in any way tired or stressed; both of these were signs of weakness.

"What I'm suggesting is that a lowly Goblin guard would not be stupid enough to go and kill the person he's supposed to be protecting," he began.

"Exactly!" added his general.

"But what if," continued the Lord Protector, "he received the order from someone else; someone higher up."

The three generals all looked at each other, as if to reassure themselves that none of them knew what he was talking about.

"But he's a member of the royal guard," replied Lang at last. "Surely the only orders he can obey would have come from the prince himself?"

"Yes, the Prince. Or the King," muttered Higarth.

Chandimer swallowed; Litmus just stared.

"No, I still don't buy it," said General Lang. "The King is hardly going to wander up to the guard and say 'excuse me, would you mind going and killing my son? You know, the one you're paid to protect with your life? There's a good chap'."

"Yes, alright!" barked Higarth. "He wouldn't make it that obvious. But all he needed to do was to distract the guard; or order him to leave his post if only for a moment."

"Just to give enough time for his assassin to sneak in, give the prince a little stab in the throat and walk out again," said Chandimer.

"Precisely", added Higarth.

"It still seems unlikely," said Lang, shaking his head. "Why would he do it, for a start?"

"I don't know. Maybe he found out about the plan to poison him. Maybe he feared his son was up to no good for years. Or maybe he just found him a bit annoying and wanted to liven up the party. And of course, maybe he didn't do it at all."

Lang nodded.

"My point is," continued the Lord Protector. "That we may be underestimating the slimy light green Monarch."

General Litmus glanced at the door. "So what do we do now?" he asked.

"Nothing," replied Higarth. "At least, nothing yet. King Grieber still ingested the poison, and he'll be dead in a matter of days."

"And we had nothing to do with the death of the prince," added Lang. "So when we're questioned, we just have to tell the truth."

"That we were only involved in one assassination, rather than two?" remarked Litmus.

"Yes. Obviously we don't tell the whole truth," growled his Lord Protector.

Suddenly the door swung open. Chandimer, who was nearest, jumped up from his seat. Warlord Sepping entered with a fierce look on his face.

"Gentlemen, you seem to be taking a rather long time in the bathroom. I trust you are ready to return to the Drugen quarter?" he said, catching each one of their eyes in turn.

"Yes of course," replied Higarth quickly. "We were just about to leave."

"Follow me," said Sepping.

They duly obliged, and followed the Warlord up two flights of stairs and along a short corridor. Nobody said a word; they were rather beyond small talk at this point.

The Drugen quarter was really just a small room. Warlord Drugen was one of the finest military tacticians of the 12th age, until the famous battle of Lumbar rock where an army of Pixies outnumbered the Goblins by more than twenty to one. As the battle began the Warlord caught an arrow in the eye, and a second one followed in the other eye soon after. With his last breaths he was just about able to shout 'I may be blind, but I can still see victory!' Unfortunately what he couldn't see were the rest of his army, who had now deserted him and were fleeing the other way.

After this, it was generally accepted that Drugen deserved to at least have a hall named after him in the Royal Hollow. Of course all the good ones had already been named, so he was left with a rather small room. The Goblins called it a 'quarter' just to make it sound a little fancier.

Lord Protector Higarth looked around the room as they entered. Everyone who had been at dinner the morning before was there. Queen Afflech was in the corner looking in a state of shock; the King sat next to her with a hand on her shoulder. Prince Nutrec was to his right, looking as pale as a Goblin could look. Which is a sort of light green minty colour.

Warlord Uoro was also sitting down, alongside a number of guards, waiters and other general staff. This was indeed everyone who had been in any way involved with the dinner.

The Lord Protector of the Ogres took a seat on the other side of the room in silence, followed by each of his generals.

Warlord Sepping on the other hand simply marched to the middle of the room and stood there, surveying the scene. After a few long and awkward seconds, he began to speak.

"By the orders of the King, nobody will leave this room unless they are either instructed to, or they have been given permission," he said.

He looked around the room, as if expecting a response from someone. Higarth gritted his teeth; ordinarily he would sooner cut off his own limbs than receive orders from a Goblin, but on this occasion he simply had to accept it.

"The questioning will begin now," continued the Warlord. "Each of you will follow me, one by one, to the interview room."

The interview room was apparently smaller than the Drugen quarter, and wasn't even considered worth naming after someone.

Another silence followed. Most of the Ogres and Goblins were staring at the floor, doing anything they could to avoid making eye contact with their peers.

"Drucza," barked the Warlord. "You will be first. Please follow me."

A startled looking young Goblin slowly rose to her feet; evidently she was some member of staff who had no idea what was going on. She followed the Warlord's instructions and nervously left the room behind him. Everyone else stayed deathly silent.

Higarth let out a deep breath and glanced at his three Generals. Who would have thought one simple attempt to poison a King could end up causing this much commotion.

Chapter 27

"So you're nobody important then?" said one of the guards, looking down from his pedestal.

"We're very important!" replied Samorus indignantly. "We just can't tell you why, or how."

"You just have to believe us," added Petra.

"Believe you about what? You haven't told me anything," replied the guard, who seemed to be enjoying this a little too much. There were two of them, both standing on small pedestals outside the gates of the White Castle.

Samorus however was not enjoying himself. They had been walking for days, stopping only to eat, sleep and have the occasional sit down. But there hadn't been enough of these occasions, and the old Pixie was tired.

"Look, we can't tell you anything. But we need to see the Queen!" he snapped.

"Oh, you need to see the Queen! Well why didn't you say so?" replied the guard. "I thought you were just here to wander round and chat to us guards."

Samorus gave him a cold hard glare.

"Okay enough of this," continued the guard. "I can't let you in, so you may as well just move along."

"All right," said Samorus.

He reached into his pocket and pulled out a couple of silvers. He handed one to both guards without making eye contact.

"Thank you very much," said the guard they were talking to. The other one remained silent, though seemed to be smiling to himself. "We still can't let you in though, but well done for trying."

The old Pixie shook his head. "You're going to keep that, aren't you?" he said, gesturing to the coin in the guard's hand.

"Yes, I think so," he replied. "We only get four of these a week, it's a rather generous tip."

Samorus gave him an even colder, harder glare. He even

made a move towards him, but Petra quickly tugged on his arm.

"I think we should go," she said. "This clearly isn't working."

The old Pixie sighed. She was probably right, but what in the Known World were they going to do now? He couldn't believe that in all the time they had spent walking here, it hadn't occurred to them to think of a plan for getting into the castle. Apparently just turning up and asking to be let in wasn't quite enough.

As he turned round, he couldn't resist having a last pop at the guards.

"You two think you're so tough don't you, standing on those fancy pedestals to make yourselves look slightly taller than us," he said. "Have either of you even done any real fighting?"

"Nope," replied the guard, "that's far too dangerous. We prefer just to stand here and make ourselves feel big. Have a safe trip home."

As he said this, he turned his gaze slightly behind the old Pixie. Someone fairly young and important looking was making his way towards them.

It was obvious that he was important from the clothes he wore; he had a tunic of bright purple, the kind of colour that is only possible to make using rather expensive dyes, or an impressive amount of magic. His belt even seemed to carry the air of importance; a dark shade of leather tied together in an important looking knot, and embellished with some rather important looking metal studs. His shoes looked fairly average, but you can't have everything.

His hair was jet black, and he sauntered up towards them in a casual way that suggested he had been to the Queen's castle many times before.

"Good day to you sir," said the guard as he approached them.

His smug and sarcastic tone seemed to have vanished at the flick of a switch; he even seemed to be standing up straighter than a few moments ago.

"Good day indeed," replied the Pixie in an important manner.

"Now if you don't mind," the guard gestured to Samorus

and Petra, who still stood there rather awkwardly, with no idea what to do next. "Would you kindly be on your way."

The important looking Pixie glanced at the two of them. "Nonsense," he replied. "They are with me. This way."

The guards, both looking rather taken aback, hastily opened the wooden doors on either side. The Pixie marched straight through without giving them another glance.

Samorus and Petra stared at each other blankly, before shrugging and hurriedly following their new friend.

The interior of the White Castle was quite impressive. The atrium was long and well lit, covered in an array of paintings which must have all had their own story to tell. Of course the two Pixies didn't have a lot of time to look around; they were both fixated on the person in front of them, who was now walking at a rather brisk pace without bothering to turn around or acknowledge their existence.

It turned out they didn't have to walk for long. The Pixie suddenly stopped at a door to his left.

"Here we are," he said, as he opened it briskly and gestured to Samorus and Petra to step inside.

It was a small room, but no less impressive than the rest of the castle. The walls were decorated on every side; hours of careful craftsmanship must have gone into every inch of this place.

The two of them sat down, not knowing what else to do. The dark haired Pixie did the same, and for a few moments they all sat in silence.

"Well?" said Samorus at last. "Why did you do that? How do you know who we are?"

"Oh I don't," he replied. "I was just bored."

Samorus's eyes widened in disbelief.

"You were just bored?" he stammered.

The Pixie began to chuckle. "Don't be silly, of course I know who you are. You're Samorus Enteley, one of the masters of wizardry. I used to watch you, years and years ago when I was only a child. Although you probably don't even remember me."

Samorus smiled and slowly shook his head.

The Pixie turned to Petra.

"Honestly, the things this guy can do to animals. You would be amazed. One time, he managed to levitate a badger, and turned it bright green."

"I think maybe I just made it feel sick," replied the old Pixie. "Though unfortunately my powers aren't quite what they used to be."

Petra was amazed. There was so much about her mentor that she still didn't know.

"You used to work at the White Castle?" she said to him.

He nodded. "In a different time," he said. "It feels like a distant memory now."

Samorus wasn't interested in telling old stories. He was more intrigued by the Pixie sitting in front of him.

"So you were a child, here in the White Castle?" he began. "Does that mean…"

"Yes," interrupted the Pixie. "I'm Prince Vardie."

Petra stared, open-mouthed.

"You're Prince Vardie? One of the Queen's sons?" she stammered.

"Well yes, if you want to put it like that," he replied. "And I'm fifth in line to the throne. Not that it matters."

"Of course, I remember you now!" said Samorus. "The young Prince, the one who was always getting up to mischief."

The Prince laughed. "Something like that," he said. "I'd like to think I've matured a little since those days."

"Well yes, of course," replied the old Pixie. "It's a real honour to see you again sir."

"Likewise!" said Prince Vardie. He turned his gaze to Petra. "So tell me, what brought you and your friend here to the White Castle? What could possibly be so vitally important as to almost get you into a fight with two armed guards?"

Samorus sat back in his chair. "Before I tell you, I think we need reassurance that you will speak of this to no-one."

The prince seemed intrigued. He even stroked his chin slowly in a way which made him look particularly curious.

"Of course," he shrugged. "Nothing leaves these four walls."

The old Pixie took another glance at Petra, and began.

"Well. Just now, you called me a master of wizardry. I don't like to blow my own trumpet, but I do admit that back in the day I had a certain level of skill."

"A rather high level," added Prince Vardie.

"But the thing is, the girl sitting beside me has ten times more talent than I did, even in the prime of my wizarding life."

Petra began to blush.

"You could take Cordelle, Mahuzi and Liliana, pile them all on top of each other and they still couldn't do half of what she can."

The Prince raised an eyebrow.

"High praise indeed," he said. "So why did you bring her here? Does she want to work at the White Castle as our lead wizard?"

"No, I don't think you quite understand," said Samorus. "Petra can do things that no other wizard in the history of the Known World can do."

"I see," said the Prince. "What kind of things are we talking about?"

Samorus lowered his voice. "My Prince, she has the power of infernication."

Prince Vardie nodded. "Infernication?" he said. "Interesting."

He turned to Petra and then back to Samorus.

"And what is infernication?" he added.

"Well it means," continued Samorus, "that she can create fire, purely through flicking her wrists."

The Prince's eyes widened. "Fire?" he exclaimed. "What? How? Is she half dragon?"

Samorus frowned. "Does she look half dragon? Wait, there's no such thing! How is it possible for anyone to be half dragon?"

"Yes well it's not possible," replied Prince Vardie. "But neither is it possible to create fire by magic."

"She can do more than that," said Samorus smugly. "She doesn't just set things ablaze; she can make them combust in an instant. I've seen her turn live animals into dust in a matter of seconds."

The Prince was clearly still struggling to comprehend what he was hearing. He turned to Petra. "Is this true?" he said.

Petra nodded. "Yes, it's true," she said. "And before you ask, I couldn't even begin to explain how I do it. It's just something I discovered one day while I was training."

"But this is unbelievable!" said the Prince. "If this is really true, then this has the power to change the world. Just think about it; we would have fire whenever we needed it. The long, dark nights could be filled with light; the coldest parts of the realm could feel nothing but warmth! The coal industry would probably take a hit, but think about the benefits!"

Petra smiled and nodded again.

"Of course," continued Prince Vardie, "there would also be huge risks."

"Exactly," replied Petra. "And that's why we have come all this way. Not everyone in the Known World would want to use this kind of thing for good."

"Yes, the Ogres would go green with envy for one thing," continued the Prince. "They use torches more than fish use water. The idea of an infinite supply of fire would simply be too much for them to ignore."

"We know," said Petra. "We were thinking the same thing. It's simply not safe."

Vardie paused for a minute, maybe more, deep in thought.

"Does anybody else know about this?" he asked.

"No," said Samorus. "Nobody at all. Apart from these two Humans we met a few days ago."

"What Humans?" said the Prince.

"They were travelling to the Goblin Realm," said Petra. "Traders, simple folk really," she added.

"Any particular reason why you decided to tell these two Humans such a vital and dangerous secret?"

"Obviously it wasn't on purpose!" interjected Samorus. "It just happened."

The Prince looked quite taken aback. "But they were going to the Goblin realm? Who knows what could have happened by now, or who they could have told?"

"They won't have told anyone," said Petra. "We told them not to."

The Prince buried his head in his hands for a second, struggling to take in everything he was hearing.

"Look..." said Samorus. Prince Vardy raised his head once more and interrupted the old Pixie.

"Do you trust them?" he said. "Actually, it doesn't even matter. If everything you have told me is true, we have something that no Ogre or Troll can compete with. And we have to use it to our advantage."

"What are you saying?" asked Petra.

"I'm saying, that you might just be the greatest hope for defending our proud people; for defeating the Ogres, Trolls or whoever may threaten us. For achieving peace in the Known World. We should not just use this gift for warmth or lighting; we have to use it to fight."

"Blimey," said Samorus. "Are you saying you want Petra to be a guard?"

The Prince shook his head. "I don't know what I'm saying. What I do know is we need to act quickly."

He stood up. "I don't trust those two traders, whoever they may be. But there is one Human I do trust; and we must consult with him at once."

Petra and Samorus both rose to their feet. The Prince continued in a firm tone.

"We ride north for Peria. I'll send word to King Wyndham that we are coming."

Petra nodded.

"Although I need to speak to Queen Vernipula before we go," added the Prince.

"You mean, you need to check with your mother first?" said Samorus.

"Yes," replied Prince Vardie. "You know, just to make sure she agrees."

Chapter 28

The Lord Protector of the Ogres surveyed the room. It seemed like nobody had spoken for hours; probably because nobody had spoken for hours. All he saw were tired and worried looking Goblins sitting around the Drugen quarter, attempting not to make eye contact with each other.

He turned back to the empty space next to him. Two of his Generals had come and gone and now it was Chandimer facing interrogation by Warlord Sepping, the jumped up Goblin who seemed to be enjoying this a little too much.

There was something mysterious about all this, and not just the mystery of who killed Prince Grumio. Why, for example, did they do the questioning in such a specific order? Every one of the Goblins had been questioned before they even turned to his Generals. Was it really a coincidence that they were saving him and his Ogres until last?

And what about the timings? The Goblin King seemed to have reappeared in an instant; the Warlord must have barely had time to ask him his name. Well, he already knew his name, but that's not the point. His Generals on the other hand, had been in there twice as long as anyone else. What were these Goblins up to? It was very mysterious.

The door opened. A straight faced Warlord Sepping entered followed by a rather more wobbly faced General Chandimer who hurriedly took his seat again, lending a quick glance to his leader as he did so.

"Lord Protector Higarth," said Sepping in a monotone voice.

The Lord Protector casually rose to his feet. He trudged slowly over to Warlord Sepping. He wasn't going to give the Goblins any satisfaction by looking tired or confused. Both of those, naturally, were signs of weakness.

He followed the Warlord out of the Drugen quarter and across the hall. The 'interrogation room' was only a few yards away. It consisted of two chairs, a table and a couple of small torches. The Warlord locked the door behind them.

173

They both sat down. He locked eyes with the Warlord and neither of them spoke for a couple of minutes. It was Sepping who broke the silence.

"Lord Protector Higarth," he began. "First and foremost, allow me to apologise for this unfortunate circumstance we find ourselves in."

"No need to mention it," replied Higarth mechanically. "My deepest condolences once again."

"Well thank you," added Sepping. "And I hope you understand that this is simply a standard procedure. In circumstances such as this we have to follow protocol to the letter."

The Lord Protector nodded. "Of course. And again, no need to mention it. I suppose it is also your procedure to interrogate Ogres far more intently than any Goblin," he replied.

"We treat every person with the exact same level of scrutiny," said the Goblin Warlord, as if prepared for this question.

He glanced at the door to check that it was still locked before continuing.

"Please describe your relationship with Prince Grumio."

Higarth took a breath. "He was a member of the Goblin royal family. As leader of the Ogres, we were obviously well acquainted."

"So you would say you knew him well?"

"Do you not know what 'well acquainted' means?" said the Lord Protector.

"Well yes, all right then," said the Warlord. "And how long have you known the Prince?"

"All his life, obviously. I knew the Goblin King before his son was even born" he replied. "Do you know how old your Prince is or do you need me to tell you that too?"

Warlord Sepping rolled his eyes. "Let me ask you a harder question then. Can you think of any reason why you or your fellow Ogres would want Prince Grumio out of the picture?"

"That's not a harder question," said Higarth. "The answer, obviously, is no."

"No reason at all?" said the Warlord.

"Of course not. You know full well that Ogres and Goblins are the closest of allies. What could we possibly have to gain from the death of the Goblin leaders?"

Quite a lot, obviously. But the Warlord didn't have to know that.

"And you speak for yourself and all your Generals when you say that?"

"I do indeed," said Higarth. "Although actually, you have already spoken to all my Generals so I don't really see why I need to."

He looked down at the table between them, and a thought suddenly occurred to him. "You're not taking any notes here, are you?"

"I'll ask the questions, thank you," replied the Warlord.

"You aren't though, are you? There's no quills, not even any paper."

"As I said, Lord Protector. I'll ask the questions."

Higarth glanced around the room. "Come to think of it, isn't it a bit odd that you're the only one here? There's nobody taking notes, and nobody to back up any of these answers. How are you even going to keep a record of all this?"

"I have an excellent memory for one thing," replied the Warlord, forgetting he was supposed to be the one asking the questions.

"I'm sure you do," said Higarth. "And I'm sure that's the protocol in the Goblin Kingdom. If someone is murdered, don't make any records, and leave all the investigating to one Goblin who has an excellent memory."

"Yes and perhaps we should be getting back to the investigating," said the Warlord impatiently.

Higarth paused for a moment. "And how has the rest of the investigation been going?" he said.

What seemed to puzzle him earlier was suddenly becoming remarkable clear.

"A member of the Goblin royal family dies, under suspicious circumstances," continued the Lord Protector. "And the entire investigation is done in a small room by a single Goblin. There are surely only two reasons why this would be handled so incompetently."

The Warlord glared at Higarth. He continued regardless.

"Either the Goblins really are the most ridiculous and senseless race in the entire history of the Known World," he looked up at the ceiling to avoid a further glare from the Goblin Warlord.

"Or," he continued, "you already know the answer."

Sepping continued to glare.

"Or both, of course," added the Lord Protector, unable to resist another dig.

The Goblin Warlord finally snapped.

"Whatever it is you're accusing me of," he growled at the Ogre, "I would think carefully before coming out and saying it. May I remind you that I'm a Warlord of the Goblin realm. Any insult to me, is an insult to every Goblin alive!"

"I just called the whole of the Goblin realm ridiculous and senseless; somehow that doesn't bother me," replied Higarth. "But anyway, I haven't accused you of anything. Whatever this is, I think it is greater than one Goblin. Even if he is a Warlord."

"And what exactly are you suggesting?" said Warlord Sepping.

Higarth stared at the Goblin. The fire in his eyes was still shining back at him. The grey hairs on his head were standing as upright as soldiers. As he continued to stare, he could see that the Warlord was shaking.

"As I said, I'm not accusing you, or any of the other Goblins of anything," began the Lord Protector. "But let's just say, hypothetically, that I was the King of the Goblins. And I had a son. A son who would one day take over from me when I'm old and grey, to carry on my legacy."

Warlord Sepping sat back in his chair; apparently accepting that the questioning was taking a back seat for the moment.

"But suppose, again hypothetically, that there was a problem. My son didn't agree with me on anything. He saw the relationships I had forged with other races, and he resented it. Suppose he wanted to take the Goblin realm back to what it was; break relations with the Humans and the Pixies. And for some reason, I thought this would be a disaster."

"Are you suggesting that King Grieber wanted to kill his first born son?" snapped the Warlord.

"I said nothing of the sort!" replied Higarth instantly. "But anyway, as the hypothetical King of the Goblins, suppose I wanted to kill my hypothetical son. I wouldn't like the idea, but after years of trying to reason with him, I eventually came to the opinion that there was no other way. For the sake of the Goblin realm, he had to be dealt with."

"I simply can't believe what I'm hearing," said the Warlord, who nevertheless continued to listen.

"Now of course, as King of the Goblins I could do whatever I wanted. I could hire an assassin on the sly; have him subtly brutally murdered and then back to business as usual. Who would possibly suspect a King had murdered his own son?

"But that would still be too risky; after all, if the King didn't kill his son then who did? As the hypothetical King of this hypothetical kingdom, I would need a scapegoat."

"A hypothetical one?" asked Sepping, now covering his head with his right hand.

"Exactly," replied Higarth. "So the question is, who? Of course it would be pretty easy to find some random peon and blame the assassination on them; say they were crazy or wanted to abolish the Monarchy. But then what? The Goblin prince would die a hero. People might start to agree with his views; undermine the King."

"Which is you; don't forget you're the King in this hypothetical scenario," Sepping added.

"Yes. And as the King, I couldn't have that. For some reason, I firmly believe that a close relationship with the Humans, and the Pixies, is what's best for my Kingdom. So I should try to undermine those who disagree. If I need a scapegoat for the death of my son, how about someone who also shared his views? Or better yet, a whole race of people? A race of people who, since the dawn of the Known World, have had nothing but hatred for the race of Humans. The Ogres."

He paused, waiting for the Warlord to respond. He didn't. So Higarth continued.

"Now of course, the Ogres are the strongest and most powerful race in the Known World. I could hardly try to frame one of them for murder; or even go about accusing him of anything of the kind. But I wouldn't need to. I would just let people think what I wanted them to. Invite the Lord Protector of the Ogres to Nuberim, and a few of his Generals. The first night they arrive, the Goblin Prince dies. Then, I just let people put two and two together."

"So you kill your own son, and let people think the Ogres did it," said Sepping.

Higarth began to grin. "I'm right, aren't I? Everything I've said is absolutely right."

"Are we still speaking hypothetically?" said Sepping.

"Yes, of course," said The Lord Protector. "But what I don't know is the next step in this hypothetical plan. Although I'm guessing it's quite simple. I just wait. Let the whole realm go through the mourning process; hold an inconclusive investigation and draw a line under the whole thing. Then, continue to rule the Goblin Kingdom, and one day pass it onto my second son. One who I trust to carry on my legacy."

"And the final question," sighed the Warlord, "is what would happen if people found out about this devious plan."

Higarth grinned once again. His yellow teeth began to show; it was really rather revolting.

"I wouldn't worry. They wouldn't say anything, even if they were the Lord Protector of the Ogres."

The Warlord let out a breath.

"After all, what would it achieve? I doubt anyone would believe them. And imagine the tension it would cause between the Ogres and the Goblins? It could end in an all-out war!"

"Well exactly," replied Sepping.

"Although something tells me that might be happening anyway."

The Warlord turned pale in an instant. Higarth just laughed.

"I think this investigation is over, Warlord Sepping. Don't you?" he said.

Warlord Sepping just nodded blankly.

The Lord Protector got up and left the room, marching straight back towards the Drugen Quarter. He couldn't have anticipated anything like this. He knew the Goblin King was a traitor; a weakling; a filthy Human friend. It was hard to believe he was capable of something like this.

Surely it was something the King would regret for the rest of his life. Which, of course, was only another few days since the poison was now working its magic.

Chapter 29

There's no place like home. Especially when your home is a massive palace with guards on the outside and servants on the inside.

King Wyndham's home for the last few weeks had been a combination of travel taverns and hastily constructed camp dens. He had missed the firm bedding and roaring fires from his royal chamber. He had missed the ripe meat off the bone and the fine wines from his cellar. He had missed everything about this place. And his wife, of course.

It was rather hard to put his trip into words. He had personally travelled all the way up to Lanthyn, only to be told by the Elves that there was nothing they could do to help. And then he had travelled further, to the very edge of the Known World to see the Oracle once again. She had been mildly helpful, but the King was still trying to understand what she meant.

Was King Grieber really in trouble? The Oracle had said she saw Goblins; and a golden crown fall to the ground. Unless someone was playing fancy dress, that could surely only be the Goblin King. But what could he do to help? He had sent a messenger, although no word had come back since. Perhaps the messenger hadn't even made it to Nuberim yet; it was half way across the Known World, which is rather a long walk, even for a horse.

Of course that wasn't all the Oracle had said. The 'olive branch of peace crumbling into dust' had been worrying the King even more. Surely that couldn't mean the end of peace between their realm and the Goblins; that possibility wasn't even worth thinking about.

And yet all he had done on the journey home was think about it. Perhaps he needed to go to the Goblin realm himself, just in case. To make sure the King was safe, and their friendly relationship could continue. But even that seemed like overkill, after all what was he supposed to say. 'Oh hi, I visited an Elf who can see the future and suggested that possibly something bad might happen to someone matching your description. So I just wanted to check you were okay'.

Hard to justify it really; the messenger would have to suffice. Besides, King Wyndham was tired. He had finally made it back to Peria and had no intention of leaving again for a while.

One thing he hadn't missed about the city was the politics; the constant need to make decisions about the smallest little detail. But it was all necessary, and there was one decision in particular which he finally felt ready to make.

"We have to withdraw from Carlom," the King announced.

"Shouldn't we wait for the Lord of War to get here before discussing this, sire?" asked the Lord of Religion hastily.

"We can't," replied King Wyndham. "The last message I heard was that he's still at the fortress; we won't be seeing him back here again for a few days at least."

"Well perhaps we should wait a few days? I would think Cecil would have something to say about this. Surely we need him here," said the Lord of Religion. "And welcome back to Peria by the way, sire," he added, sensing the King was not overly impressed by his answers so far.

It was the first Meeting of the Lords since Wyndham's return. Of course the Lords had held many meetings while he was away; but without the King here they didn't technically count as a Meeting of the Lords.

Not that it really mattered; although the Lords did once debate what to call their meetings when the King wasn't there. They eventually agreed that a Meeting of the Lords was still an appropriate name for a meeting without the King. Although since the King wasn't there it didn't technically count as a decision made at a Meeting of the Lords, so the name was never officially changed.

"I'm inclined to agree with the Lord of Religion," said the Lord of the People. "We have many pressing issues to attend to; perhaps the question of war should wait until the Lord of War has returned?"

"This question," snapped the King, "is the only question that matters."

There were seven Lords in the Kingdom of Humans. They were all considered to be of equal importance and power; in the sense that each of them thought they were more important and powerful than the others.

But on the question of the battle with the Trolls, it was probably fair to say the Lord of War was the most relevant advisor. Except perhaps for the Lord of Peace.

"If we're going do this," continued the King, "then we have to act quickly. The longer we wait, the greater the risk of further casualties."

"But we've discussed this many times, sire," said the Lord of Peace. "Our men have a right to be there. And what about the Ogres? It makes us look weak."

"So does losing battle after battle against the Trolls."

"We haven't lost a battle in over a month," added the Lord of Peace.

"Yes, not since the last battle. A month ago," replied the King.

"Think about the cost though sire," added the Lord of Gold. "Withdrawing all those soldiers from Carlom and bringing them back here. It would be expensive."

"Any more expensive than keeping them over in Carlom?"

"Well no, I suppose not," replied the Lord. "The cost is probably lower actually. And to be fair, there can't be many people we would need to bring back. That is sort of the benefit of losing so many battles. The more soldiers you lose, the cheaper it becomes."

King Wyndham leant back in his chair. Of course his chair was higher than all of theirs, so he still maintained his commanding presence regardless of how much he slouched.

"What did the Oracle tell you, sire?" asked the Lord of Peace.

He was beginning to enjoy the fact that his counterpart was not at the discussion; it made him feel a lot more important than usual.

The Lord of Peace was a highly respected title; one which Elgin had held for over 22 years. In fact the role had been passed down from generation to generation for as long as anyone could remember. Each father would pass on the wisdom to his first-born son; teach them the skills required to be a successful Lord of Peace. The main one of course being the ability to claim no responsibility when a war breaks out; but still take all the credit when it ends.

"What happened between me and the Oracle is private," said King Wyndham.

"You mean you two had a thing…"

"Not like that!" snapped the King. "I mean that everything I saw was for my eyes only. Everything I heard was for my ears only. And I do not wish to repeat it."

"That's fine, of course sire," said Elgin quickly. "I simply wanted to make sure that you were taking on board any advice you were given. After all, it's a hugely important decision."

"You all seem to be under the impression that this is a consultation," said the King. "It isn't. I have made my decision. The war with the Trolls is over. We have lost it."

There was a sour silence.

"Again sire perhaps we should check with the Lord of War before we…"

"Enough!" growled the King. "The Lord of War will be informed of this at once, and then we will surrender."

"You mean, begin our strategic redeployment of forces to suit our ongoing military needs?" suggested the Lord of Peace.

"Yes good point," added the King. "I think we can avoid terms like withdrawal and surrender since we all know what we're talking about."

"Indeed," continued Elgin. "After all, this isn't merely a surrender. We have had a presence in Carlom for hundreds of years, and done all we could to defend it."

"Quite," said King Wyndham.

"Battle upon battle we have fought and lost over the last few years. Many people would have given up long ago when it became blindingly obvious we were never going to win. But not us, sire, we kept our soldiers fighting despite all the naysayers; despite all their common sense and rational arguments."

"Well I wouldn't say it quite like that…" replied Wyndham.

"What I mean, sire, is that if this a surrender, then it is a brave one. A great surrender, if you will."

"A perfect surrender, even," added the Lord of the People.

"Again, I think we should just stop saying the word 'surrender'," said King Wyndham.

This was something that all the Lords agreed on. In fact, given the circumstances the room seemed very upbeat. The King and his Lords were almost congratulating themselves on making this decision.

One Lord however had been very quiet during this whole discussion. The Lord of Science tilted his head down, and stared blankly at the table in front of him. All these years he had been waiting for the war to end, yet now he simply couldn't feel happy about it.

He had been convinced it would never happen without drastic action. He never would have done it otherwise. All he was thinking about now were the two men he had sent on a perilous mission to the Goblin Realm. If they succeed, the Goblin King would be killed. If they fail, it wasn't even worth thinking about. But it was all justified, for the sake of ending the war.

Although now of course, it wasn't. The war was about to be over; and now he had quite probably sent two men to their deaths for absolutely no reason.

It was too late for him to call it off at this point; they must be near Nuberim by now, and how could he possibly get hold of them anyway? All he could do was sit there, and hope that somehow everything would work out. Or if it didn't, that nobody would figure out he had anything to do with it.

Chapter 30

"It's all going to be worth it in the end," said Ridley. "I'm really starting to believe that now. The money helps, but deep down I don't think it was ever about the money."

"Of course it wasn't," said Fulton, smiling. "We could be the two people who single-handedly ended the war. I mean, that's pretty amazing."

They were in high spirits, despite the tiresome journey they had both endured. The last few days had been particularly strenuous; they had walked quickly, taking very few stops. And more importantly they had spoken to no-one; it was too risky in this part of the Known World.

As a result, the two men had managed to make it to the Goblin Capital. And they could certainly tell they were in the right place; despite using side entrances and thin tunnels, they could still feel the resplendence of Nuberim as they made their way through the city. There was an abundance of light, with torches on all sides. Even the thinnest of tunnels had plenty of space and high ceilings. At times, it was easy to forget that they were underground at all.

It was also rather difficult to tell whether it was day or night. On the surface it's quite easy; you look up, and see whether it's light or not. So those of us who live on the surface tend to take this luxury for granted. But underground, how were they supposed to know?

The Goblins must have known, but stopping to ask them would make them look suspicious. Or stupid. So the best way to judge was by how many Goblins were walking around. They don't come out during the day time, so if there were loads of them in the tunnels it must be night time.

And it seemed to be getting that way. They must have been walking through Nuberim most of the day, as the empty tunnels were now beginning to fill with Goblins. The fifth and final night of the Dernbach festival would soon be upon them.

They surely did not have long until the King's speech.

They had to make it to the Citadel and find a good hiding place. Scratch that, an excellent hiding place. But before they could find that, they had to actually find the citadel.

The map from the Lord of Science had been surprisingly helpful. Ridley was in no doubt that they couldn't have made it to the Goblin capital without it. It even had a separate map of Nuberim itself, with bold lines marking the main tunnels and arrows showing the entry points.

Of course a piece of parchment can only go into so much detail, and reading it underground can be tricky even with all the torches around. That's why the two men were quite taken aback when they suddenly came in contact with the open air.

It was a clearing; a huge clearing in the middle of the city. They came to the end of the tunnel and stopped, surveying the scene around them. It was eerily breath-taking. Theirs was one of many tunnels, all leading to this same place. While they had been underground only seconds ago, now they could see clear skies above.

"Is this it?" said Fulton. "Surely this is it," he added, answering his own question, which meant Ridley didn't bother to reply.

He just nodded. It wasn't quite what he expected, although he hadn't been sure what to expect. Wilfred had described the Citadel as a bucket, and in some ways he wasn't far wrong. Down below them was a flat space, circular, and perhaps two hundred feet wide. Stone terraces then stood all around it, rising steeply upwards to the very top of the rock. If the place was wooden, and a thousand times smaller, then it probably would look like a bucket.

But it was grander than Ridley had expected, and better made. The stones all looked fairly new; the only gaps were for tunnel entrances. There was probably space for fifty thousand Goblins here, and more importantly, there were no caves or obvious hiding places. How in the Known World were they going to find a place to shoot an arrow at the King, without being spotted?

"Wilfred did say he had been here before, didn't he?" muttered Ridley.

"Yes, many times in fact," said Fulton.

"So presumably, he knew the layout of this place quite well."

The Magic Fix

"I would assume so, yes," replied Fulton.

"So you would think he'd mention the fact that there aren't actually any hiding places. Where are we supposed to go?"

"Hmmm," said Fulton, in a way which made it sound like he was thinking hard and about to say something clever. And as it turned out, he actually was.

"What the Lord of Science said, is that we should position ourselves near the top of the bucket. I mean citadel," he began.

Ridley looked round again. As it happened, they were already fairly near the top; apparently they had not been as deep below ground as he thought.

"I think we actually need to be at the very top," he continued. "So we can get away as quickly as possible. Instead of escaping back through a tunnel, we just go on top. We don't run through the city; we run over it."

Ridley smiled. "I think you're right," he said. "But there is one small problem. Have you seen what's on the top of this thing?"

It was the first time they had properly studied the upper tiers of the citadel. The terraces looked no different from anywhere else; the same stone pattern continued all the way to the top. But on the top, was a wall. It looked quite imposing, with several turrets positioned all around it.

Fulton sighed as he looked up. There were plenty of unguarded exits from the city; why did this one have to be so heavily fortified?

"Well we'll have to climb it?" he said.

"It doesn't look that easy," replied Ridley. "So we shoot an arrow, kill the Goblin King, and as everyone's in shock looking for the culprit they see two Humans trying to climb a twenty foot wall? I feel like we wouldn't be able to do it quickly enough to escape, and it might look a little suspicious."

Fulton glared at him. "So how about we climb it before we 'do the deed'? Then all we have to do is jump down the other side and run."

"I don't know," replied Ridley. "I still think we would stand out; anyone would be able to see us."

He thought for a moment. "The turrets are the answer," he said at last. "We have to get inside one. They must have a great view of the ground below; and we would still be fairly hidden."

Fulton looked up. The turrets looked rather daunting above them.

"Won't there be guards? Isn't that the whole point of the turrets?"

"Yes, I expect so. But they look empty to me right now. All we have to do is get in there first."

Fulton raised an eyebrow. "That's all we have to do, is it?"

"Well yes. And then kill the guard or guards who try to enter it, obviously."

"Yes, let's not forget that minor additional detail," said Fulton. "I was sort of under the impression that we would do as little killing as possible. One arrow; one Goblin; that was all it took. After all, we're trying to bring about peace and save lives here, not the other way around."

Ridley sighed. "There's no other way," he said, as he continued to gaze at the turrets above them. "Now come on, we have to make it up there as soon as possible. Any moment this place could be swarming with Goblins; and all it takes is one of them to spot us."

They both pulled their cloaks above their heads and made their way up the terraces. The nearest turret was only above a hundred rows away; and once they made it there, all they had to do was wait. And assassinate a King. And any number of Goblin Guards. And then run for their lives. Simple.

Chapter 31

The last few days had seemed like months to Higarth and his Ogres. Stuck in Tygon Hollow with these insufferable Goblins. There was nothing they could do to help the disastrous situation they found themselves in. All they could do was wait. Wait until enough time had passed that they could go back to their own realm without looking unsympathetic.

The Lord Protector's whole plan was founded on the basis that Grumio would become King; he would stop cosying up to the Humans and bring back the Ogre-Goblin relations from the past. Unfortunately he was now dead, so his chances of becoming King were quite remote.

The investigations into his death continued, but had pretty much fizzled out after the first night. Unsurprisingly, Warlord Sepping hadn't found the killer, since he already knew who did it. The last few nights had involved quiet meals and muted discussions; people making every effort to be as diplomatic as possible and not say anything stupid.

This was the quietest of all the quiet meals; three Ogres and three Goblins were sitting in a stone hall. Nobody had said a word, and Higarth had no desire to break the silence. He sat there nibbling at a turkey leg, wondering how they got into this state; and whether the Goblins would ever learn how to properly cook their food. Honestly, it tasted like sawdust.

The one positive from all this was that the plan to kill King Grieber was working. The King had apparently been confined to his bed for the last two nights, too sick to join in the festivities, or lack of festivities. He may have just had a virus, of course, but the Lord Protector was fairly confident that any day now they would hear the news that the poor King had passed away. A messenger could come in any minute now. Any second now.

"My apologies for interrupting," said a young Goblin, bursting through the wooden doors. "But I have some terrible news. His Royal Highness is... I mean, he has been found... dead!"

The three Goblins in the room shot to their feet.

"Dead?" cried Sepping. "It can't be! He has been sick these past few days, but surely nothing fatal!"

"This is a tragedy," added Higarth, who had also risen to his feet. "How? How could this have happened?"

The young Goblin shook his head slowly and faced the floor. This must have been the worst message he had ever had to give, and he clearly wasn't enjoying it.

"Please follow me," was all he could muster, and the six of them did so without further questions.

They were led out of the doors and across a long tunnel, up a set of stairs and then across a shorter tunnel. Tygon Hollow really was a maze; they could surely have designed this place better. Though this was probably not the time to bring that up.

Eventually they made it to the Royal Quarters, where they came across a very pale looking Prince Nutrec. He seemed to be frozen on the spot; in fact it was quite possible he hadn't moved for hours.

This was not surprising, really. The poor Goblin had seen his father and older brother both die in a matter of days. The consolation, of course, was that he was the next in line for the throne. Rather exciting really, but again probably not the time to bring that up.

"My deepest condolences, Prince Nutrec," was all the Lord Protector said.

"Indeed, our deepest condolences," said General Lang.

"Deepest condolences," added Chandimer.

"I can only imagine how you must be feeling," said Warlord Sepping.

The Prince said nothing. He still seemed to be barely moving, barely even acknowledging their presence.

"This must be a terrible shock," added one of the other Goblins; evidently running out of comforting phrases to say.

"Perhaps we should come back later," added Sepping.

"No, stay," replied Prince Nutrec. "I need you here. I've been sitting in this room for hours, although it's felt like nights."

"Of course," said Sepping.

"I think there is a lot we need to discuss," continued the Prince.

Higarth was quite impressed. He knew very little about Prince Nutrec, but the young Prince seemed to be handling this remarkably well. Maybe he was one of the few Goblins who actually had some strength inside him.

"What have the apothecaries said?" said Sepping. "How do they think it happened?"

"They don't know," replied the Prince mechanically. "From all they can tell, it was natural causes."

"These things happen," said Warlord Ouro, before adding "Such a tragedy," in case that sounded a bit careless.

"Of course they do happen," said Sepping. "But can it really just be a coincidence that this happens only a few days after Prince Grumio is killed?"

"Yes, it must be a coincidence," replied General Chandimer. Before adding, "Such a tragedy though," in case that sounded a bit suspicious.

"Well I don't know," said Ouro. "But I do know that we'll get to the bottom of this. Whatever happened, we will find out."

"Thank you, Ouro," said Prince Nutrec. "I am sure you're right. But right now we have more pressing things to discuss. After all, we all know what tonight is."

And they all did know. Even the Ogres knew the importance of tonight. The fifth night of the Dernbach festival; the culmination of five days and nights of celebration in honour of their Gods. An ancient tradition that dated back before the first age, probably.

And with this tradition of course, comes the speech. When the King stands in front of thousands of Goblins and gives his yearly message.

The King who was now dead. Prince Grumio could have gone in his place, but he was now dead.

"We only have a couple of hours," continued Prince Nutrec. "The people will already be gathering in the Citadel. Somebody needs to address the realm. Somebody needs to tell them what's happened. And I think it has to be me."

"Are you sure, my prince?" said Warlord Sepping. "You could always let me go in your place."

The Prince shook his head. "Noble of you to offer. But no, it is always the King who addresses the realm. It's an ancient tradition that dates back before the first age, probably."

The Goblins all nodded.

"But I will need your help. Thousands of people are in Nuberim, celebrating in blissful ignorance. Unaware of the tragic fates of their King and his eldest son. We need to find a way of breaking the news; but still reassure the realm that they are safe; that everything will be okay. They need to know that they still have a King. They still have a leader. I'll need his robes. And his crown."

Higarth also nodded; he was still finding this all quite impressive. The poor Goblin had only just lost his father.

Prince Nutrec turned to him. "Lord Protector Higarth, I am truly sorry that you had to be here during such difficult circumstances."

"Please, do not apologise," answered the Lord Protector. "I am just sorry that such tragic circumstances have happened."

He looked around the room, and sensed an opportunity to leave this awkward situation.

"And if there is anything that I, or any of my Generals can help you with, don't hesitate to ask."

The Prince feigned a smile as Higarth made his way to the door. The other Ogres followed him.

"What do we do now?" asked General Lang, as they walked back along the tunnel. "Where are we even going?"

The Lord Protector looked around as they walked.

"I don't know," he said. "We just need to go somewhere quiet, and let this whole thing unfold. Let the Goblins sort out their own mess, we'll just sit back and see what happens."

"So what do you think is going to happen?"

Higarth thought for a moment. "I think the Prince is going to go out there and give a great speech. And soon enough, he'll be the new King. I have no idea what kind of King he'll be, but it can't be any worse than the last one."

Chandimer nodded. "I think he could be a great King. You know, the right sort of Goblin leader."

"You might be right," said the Lord Protector. "And if he isn't, we can always go get some more poison."

Chapter 32

Ridley breathed. There were no lights inside the turret; the only sources of illumination came from the torches in the rows below. The Citadel was now filling up. The two men could see Goblins wandering across the stone steps and taking their seats.

There was clearly a buzz around the place. People were chatting, laughing and shouting to each other. The general background noise was almost comforting; Ridley felt he could speak freely with Fulton in the turret without somebody overhearing. Of course he still didn't say a word to him, partly because it was too risky but mainly because he really didn't want to.

So instead he just kept breathing, and watching the rows below him. The turret gave him a great view of the main stage. After all, it wouldn't have been a very pointful turret if it didn't. The roof was its best attribute; a few simple tiles but it clearly did the trick. They both felt hidden. Sheltered. Almost safe.

The only downside was the space. There was just about room for the two of them at the top of the ladder. Fulton was sitting down by the entrance, while Ridley stood next to him, staring out of the viewing gap. And of course breathing.

"Can you hear something?" whispered Fulton.

"What?" he replied.

"I said can you hear something?" said Fulton again.

"I know, I mean what?" said Ridley.

Fulton closed his eyes. "I think I can hear footsteps. Close ones. Getting louder."

The two Humans stopped for a minute. There was white noise; people talking and walking around. But nothing more.

"It's probably just your heart beating," said Ridley sarcastically. "Try to relax."

And with that, he turned his head back to the main stage. It looked quite beautiful, in a hideous Goblin-like sort of way. There were great high torches dotted around the circular platform, all of them now lit, sending white smoke up into the dark skies above them. There were five statues evenly spread out around the edges; presumably representing the five Gods of the Goblin religion. From Ridley's viewing point they all looked exactly the same, and he didn't really see the point of them besides to block the view of some poor sods who probably paid big money for a front row seat. Mind you, they would have worse things to complain about by the end of the night.

"Ridley!" snapped Fulton suddenly, in a tone that sounded like he was trying both to whisper and shout at the same time.

"What?" he replied. He then recoiled in horror as he turned only to see a Goblin's head staring straight back at him, peeping up through the turret's entrance.

It wasn't moving. Was he dead? It took Ridley a moment to see the dagger in his neck; and a moment longer to see a young Human's hands still wrapped around it. He then saw the face of the young Human; pale as an albino ghost who had just fallen into a bucket of white paint.

"What have you done?" said Ridley, in the same whispery shouting tone that Fulton had used just a few moments ago.

The young man could barely speak. But he managed.

"I just saw the head appear out of nowhere," he said. "I didn't have time to think. I didn't think. I just stabbed him."

"Yes I can see that," replied Ridley.

His heart was pumping fast, but a slight sense of relief was now pouring through him. Clearly the Goblin was dead; there was no doubting that. Fulton's swift action had saved them. And not only that, he had somehow done it so quietly that nobody else noticed. Not even Ridley!

"Well done!" was all he could think of to say. "You've just killed a Goblin soldier. A couple of seconds later and it could have been us."

The colour was quickly returning to Fulton's cheeks.

"But what now?" he gasped. "What are we supposed to do with him?"

He still had his hands around the Goblin's neck. If he let go, the Goblin would probably fall back down the ladder.

"Should I let him fall?"

"No!" cried Ridley; again, in a whispering sort of tone. "People might find it a little suspicious if they suddenly see a

Goblin's body come crashing down from one of the turrets!"

He moved towards Fulton and grabbed the Goblin's shoulders. They were armour plated of course, making him twice as heavy, although they at least gave Ridley something to hold onto.

"Quick, help me hoist him up here," he said.

Fulton put one hand under the breastplate, and they both heaved the body up onto the platform.

"But what do we do with him?" asked Fulton. The turret was small enough as it was; now with a great Goblin in between them there was barely room to breathe.

"Nothing," replied Ridley. "What else can we do?"

"Why don't we hoist him onto the roof, and then throw him off the back? When the time comes to escape, at least we'll have something to cushion our fall."

"Cushion our fall? He's a Goblin soldier covered in armour! Why don't we just throw a couple of spikes down there too for good measure?"

"It was just an idea."

"No, besides it's too risky. What if someone sees it?"

Fulton accepted he had a point.

"I think we're just going to have to sit on him," continued Ridley.

He manoeuvred himself so he could drag the body round, and laid it out horizontally under their bags. Fulton watched, and the two men then tried to make themselves comfortable. Or as comfortable as possible when you're sitting on top of a Goblin soldier in a cramped turret.

They sat there in an awkward, satisfied silence for a long while. Then Ridley slowly moved his head back towards the eye of the turret, once again staring down at the main stage.

It seemed like the event was finally getting started. A couple of Goblins were now walking across the circle, inspecting the torches and looking out into the crowd. Another one was sprinkling flowers around the stage. Or something that looked like flowers; it wasn't easy to tell from Ridley's position.

The Goblins left the stage, and the crowd then fell silent. Once again, he could hear himself breathing deeply.

Four trumpet players took to the stage, each one dressed in shining blue robes. Even at their height at the top of the citadel they could still hear the music. It sounded soft, soothing. He looked at Fulton, who almost seemed to be enjoying it.

The trumpets didn't last long. Once they had stopped, the musician nearest them started to speak. He bellowed out, clearly making an effort to reach every one of the thousands of people in the crowd. It didn't work for Ridley; he could hear noises but had no idea what the trumpet player was saying. That was, of course, until the crowd suddenly erupted with cheering and the four trumpet players moved off the stage.

Ridley leant down and pulled the bow out of his bag. This was it. This was surely it.

A majestic looking figure made his way slowly into the middle of the circle. His robes were a white gold; on his head was something that clearly resembled a crown. The Goblin King had arrived.

Ridley picked up an arrow with his left hand and placed it squarely onto his string. Trembling slightly, he prepared to draw it back.

The crowd was deafening. They cheered. They applauded. They all seemed to be talking at the same time.

The King waved. He moved around the stage, nodding to the crowd in every direction as he did so. Ridley waited. Poised. Ready to strike.

"Stand still, your highness," he whispered under his breath.

The Goblin King continued to wave. But now he was making his way back to the centre of the circle.

"Patience," muttered Ridley, "you've done this a thousand times before."

He drew his bow back fully, feeling the tension of the string in his hand. His left thumb followed the King across the circle. Any trembling in his hand had now disappeared. He was as cool as a cucumber. As solid as a rock. As focussed as a turnip. He may as well have been back at the archery range. That's all this was; just one simple target to aim at.

The King began to speak.

"My friends," he said, or something to that effect.

It didn't really matter, since the rest of his speech was cut short rather abruptly by an arrow shooting through his skull.

The Magic Fix

It must have been the shortest speech ever given at the Dernbach festival, but almost certainly the most memorable. Which is often the way with short speeches, isn't it?

Ridley knew at once that he had hit his target. There was no time to wait around to be sure.

"Go!" he snapped to Fulton, who instantly sprung up through the eye of the turret and onto the roof.

Ridley passed Fulton the two bags and then manoeuvred up onto the roof himself. Their dead Goblin soldier friend stayed put.

It was pandemonium in the citadel; all Ridley could hear was shouting and screams. The two men were clearly visible now on the roof of the turret. But they couldn't afford to look back. They crouched at the edge of the building and stared down below them.

It looked far. Too far. Ridley kicked himself for not checking this first. The citadel was basically a hole in the ground, and they were at edge of it. It was only a small wall at the very top. So therefore he assumed, it should only be a small jump. But it didn't look small. Not now.

"Throw down the rope," he said in a low voice.

Fulton nodded. He rapidly pulled the thick thread from one of the bags and threw it straight down to the ground. It landed in a pile right below them.

"Ah," he said. "You meant throw down one end of it, and tie the other?"

Ridley was breathing fast now. The turrets of the wall were lit up, and people could surely see them on both sides of it. He could feel the sweat running down his neck.

"Well now we have no choice," whispered Ridley. "Jump!"

Fulton flung both the bags down. There was an uncomfortable second before they heard them hit the ground.

They looked at each other. This was their only chance.

They jumped. Then the jump became more of a fall as Ridley felt the cold air against his face. Then he felt the ground. And it hurt. It really hurt.

He felt a silent scream but couldn't make a noise. Was it his foot? His ankle? He couldn't even tell.

Fulton turned round; he was already about to run.

"What's going on? You okay?" he said.

A panicked look suddenly appeared on his face. He knew

197

the answer to that question.

"I can't move," Ridley yelped.

Fulton leant down and grabbed his shoulders.

"No, leave me" he said. "I'm done. You may only have a few minutes. You've got to run."

"What? I can't go without you!" cried Fulton.

"This is not the time to be noble," said Ridley.

"I know, but I can't go without you. I don't know the way!" he replied.

Ridley winced. The pain was unbearable, wherever it was coming from.

"You'll be fine. Just run."

Fulton tried in vain to grab his shoulders again. Ridley fought him off.

"Run!" he shouted.

But Fulton didn't even have time to turn around. Ridley saw three Goblin guards appear from the shadows, surrounding the two of them in an instant.

With the wall behind them, they were surrounded. There was nowhere to run. Not that it mattered since Ridley couldn't even walk.

Chapter 33

"Lord Protector! The King has been killed!" cried General Lang, bursting through the door to his room.

"Well yes Lang, we know. That was the whole point of this! What's wrong with you?" he replied.

"No my Lord Protector. Not Grieber."

"Yes, Grumio. We obviously knew that too."

"Not him either," replied the General. "It's Nutrec. He's been shot with an arrow!"

The Lord Protector's eyes widened.

"What?" he shrieked.

"It's true. Shot with an arrow! Just as he was about to give his speech!" said his General.

Higarth rose to his feet. This was supposed to be a quiet few nights; they were keeping their heads down and waiting for everything to blow over. But this was rather the opposite of blowing over. Everything was well and truly unblown.

"But how? Who by?"

General Lang simply shook his head.

"Nobody knows. Some random Goblin I guess!"

The Lord Protector scratched his head.

"None of this makes any sense," he said. "We came here to assassinate the King."

"Which we did, Lord Protector," added Lang.

"Yes. But then Grumio gets assassinated first."

"Indeed. Before he could become King."

"Yes. And then Nutrec takes the place of the King to make the speech," continued Higarth.

"And gets assassinated," said Lang.

"Right," replied Higarth. "So what's the common link?"

General Lang stopped for a moment.

"Assassination?" he said. "Goblin Kings? Goblins?"

"Yes. Okay there's more than one common link."

Lang nodded. "At least three, I would have said, My Lord Protector. But anyway, I don't think now is the time to discuss it. We have to go and see the Goblin Warlords and

Nobles; offer them comfort; make it look like we had nothing to do with this."

"But we did have nothing to do with this!" barked Higarth. "We had no involvement whatsoever in two of the three assassinations!"

"Exactly. We're completely innocent," replied General Lang, making his way back to the door. "So now I think we have to go and console the Goblins. We can figure out the rest of this mess later."

"Yes, we can," replied the Lord Protector. He followed his General out of the room. "And we will, if people could stop assassinating each other for about five minutes."

They went back the way Lang had just come; down the steps and into the Irk Atrium. It was a rather wide hall with quite a sinister feel, though obviously more sinister than usual given the circumstances.

The room was full of Goblins, all looking shocked, confused, angry and frightened at the same time. Higarth saw a few familiar faces, including of course his other Generals; Litmus and Chandimer. Both were looking equally as perplexed as everyone else in the room. As well as shocked, confused, angry and frightened of course.

Warlord Uoro was sitting at one side, comforting Queen Afflech, who looked like she had just been shot with an arrow. Although probably not quite as bad as her son, who actually had just been shot with an arrow.

Higarth cleared his throat quietly. What can you possibly say to someone who has just seen her husband and two sons killed in the space of a few days?

"I'm sorry for your loss," said Lang, before getting a glare from the Lord Protector.

"Your Highness!" added Higarth. He wouldn't of course usually use the term; but if there was ever a time to be polite, this was surely it.

"I know that nothing I can say will comfort you right now; but rest assured we will find out who did this. We will find out who did all of this, and ensure that justice is done!"

The Queen barely acknowledged their presence, save for a faint nod.

"I think that for the moment, her Highness needs to be alone," said General Uoro. They both got up, and he escorted the Queen out of the Atrium. "We will be in the royal chambers if anyone needs us."

As the door closed behind them, the Lord Protector of the Ogres turned to the only other Goblin Warlord in the room he knew. There was no time for mourning; he had to figure out what in the Known World was going on. He sensed that Warlord Sepping was thinking the same thing.

"Well?" he said, as he approached the Warlord.

"Not overly well, Higarth," replied Sepping.

"Indeed," said the Lord Protector. "I can only imagine how you must be feeling."

The Warlord nodded. "I was there," he began. "I was there when it happened. We all were."

He gestured around the Irk Atrium at the many downtrodden faces.

"I was crouched in the front row; looking up at the crowd. They were laughing; cheering; every kind of celebrating. And then I saw it. Quick as a flash. The arrow shot over my head."

The Warlord sighed. "I didn't even need to look round. I knew in an instant what had happened."

"And what did you do?" asked Higarth.

"I ran to him of course," said Sepping. "A few of us picked him up and rushed him straight down to the Healing Centre. But I felt no movement at all as I carried him; the apothecaries only needed to glance at him to know. The arrow went straight between the eyes. No healing treatment in the Known World could have saved him."

The Lord Protector nodded. "And where is he now?"

"He's still in there. Lying there. At peace," replied Sepping. "And now I don't know what to do. I have half of my soldiers out there looking for the killer."

"Only half?" replied Higarth.

"Yes, well it is the Dernbach festival. A lot of people like to take the night off for it."

The Lord Protector frowned.

"Although obviously, their night off has now come to an end."

Higarth leaned closer to the Warlord and lowered his voice.

"Do you have any leads at all? Any idea who could have done this?"

Sepping gave him a cold stare. "None at all," he whispered.

"Who could possibly have planned something like this?"

"My Great Warrior," called a young Goblin, entering through the side door. "There is a messenger to see you. A messenger from the realm of Humans."

"What?" growled Higarth in response.

"Send him in," said Sepping calmly.

A well-dressed young Human appeared; his dark hair slightly dishevelled with a smile on his face. Two heavily armed guards accompanied him on each side.

"Good evening," he began, addressing Warlord Sepping directly. It was fairly obvious who the most important Goblin in the room was.

"I am Farthing, a messenger from the Kingdom of Peria. I bring word directly from the King of Humans."

Higarth and Sepping just stared at him; as did all the other Ogres and Goblins in the room.

"He says to take extra care. Because the Goblin King's life may be in danger."

Warlord Sepping rose to his feet, with a look of both anger and complete puzzlement on his face.

"Did he by any chance say which one?" he bellowed.

The Human looked taken aback. "Which King, you mean?" He swallowed as he spoke. "But there is only one Goblin King. King Grieber!"

"Yes. Well there was, until he died a couple of nights ago!" added Higarth.

The messenger had not noticed the Lord Protector of the Ogres until now. His expression changed; his face grew visibly paler.

"So the Oracle was right!" gasped the messenger.

Sepping scratched his head, struggling to take in all this sudden information.

"So the Oracle predicted this?" he said. "That's why Wyndham sent you down here?"

Higarth shuddered; the fact that the Warlord referred to the King of Humans by his first name, it almost made them sound like friends.

"Yes," replied the messenger. "King Wyndham sent me straight here to warn you. The Oracle saw the death of the Goblin King."

"Well the Oracle got it doubly right this time. Triply in

202

fact!" snapped the Warlord. "Not only has it happened once; it's happened three times!"

The Human looked taken aback, once more. "You mean he died three times?"

"He only died once, you fool," growled Higarth. "As did Prince Grumio; and now Prince Nutrec."

The Human's eyes widened. He drew breath, unable to speak. And then he spoke.

"But how? I'm... I'm so sorry!" he mustered. "If only we could have come sooner. If only!"

Warlord Sepping was at the end of his tether. "Is there anything else you wanted? Otherwise, the door is right behind you!" he growled.

"Ah well that was only the first part of the message," stammered the Human, with a pale yet red glow covering his cheeks. "He also sent these two guards as an offering. For protection, until we know the Goblin King is safe."

He visibly shook as he caught the glare of about twenty Goblins at once.

"But perhaps, their services are no longer needed."

The young Human awkwardly made his way towards the door; opened it slowly and walked out without saying another word. His two guards followed.

"Should we stop him?" muttered General Lang.

"Oh let him go," said Sepping. "He was just a useless messenger; clearly he had nothing to do with these murders."

"No, of course he didn't," said Higarth. "But don't you think it's a little suspicious; the King of Humans sending us a warning about the Goblin King dying?"

"After it actually happened," added Lang.

"Well yes," replied the Lord Protector. "But let's suppose that the messenger was meant to arrive a few nights earlier. Maybe Wyndham really did visit the Oracle and receive this prophecy. Or maybe he knew the Goblin King was going to be killed; because he planned it."

Sepping scratched his pale green chin.

"So you're saying that the King of Humans had a plot to kill the Goblin King. And he thought it would be a good idea to warn the Goblins that he was about to do this. And he sent us some of his own armed guards just to make it more of a challenge?"

"Yes all right," snapped Higarth. "But what if he only did it as a cover? Send his own guards to make it look like he could have had nothing to do with this."

The Warlord shook his head.

"I just can't see it. Wyndham and Grieber were good friends; why would he possibly want to kill him?"

"Maybe he didn't," replied Higarth. "Maybe he wanted to kill Grumio. Or Nutrec."

"But why? It still makes no sense to me," said the Warlord. "What was the motive? What reason did he have? I just can't see the Humans being involved in this."

"My Great Warrior!" called a Goblin guard, bursting into the room. "We have caught them. We have caught the assassins!"

"What?" cried Sepping; rising to his feet.

"We found them behind the wall of the citadel, trying to escape," continued the Goblin guard. "Two Humans!"

"Humans? Really, how fascinating," muttered Higarth, as he swiftly followed the Warlord out of the door.

Chapter 34

It was amazing how different the second leg of their journey had been. The trip to Peria was actually a fair bit longer than their walk from Madesco, but somehow it had seemed so much shorter.

The horses had helped. Petra had never ridden one before; in fact very few Pixies did these days. Most horses were far too big for a Pixie, and just managing to get on top of one was a feat in itself. You either had to use some sort of pole-vaulting technique, construct a sturdy ladder, or coax a horse to come right by the side of a building and jump on top of it from the roof.

Quite frankly, in the time it took to get on top of the horse, you might as well have just walked to wherever you wanted to go.

These horses of course were different. The White Castle had many Pixie sized horses, specially bred to be just the right height. They were mostly a snowy white colour, and surprisingly obedient.

It wasn't just the horses of course; the provisions helped. They weren't having to settle for the grain and raw cabbage that Samorus took with him (apparently he couldn't magic them into anything nicer). Now they had enjoyed the finest meat, fish and vegetables; only the very best for Prince Vardie and his companions.

And speaking of companions, the company had been rather good too. It wasn't just the three of them; they had a whole team of guards and servants. It almost felt like a party. As Petra laughed with the Prince, while sitting on her horse and crunching a rather nice apple, her old life in Samorus's hovel couldn't have felt further away.

Of course, now they were in Peria there was no time for laughing. They were here on serious business. Their appointment happened to be just after the Royal Jester, but that was purely a coincidence.

Petra sat in the meeting room with Samorus and Prince

Vardie; slightly in awe of the situation but doing her best to remain in control. She had spent the last few days with the Prince after all, so the King of Humans was sort of just another person to her now.

King Wyndham looked imposing, with two Lords seated either side of him. The Lord of Science; looking old, wise, stroking his white beard. And the Lord of War; looking young, presumably less wise, stroking his bare chin.

As Petra looked from one to the other, she realised that nobody had spoken for a good five minutes.

"Any further questions?" she asked, somewhat sarcastically.

They had been sitting there for a long time now. Petra had done her party trick; it was all getting rather mechanical by now. They had brought in a rat; she had turned it to ashes with a flick of her wrist. And then the three Humans had sat around in amazement, asking her every question under the sun.

"Who else knows about this?" asked the Lord of Science.

At least they had stopped asking if it was a trick; and moved onto something a bit more useful.

"Nobody," butted in Prince Vardie, before glancing at Petra. "Nobody but us three and Queen Vernipula. Even the rest of our escort don't know why we're here."

Petra looked back at the Prince. She didn't know why he had lied to them, but almost felt relieved that she didn't have to come clean. Ridley and Fulton knew everything about it; but they were somewhere in the Goblin Realm by now. She would probably never see them again. But no, she might. There was always a chance that she might.

"What do you think, Sire?" said the Lord of Science, turning to his King. Wyndham had been sitting there, quietly contemplating the situation.

"Well, I don't even know where to begin," he began. "It just doesn't feel real. Right now I'm torn between excited and terrified. Excited at the thought of what this gives us. This young Pixie could save lives; thousands of them."

Petra smiled softly. It was rather hard to justify being called a lifesaver when all she had done so far was burn a few rats to death.

"But if the Ogres found out about this; or even worse, got

hold of her," continued Wyndham. "Well, it doesn't even bear thinking about."

"Exactly what I was thinking," said Prince Vardie. "And as I said, that's why we're here. We need a plan. We need a strategy."

The King nodded. "Well to start with, let's state the obvious. Nobody else is to know about this; not until we have a clear idea of what to do next."

"What about the Lord of Peace?" said Cecil, the Lord of War.

Wyndham thought for a moment. "No, not even the Lord of Peace. We can't risk it."

Cecil looked shocked. "Or the Lord of Gold?"

"Not even the Lord of Gold."

"What about the Lord of…"

"Nobody else is to know!" growled the King, wondering why he had brought these Lords along in the first place.

"Agreed," said Prince Vardie in return.

The King turned back to Petra. She smiled. He didn't.

"And I think before we make a decision about anything else, we need to understand just what Petra is capable of."

"We already know that," said Samorus.

"Sorry, who are you again?" asked King Wyndham.

Samorus didn't reply. In fact he didn't talk again for a while.

"What I mean is," continued the King, "that we need a full understanding. From what I have heard so far, we know that Petra has unbelievable powers. We know she can turn small objects and animals into flames, into ashes even, in the blink of an eye."

"That's right," said Vardie.

"But what about on a larger scale. What about trees? What about buildings? What about… people?"

"People?" gasped Petra. She turned to Vardie, who didn't look quite as shocked.

"Well that we don't know," he turned to Petra. "King Wyndham's right. We are not asking you to do anything, but we need to know what you're capable of. We need to know, for example, if an Ogre or a Troll came running at you, whether he would defeat you, or whether you would turn him to dust."

7

8 ly.

Petra frowned. A lot of her time here had felt like a dream. But right now, this felt very real.

"And what if I am capable of turning them to dust with my bare hands?" she asked. "Would you then be asking me to fight in the war?"

"We're not saying anything of the sort," said Cecil. "Besides, we're not even at war right now."

"What about Carlom?" said Prince Vardie.

The King sighed. "It's over. Our people are withdrawing from the city."

"A tactical redeployment," added the Lord of War.

"Our settlers will be finding new homes closer to the capital. All the soldiers returning. Carlom will once again belong to the Trolls."

Prince Vardie looked shocked. "What changed?" he said. "What happened to never giving up? Never retreating?"

"Tactical redeployment," said the Lord of War again.

"We were fighting a losing battle," said King Wyndham gravely. "We had no support from the Elves. And I fear any support from the Goblins may have been coming to an end."

Wyndham stopped himself short. He hadn't meant to mention his discussion with the Oracle. The message had been sent to Nuberim; nobody else needed to know what the Oracle had told him.

And then of course it came to him. He couldn't believe he had missed it until now. He repeated the Oracle's words in his head. 'A pair of magic hands on the smallest of creatures'. The magic Pixie!

He looked down at Petra; her fiery green eyes shone back at him, and the King couldn't turn away. The Oracle was right. It all made perfect sense. Sort of. In fact, none of it made sense at all. If she was right about this, did it mean the Goblin King was going to die? Maybe he was already dead. Maybe Petra could save him. Or save the world. Or destroy the world.

Yes, none of it made any sense. He needed to see the Oracle again. Why did she have to live on the other side of the Known World? Well, not quite the other side, but very far away!

Chapter 35

"At least they put us in the same cell," said Fulton. He feigned a smile as he spoke, but Ridley could see that even his trusted young companion was struggling to see the positives in this situation.

Ridley could feel the metal chains digging into his wrists. One of his legs had now gone numb, but he could still feel a stabbing pain in his right ankle. Something was broken, he was sure of that.

His throat was dry; he could hardly remember the last time he had a drink. Well, it must have been a few hours ago, before he had shot that arrow. But still, it felt like a long time ago now.

The prison cell was only a few yards wide, although it was so dark that it was pretty hard to tell. The only light came from the torches at the other side of the corridor, illuminating three Goblin guards who were sitting in the alleyway, engaged in conversation and taking it in turns to glare at the prisoners.

Ridley couldn't see the other prison cells. He knew there were others but he could hear no noises coming from them. He guessed they were the only prisoners in this block. After all, the two Humans had just done something pretty big. They were surely now the main attractions in this prison. The VIPs; so special that they got their own cell block.

Fulton glanced at the guards, then turned back to Ridley.

"What do you think they're going to do to us?" he asked.

Ridley shook his head. "I don't know," he said.

He really didn't. The Goblins had pounced on them. Two Humans, trying to run away just after the Goblin King had been shot with an arrow. There was no need for a detective; they might as well have had a sign above their heads saying 'we did it guys'.

The guards had dragged them straight back to the citadel; then down a series of tunnels. Then down some more tunnels. And then down some steps. And then some more tunnels.

Ridley didn't know where they were; but they must have been deep underground. About as deep as it gets.

He suddenly heard a movement outside.

"They are in the end cell, my Great Warrior," came a voice in the alleyway.

Ridley and Fulton both pressed their heads against the bars. They could see the guards were on their feet. Someone, or something, had joined them.

It was someone, obviously. Ogres and Goblins were people too; just not people who were very nice to look at.

In fact it was two people; a tough, angry looking Goblin, and a tougher, angrier looking Ogre. They both carried torches, and as they walked slowly to the edge of their cell Ridley could almost see the fire reflecting from their eyes. He glanced over at Fulton. He was visibly shaking.

Soldiers brought across two stone chairs; the Ogre and the Goblin both sat down, directly in front of the cell. They sat so close that Ridley could almost reach his arm out through the bars and touch them. He didn't try, obviously; that would be weird.

"Who are you?" growled the Goblin.

The two Humans just stared.

"We didn't do it," said Fulton at last.

The Goblin almost seemed to chuckle. The Ogre just continued to glare.

"We know you did it!" bellowed the Ogre. "You were caught trying to flee, from the exact point where the arrow was shot."

"Yes. With a bow and arrow in your bags," added the Goblin.

"Hmmm on reflection we probably should have left that behind," admitted Ridley.

"But they would have found the bow," said Fulton. "What if they had traced it back to us?"

"Yes well maybe we just shouldn't have got caught!" replied Ridley.

"Maybe you just shouldn't have done it in the first place?" said the Ogre.

Even he was looking fairly calm now. Evidently he couldn't believe how easy it was to get a confession out of them. Not that they needed it.

The Goblin smiled and nodded. "I'm Warlord Sepping by the way. I'm one of the four Great Warriors of the Goblin Kingdom."

"And I'm Higarth; Lord Protector of the Ogres," said the Ogre.

Ridley took a breath. "But, you can't be? You're Lord Protector Higarth? You're the leader. The leader of the Ogre realm! Why have you come here yourself? And the leader of the Goblins too?"

"I'm not quite the leader," said the Goblin. "We had a leader; but you killed him."

"Ah yes," said Ridley, deciding not to say anything more.

Higarth stared at him once more.

"We came here because we wanted to hear your answers with our own ears," he said. "We know you killed Prince Nutrec. But we need to know why."

"What makes you think we're going to talk!" said Fulton defiantly. "Wait... Prince Nutrec? But, surely you mean King Grieber? He's the one we killed."

Ridley sighed; although now it didn't really matter how many times they admitted to the killing. Although he was equally confused. Prince Nutrec? What did he have to do with anything?

"Prince Nutrec. He's the one you killed," said Sepping.

"You really didn't know that?" said Higarth. He couldn't believe what he was hearing. "Well, I guess we know why they did it then! They thought he was the King."

Warlord Sepping nodded. Clearly these two idiots weren't lying. But they clearly were idiots.

"So then the next question," he said. "Why were you planning to kill the King?"

Ridley was beginning to feel faint. He didn't know what to do, or say any more.

"What if we don't tell you?" said Fulton. "Are you going to torture us?"

"Yes, probably," said the Warlord. "But we'll most likely do that anyway," he added.

"We haven't decided yet," said Higarth. "So I would say it's in your interest to tell us everything you know. Wouldn't you?"

"Well yes," admitted Ridley. To be fair, they had done a

pretty good job of telling them everything so far.

"So why were you planning to kill the King?" said Sepping again.

Ridley sighed. "It's complicated. We wanted to bring about peace."

"Peace?"

"To end the war in Carlom, yes."

Warlord Sepping frowned. "So you wanted to kill the King, in order to *end* the war?"

Ridley nodded. "Yes," he said. "The Goblins were supporting the Humans out there. King Wyndham wouldn't back down unless he lost their support. So we had to kill the Goblin King. It was the only way to make it happen."

Even in the dimly lit corridor, Ridley could make out the look of puzzlement on the Warlord's face.

"You're serious, aren't you?" he said. "That was genuinely the reason you came here."

"Yes," said Fulton.

"So King Wyndham didn't send you?"

"Oh Gods no," replied Fulton. "The King would kill us if he found out what we were doing!"

"There's a chance he might find out now," replied the Warlord sarcastically. "Although I wouldn't worry; I very much doubt that Wyndham is going to be the one who kills you."

"Well that's reassuring," muttered Ridley.

Sepping turned to Higarth. "What do you make of all this?" he said.

"It doesn't make any sense," said Higarth, shaking his head. Of course, it actually made perfect sense; he had planned the exact same thing. The only difference was, he had actually achieved it.

"We were paid to do it, too," added Fulton. Ridley sighed. Apparently they were now giving away information without even being asked.

"By who?" said the Warlord.

"I can't tell you that," said Fulton. The Warlord glared at him, and gestured as if he were about to get up. "Wilfred, the Lord of Science!" cried Fulton.

"Well done," said Ridley. A slight glare from the Goblin was clearly enough torture for the young Human.

"The Lord of Science?" said Higarth. "But he's close to the King of Humans, surely."

"He's a rebel," replied Ridley. "The King knew nothing. He had no part in this plan. Why would he? Wyndham and King Grieber are friends."

"Well that's certainly true," said Higarth bitterly.

"You mean they were friends," added Warlord Sepping.

"What?" said Ridley. "You said we killed the Prince."

"Oh you did," said the Warlord smugly. "King Grieber was already dead. He died a couple of nights ago. Poison. Or natural causes. We still don't know which."

Higarth smiled at the two prisoners. "It must be reassuring for you; that you came all this way, ending up in a jail cell having failed in your task. And the King was going to die anyway, so you needn't have bothered at all. Just something to think about when you're rotting away in this cell."

The two men didn't respond.

Sepping nodded. "I think we have heard enough for tonight," he said slowly.

"I agree," said Higarth, rising from his seat. "We need to think this through; consider our next steps."

"Well if you need anything more, you know where to find us," muttered Ridley.

The Goblin Warlord and Lord Protector of the Ogres took their torches and made their way back across the corridor.

"What do you think?" asked Warlord Sepping, once they were both alone.

"Well they seemed to be telling the truth," said Higarth. "But something about this just doesn't seem right. They said the King of Humans had nothing to do with this, but what if they were lying? What if it was a part of his plan all along; to make the Goblins weak? What if the Humans are planning something bigger? Maybe even an all-out war against the East of the Known World."

Warlord Sepping stared at him. "You really think that's possible?" he said.

"Of course it's possible," replied the Lord Protector. "I'm not saying I believe it. I'm saying that we need to be careful. Not just me and you; everyone from both our realms. Throughout history, Ogres and Goblins have always stood side by side. In these perilous times, we need to remember who our friends are. And our enemies."

Sepping nodded, looking straight ahead of him as he walked.

Higarth smiled, the toothiest and ugliest smile of the night. He couldn't believe his luck. Let's face it; the last few nights had been an absolute nightmare. But for a plan that had started so disastrously wrong, and gone steadily downhill from there from one disaster to another, it had somehow ended pretty well.

Chapter 36

Petra woke up, wondering where she was. It took her a few minutes more than usual to adjust to her surroundings. The bedroom was splendid; it was certainly nice of the Humans to put them up in the Palace. Her bed was surely too big for a Human alone; but for a Pixie, it was simply enormous. The rest of the room was not to be sniffled at either; a great wardrobe, two sofas; she could probably live in this room and never have to leave. It might get a bit boring, but still.

She looked round the room for some clothes. There didn't seem to be anything except the ones she had brought. She wondered why the Humans hadn't brought her any. Maybe they just couldn't find any that would fit. Surely they could find some children's clothes somewhere? Ah well; her old ones would have to do.

There was a knock at the door.

"Come in," said Petra, putting on her top.

Samorus entered. He surveyed the room and smiled; or at least as much of a smile as Samorus ever gave.

"Not bad, right?" said Petra.

Samorus nodded. "I have to admit, these Humans have been all right to us."

"How's your room?" said Petra.

"Too big," he replied. "Far too big."

Petra laughed.

"So what do we do now?" she said.

The smile seemed to fade from the old Pixie's face. To be fair, they never lasted long.

"I have been thinking," he began. "I know this place is amazing, but I just don't know how long I can stay. I think it's time to go home."

"Home?" replied the young Pixie. "But we only just got here."

"I know that," said Samorus. "But we have been on the road for weeks. I'm old, Petra. I can't handle all this travelling."

"So maybe you should just stay here and rest?" she replied.

"Well yes, that does seem like the logical solution," said Samorus. "But that's not the only reason I'm saying this."

"You also miss your old house? All those hours making healing potion?"

"No, not that," said the old Pixie. "Well all right partly that too. But it's something more serious. I'm worried. Why do you think they put us up in such nice accommodation? Why do you think they are being so nice to us?"

"Because they're nice?" replied Petra.

Samorus sighed. "Maybe. But have you forgotten what they were asking you yesterday?"

"You mean about whether I can kill Ogres? No, I haven't forgotten. I obviously haven't forgotten."

"They want you to fight, Petra," said the old Pixie. "What if they see you as nothing more than a weapon?"

Petra turned away. She walked slowly towards the balcony door. She had spent close to an hour on that balcony last night. The view was enchanting; she could see half of the city, even at night time.

"What if they do?" she began. "The thing is, I have been thinking too. I have a gift. A gift that nobody else in the Known World has, or ever had before. And I owe it to everyone in the Known World to use it."

She turned back to Samorus. "They asked me if I can kill an Ogre. What if I can? What if I can kill every single one of them?"

Samorus stared at her. He didn't know what to say. He didn't even know what to think. He didn't even know his own name. Samorus. It was Samorus. But he still didn't know the first two. What if Petra was right?

Suddenly he heard a bell ringing in the distance. And then another; this one was a little louder. And then a couple more went off. Before he knew it, the room was surrounded by a deafening ringing. And panicked voices. He could hear panicked voices coming from somewhere.

The door flung open; a guard appeared.

"Come. Quickly!" he bellowed to the two Pixies.

They did as he said, and hurriedly followed him out of the room and down a corridor.

"What's going on?" said Petra.

"I don't have time to explain. It's the dragon alarm; people are ringing the bells throughout the city," replied the Guard, who evidently did have time to explain.

"So it's a drill?" replied Petra, struggling to keep up with the briskly walking Guard.

"Well that's just it," he replied. "We had a dragon drill a few months ago. It doesn't seem right. But it can't be a real dragon; we haven't had a dragon this far West since the 11th age!"

"Blimey!" said Samorus, trying to catch his breath. "So where are you taking us?"

"Here," said the Guard, opening a pair of large wooden doors which led them into a well-lit room.

It was huge and fairly crowded; there must have been thirty people in there. She could see King Wyndham, alongside some important looking people she assumed were his family. Prince Vardie was already there; sitting pretty close to the King.

The two Pixies went over to him.

"What's going on?" said Petra at once.

"Have you seen it yet?" replied Vardie, answering her question with another question. "It's out there."

He pointed to the window in front of them; a small slit in the wall with a view across Peria. As she looked, Petra realised that half the room were looking the exact same way.

She edged closer; squinting through the slit. It looked fine. Blue skies; the stone buildings below. What was she supposed to be looking at?

And then the whole room let out a gasp. A shape shot past the window. She saw it. The whole room saw it. They saw the frightening wings; the terrifying claws; the also-quite-scary tail.

"It's so close," whispered Petra, craning her neck to try and catch sight of it once more.

"So what do we do?" said Samorus to Vardie.

"We stay here," he replied. "That's the drill for this situation. Go to a safe room, and hide inside until the dragon flies away."

"Or until they kill it?" said Petra, who couldn't help overhearing.

"Who's going to kill it?" replied Samorus. "You can't just kill a dragon!"

"They will try. They are already trying," said Vardie.

"King Wyndham said there are at least a hundred Archers out there right now. Every tower has a bell; and at least two guards beside it."

"But can you really kill a dragon with a bow and arrow?" said Samorus.

"It's possible," replied Vardie. "But extremely difficult. Even if the arrow hits, the chances of penetrating the dragon's skin are next to nothing. Some say that to have a realistic chance, you would have to stand there shooting arrows for so long that the dragon would have died of old age anyway."

Petra frowned. "But they have to try!" she said.

"Oh, they are definitely trying," replied Vardie. "You never know. But all we can do is stay inside and hope that either it somehow dies, or flies away."

"That's not all we can do!" replied Petra. "What if it destroys half the city before it goes? What if half the people die?"

She rose to her feet and marched towards the doors.

"Where are you going?" snapped Vardie.

She didn't look back. Before the Prince could say anything else she had gone straight through the doors and disappeared from sight.

Vardie chased after her. There were two guards standing by the doors.

He stopped and turned to them. "What's wrong with you?" he said. "Why didn't you stop her? Why did you just let her go?"

"Isn't that the Pixie that can make things burst into flames with her bare hands?" said one of the Guards.

"Yes."

"That's why," he replied.

The Prince brushed them aside and marched straight through the doors. Samorus followed.

Petra was racing down the corridor. She didn't know what she was thinking. But she knew exactly where she was going. Her room had a balcony. She would have a clear view of the dragon.

She looked behind her, and saw the two Pixies rushing towards her. That wasn't all though; Humans were following behind.

They weren't going to stop her. She wouldn't let that happen. This was it. This was her chance to prove herself; to test her ability to its limits. To help people. To help the Known World.

Chapter 37

Just breathe, thought Petra, *you've done this a thousand times before.*

Of course it had always been with rats, rather than dragons, which is slightly different. And she hadn't done it a thousand times either. But still, she could do this. She could do this.

She looked back from the balcony. A crowd had gathered behind her; it was like she was doing a magic trick. Half the people in the room had followed her. Samorus was at the front, staring. It looked like he was mouthing something, but she couldn't hear what. Although she knew what it would be; presumably something along the lines of 'breathe', 'focus' and 'concentrate.'

She breathed again. The dragon flew past. It was nearer this time; she could see the colour of its wings. A dull grey. *Just like a rat*, she thought.

She looked back again. This was crazy. Why was nobody stopping her? She wouldn't have let them obviously, but it would have been nice if they had at least tried.

She turned her head. She couldn't see the beast anymore; it had disappeared to the right, obstructed by the tower.

Petra thought for a moment. She realised that she couldn't just let the dragon keep flying around aimlessly or it might never come close enough. She needed to draw it in. Just like with a rat.

Without hesitating she put her two hands up in the air and let out a jet of fire, directly above her. She heard a gasp from the crowd of people behind, and a couple of them even seemed to clap. This really was becoming like a magic trick. She should have brought a hat for people to put coins in. A 'disappearing dragon' trick was surely worth a few silvers.

She did it again. Another white blaze shot out of her hands and disappeared into the sky above her head. This time nobody gasped; all she heard was silence.

Then she saw it. The dragon was sweeping back again, even closer this time. But it was flying away from her;

clearly it hadn't got the message yet.

"Over here!" Petra shouted. Not that it would have heard her from such a great distance, but it couldn't hurt.

She shouted again, and shot one more stream of fire into the air. As she did, she looked up and wondered how close she would need to get to the dragon to stand any chance. The flames she shot up must have only gone ten yards high at most. It may have looked impressive to the idiots behind her, but was it anywhere near enough to harm a dragon?

It's just a rat, she thought to herself again. *Just a bigger rat. With wings. And claws. And a tail; oh wait, rats actually do have tails. But they don't have fierce red eyes like these ones.*

She could see the dragon's eyes, even from this distance; piercing her like needles which had been specially designed for piercing. In fact, she could see the whole of the animal's face. And that only meant one thing. It was looking at her. It had seen her.

It was now facing her head on; it was still some distance away but she could feel it moving ever closer. Its presence became more and more real. She could even feel the wind on her face from the flapping of the beast's wings.

Focus she said to herself. It was easier said than done. The dragon's gaze remained fixed on hers. She had to hold it there. In one second, the thing could swoop down and probably take out half the tower.

She held out her right hand, her palm directly facing the dragon. It was hovering in the air. It must have been about thirty yards away now. She could make out the scales on its neck. Its eyes remained as piercing as ever.

But it wasn't moving any closer. She was sure of that. Was her magic working? Surely she hadn't stopped it in mid-air. Maybe it was just waiting. Waiting to pounce.

Concentrate she said to herself. It was now or never. She flicked her hand back and thrust it forward. Nothing. Not even a spark.

She tried again. Nothing. All she could do was hold the dragon's gaze. In that instant she wanted to run, but felt frozen on her feet. It felt like the dragon was casting its own spell on her. Like she was the victim; and it was ready to pounce.

"Just breathe," she heard Samorus call, as helpfully as ever.

She closed her eyes for a second, and thought back to that first night in his hovel. That first time she had killed that rat; turned it to ashes with her bare hands. The Old Pixie was staring at her; he hadn't believed she could even hold it still.

Petra felt the frustration; the anger that had come over her that night. It had banished her fears; any hesitation had gone in an instant. She had taken those feelings and turned them all into flames.

She opened her eyes and flicked her right hand once more. It was just a rat. Just a great huge flying rat. She felt the flame as it burst from her right hand; it almost knocked her back.

The beast let out a spine-chilling scream. The white flame had struck it hard. It was falling; and burning as it fell. In a matter of seconds, it had disappeared from sight; crashing into the rock below it. *Hopefully not somebody's house*, thought Petra. Though that wasn't the main issue right now.

She turned around. The crowd behind her were gaping, none of them saying a word. She was waiting for a slow clap to start, or something, but people were simply unable to move.

Petra walked forward to Samorus, who put his arms round her tightly.

"How could you possibly have…" he began. "I mean, I've never been so terrified!"

"I breathed," she beamed. "Breathed, focused, and concentrated. After all, it's just a rat. Just a great big, flying rat."

She looked up. King Wyndham and Prince Vardie were standing in front of her.

"I don't know what to say," said King Wyndham. "You have done something which I never, in the history of the Known World, would even have thought possible. You may have just saved the city. You may have just saved the realm!"

Petra shrugged. "Well, I thought it made more sense just to go and kill the thing, instead of waiting around," she replied.

The King of Humans laughed. "On balance, I think that was the right choice," he said. "I don't know how we can ever repay you."

Petra looked down. "Can I have some clean clothes?" she asked.

Chapter 38

There was a fine sunset over the Known World that night.

Some people in Peria were saying that it was a sign; they said that every time a dragon is slain, the sky will glow a bright orange colour. Since this was the first time a dragon had been slain in hundreds of years, people couldn't really claim they were wrong.

King Wyndham sat in his study, with a sole candle burning in front of him. He had so much to think about. This Pixie was a hero; she was their saviour. She had the power to change the whole of the Known World.

But he couldn't also help but feel a sense of dread. It was no longer a secret; everybody had seen her do it. How long before the Ogres found out? How would they react when they did?

It wasn't just that. The messenger had returned today from Nuberim. Yet again, the Oracle had got it right. Not once, but three times. Three Goblin Kings dead? And even worse, they seemed to think that two Humans had been arrested for it! Humans he never knew, and certainly hadn't ordered to do this.

The King didn't know what was going on. But he knew it wasn't something good. What if the war in Carlom was just the start? The Goblins were in trouble, and the Ogres were surely behind it. Right now, there was peace in the Known World. But it wouldn't last long. The next war; a greater war; was probably just around the corner.

Petra stood on her balcony that night, the same balcony where she had stood just a few hours ago to slay the beast. People down below were working to clear the rubble, and already starting to rebuild where buildings had been struck.

"Are you still going to go home?" she said to Samorus, who stood next to her looking out.

He nodded. "It is time," he said. "I have done all I can do here. I am ready to leave."

He turned to the young Pixie. "I take it you're not coming with me?"

Petra smiled. "I think we both know that I can't go back now," she said.

Samorus nodded again. "I think you'll like it here," he said.

"Who says I'm staying in Peria?" replied Petra. "You heard what the King said earlier. Those two Humans we met, they made it to the Goblin Realm. And now they have been thrown in prison."

"What of it?" said Samorus, frowning. "You're not going to ask the King to rescue them?"

"Maybe," she shrugged. "Or maybe I'll just do it myself."

The old Pixie laughed, like he had never laughed before. Petra just smiled. Why was he so sure that she was joking?

"Do you even remember their names?" said Samorus.

"The older Human was called Ridley," she replied. "And Fulton. The other Human was called Fulton."

Higarth had woken up early, along with the rest of his company. It was finally time to return to the Ogre realm. As they departed through the gates of Nuberim, he took a moment and looked out at the orange glow around him. He could just about see Yerin tower in the distance. It was only a speck on the horizon, but it was a great speck nonetheless. And it was certainly a colour very close to black.

Of course, Ogres don't get homesick; that's a sign of weakness. But he couldn't help but feel glad to be heading back to the Ogre capital once more.

It had been quite an ordeal. Weeks and weeks spent in the Goblin Realm. The 'three for the price of one' Goblin King assassinations had been a real shock, one that he still didn't understand.

But the Goblins were weak now; as weak as they had ever been. His Ogres were only getting stronger. The plan was already forming in his mind. They would support the Goblins once again; rebuild them and mould them into their allies. So when the inevitable Great War with the Humans came along, they would know whose side to fight on.

Ridley stared through the bars of his prison cell. He wondered what time it was. Since two new guards had just replaced the old one, he was guessing it was coming up to night time. He wondered if there was a sunset that night. He bet there was. He bet it was a beautiful red one.

He turned to Fulton. "How did we get this all so wrong?" he said.

Fulton looked tired and bruised, but somehow he was still smiling.

"Did we really get it so wrong?" he replied. "When you think about it, there's a lot we can be proud of."

Ridley looked around the small, barely lit cell. It was cold, it smelt, and he could hear water dripping from somewhere.

"Proud? Really?" he replied. "Do you mean proud that we're both able to fit into such a tiny cell?"

"I'm serious," said Fulton. "We made it all the way to Nuberim, just the two of us. We killed Goblins, found a magic Pixie, ran away from a fight."

"That last one wasn't really that impressive."

"Well how about this," said Fulton. "We were given a mission to kill the Goblin King. And we did it! Okay it might not have been the right King, but we still did it! And he's still dead!"

Ridley nodded.

"We came to bring about peace in the Known World," continued Fulton. "And we might just have done that!"

Ridley couldn't help but smile. "Maybe you're right," he said. "In some bizarre, inexplicable way, maybe you're actually right."

Fulton nodded. "And besides, we did the job we were paid to do. The Lord of Science now owes us a hundred and twenty silvers each!"

Ridley laughed. "I think we might have to wait a while for that money," he replied.

THE END

Acknowledgements

I was sitting in a lecture theatre one evening after work, when my mind started to wander. That was when I came up with the idea for this novel. It had absolutely nothing to do with the subject I was supposed to be listening to, but thank you to the professor for allowing me to lose focus, and for not seeing the notes I was starting to scribble under my desk. If I had been sitting at the front, the Known World and all its characters may never have existed.

I'd like to thank my friends, family and fiancée Catherine for all their support and interest as the book developed. I couldn't have done it without your helpful comments and suggestions, such as 'is it still not finished?', 'why aren't there any pictures?' or 'I'd never thought you would write a comedy'.

And finally, a huge thank you to everyone at Elsewhen Press for seeing the potential in this book, for your expert advice and suggestions, and for all your hard work in turning it from a draft manuscript into a fully published novel.

Elsewhen Press
delivering outstanding new talents in speculative fiction

Visit the Elsewhen Press website at elsewhen.press for the latest
information on all of our titles, authors and events; to read our blog; find
out where to buy our books and ebooks; or to place an order.

Sign up for the Elsewhen Press InFlight Newsletter at
elsewhen.press/newsletter

QUAESTOR
DAVID M ALLAN

When you're searching, you don't always find what you expect

In Carrhen some people have a magic power – they may be telekinetic, clairvoyant, stealthy, or able to manipulate the elements. Anarya is a Sponger, she can absorb and use anyone else's magic without them even being aware, but she has to keep it a secret as it provokes jealousy and hostility especially among those with no magic powers at all.

When Anarya sees Yisyena, a Sitrelker refugee, being assaulted by three drunken men, she helps her to escape. Anarya is trying to establish herself as an investigator, a quaestor, in the city of Carregis. Yisyena is a clairvoyant, a skill that would be a useful asset for a quaestor, so Anarya offers her a place to stay and suggests they become business partners. Before long they are also lovers.

But business is still hard to find, so when an opportunity arises to work for Count Graumedel who rules over the city, they can't afford to turn it down, even though the outcome may not be to their liking.

Soon they are embroiled in state secrets and the personal vendettas of a murdered champion, a cabal, a puppet king, and a false god looking for one who has defied him.

ISBN: 9781911409571 (epub, kindle) / ISBN: 9781911409472 (304pp paperback)
Visit bit.ly/Quaestor-Allan

THE EMPTY THRONE
DAVID M ALLAN

Three thrones, one of metal, one of wood and one of stone, stand in the Citadel. Between them shimmers a gateway to a new world, created four hundred years ago by the three magicians who made the thrones. When hostile incorporeal creatures came through the gateway, the magicians attempted to close it but failed. Since that time the creatures have tried to come through the gateway at irregular intervals, but the throne room is guarded by the Company of Tectors, established to defend against them. To try to stop the creatures, expeditions have been sent through the gateway, but none has ever returned.

On each throne appears an image of one of the Custoda, heroes who have led the expeditions through the gateway. While the Custoda occupy the thrones the gateway remains quiet and there are no incursions. Today, Dhanay, the newest knight admitted to the Company, is guarding the throne room. Like all the Tectors, Dhanay looks to the images of the Custoda for guidance.

But the Throne of Stone is empty. The latest incursion has started; a creature escaping into the world, a kulun capable of possessing and controlling humans.

The provincial rulers, the oldest and most powerful families, ignore the gateway and the Tectors, concentrating on playing politics and pursuing their own petty aims. Some even question the need for the Company, as incursions have been successfully contained within the Citadel for years. Family feuds, border disputes, deep-rooted rivalries and bigotry make for a potentially unstable world, and are a perfect environment for a kulun looking to create havoc…

ISBN: 9781911409359 (epub, kindle) / ISBN: 9781911409250 (304pp paperback)
Visit bit.ly/TheEmptyThrone

THE EYE COLLECTORS
A STORY OF
HER MAJESTY'S OFFICE OF THE WITCHFINDER GENERAL
PROTECTING THE PUBLIC FROM THE UNNATURAL SINCE 1645
SIMON KEWIN

When Danesh Shahzan gets called to a crime scene, it's usually because the police suspect not just foul play but unnatural forces at play.

Danesh is an Acolyte in Her Majesty's Office of the Witchfinder General, a shadowy arm of the British government fighting supernatural threats to the realm. This time, he's been called in by Detective Inspector Nikola Zubrasky to investigate a murder in Cardiff. The victim had been placed inside a runic circle and their eyes carefully removed from their head. Danesh soon confirms that magical forces are at work. Concerned that there may be more victims to come, he and DI Zubrasky establish a wary collaboration as they each pursue the investigation within the constraints of their respective organisations. Soon Danesh learns that there may be much wider implications to what is taking place and that somehow he has an unexpected connection. He also realises something about himself that he can never admit to the people with whom he works…

"Think *Dirk Gently* meets *Good Omens!*"

ISBN: 9781911409748 (epub, kindle) / ISBN: 9781911409649 (288pp paperback)

Visit bit.ly/TheEyeCollectors

Some other titles from Elsewhen Press

A series of novels attempting to document the trials
and tribulations of the **Transdimensional Authority**

Ira Nayman

If there were Alternate Realities, and in each there was a version of Earth (very similar, but perhaps significantly different in one particular regard, or divergent since one particular point in history) then imagine the problems that could be caused if someone, somewhere, managed to work out how to travel between them. Those problems would be ideal fodder for a News Service that could also span all the realities. Now you understand the reasoning behind the Alternate Reality News Service (ARNS). But you aren't the first. In fact, Canadian satirist and author Ira Nayman got there before you and has been the conduit for ARNS into our Reality for some years now, thanks to his website *Les Pages aux Folles*.

But also consider that if there were problems being caused by unregulated travel between realities, it's not just news but a perfect ~~excuse~~ reason to establish an Authority to oversee such travel and make sure that it is regulated. You probably thought jurisdictional issues are bad enough between competing national agencies of dubious acronym and even more dubious motivation, let alone between agencies from different nations. So imagine how each of them would cope with an Authority that has jurisdiction across the realities in different dimensions. Now, you understand the challenges for the investigators who work for the Transdimensional Authority (TA). But, perhaps more importantly, you can see the potential for humour. Again, Ira beat you to it.

Welcome to the Multiverse*
* Sorry for the inconvenience
Being the first
ISBN: 9781908168191 (epub, kindle) / 9781908168092 (336pp paperback)

You Can't Kill the Multiverse*
* But You Can Mess With its Head
Being the second
ISBN: 9781908168399 (epub, kindle) / 9781908168290 (320pp paperback)

Random Dingoes
Being the third
ISBN: 9781908168795 (epub, kindle) / 9781908168696 (288pp paperback)

It's Just the Chronosphere Unfolding as it Should
A Radames Trafshanian Time Agency novel
Being the fourth
ISBN: 9781911419113 (epub, kindle) / 9781911409014 (288pp paperback)

The Multiverse is a Nice Place to Visit,
But I Wouldn't Want to Live There
Being the fifth
ISBN: 9781911419199 (epub, kindle) / 9781911409090 (320pp paperback)

Visit bit.ly/TransdimensionalAuthority

Some other titles from Elsewhen Press

Urban fantasy by Tej Turner

The Janus Cycle

The Janus Cycle can best be described as gritty, surreal, urban fantasy. The over-arching story revolves around a nightclub called Janus, which is not merely a location but virtually a character in its own right. On the surface it appears to be a subcultural hub where the strange and disillusioned who feel alienated and oppressed by society escape to be free from convention; but underneath that façade is a surreal space in time where the very foundations of reality are twisted and distorted. But the special unique vibe of Janus is hijacked by a bandwagon of people who choose to conform to alternative lifestyles simply because it has become fashionable to be 'different', and this causes many of its original occupants to feel lost and disenchanted. We see the story of Janus unfold through the eyes of eight narrators, each with their own perspective and their own personal journey. A story in which the nightclub itself goes on a journey. But throughout, one character, a strange girl, briefly appears and reappears warning the narrators that their individual journeys are going to collide in a cataclysmic event. Is she just another one of the nightclub's denizens, a cynical mischief-maker out to create havoc or a time-traveller trying to prevent an impending disaster?

ISBN: 9781908168566 (epub, kindle) / ISBN: 9781908168467 (224pp paperback)
Visit bit.ly/JanusCycle

Dinnusos Rises

The vibe has soured somewhat after a violent clash in the Janus nightclub a few months ago, and since then Neal has opened a new establishment called 'Dinnusos'. Located on a derelict and forgotten side of town, it is not the sort of place you stumble upon by accident, but over time it enchants people, and soon becomes a nucleus for urban bohemians and a refuge for the city's lost souls. Rumour has it that it was once a grand hotel, many years ago, but no one is quite sure. Whilst mingling in the bar downstairs you might find yourself in the company of poets, dreamers, outsiders, and all manner of misfits and rebels. And if you're daring enough to explore its ghostly halls, there's a whole labyrinth of rooms on the upper floors to get lost in...

Now it seems that not just Neal's clientele, but the entire population of the city, begin to go crazy when beings, once thought mythological, enter the mortal realm to stir chaos as they sow the seeds of militancy.

Eight characters. Most of them friends, some of them strangers. Each with their own story to tell. All of them destined to cross paths in a surreal sequence of events which will change them forever.

ISBN: 9781911409137 (epub, kindle) / ISBN: 9781911409038 (280pp paperback)
visit bit.ly/DinnusosRises

REBECCA HALL's *SYMPHONY OF THE CURSED* TRILOGY

INSTRUMENT OF PEACE

Raised in the world-leading Academy of magic rather than by his absentee parents, Mitch has come to see it as his home. He's spent more time with his friends than his family and the opinion of his maths teacher matters far more than that of his parents. His peaceful life is shattered when a devastating earthquake strikes and almost claims his little brother's life. But this earthquake is no natural phenomenon, it's a result of the ongoing war between Heaven and Hell. To protect the Academy, one of the teachers makes an ill-advised contract with a fallen angel, unwittingly bringing down The Twisted Curse on staff and students.

Even as they struggle to rebuild the school, things begin to go wrong. The curse starts small, with truancy, incomplete assignments, and negligent teachers over-reacting to minor transgressions, but it isn't long before the bad behaviour escalates to vandalism, rioting and attempted murder. As they succumb to the influence of the curse, Mitch's friends drift away and his girlfriend cheats on him. When the first death comes, Mitch unites with the only other students who, like him, appear to be immune to the curse; together they are determined to find the cause of the problem and stop it.

INSTRUMENT OF WAR

"A clever update to a magical school story with a twist." – **Christopher Nuttall**

The Angels are coming.

The Host wants to know what the Academy was trying to hide and why the Fallen agreed to it. They want the Instrument of War, the one thing that can tip the Eternity War in their favour and put an end to the stalemate. Any impact on the Academy staff, students or buildings is just collateral damage.

Mitch would like to forget that the last year ever happened, but that doesn't seem likely with Little Red Riding Hood now teaching Teratology. The vampire isn't quite as terrifying as he first thought, but she's not the only monster at the Academy. The Fallen are spying on everyone, the new Principal is an angel and there's an enchanting exchange student with Faerie blood.

Angry and nervous of the angels surrounding him, Mitch tries to put the pieces together. He knows that Hayley is the Archangel Gabriel. He knows that she can determine the course of the Eternity War. He also knows that the Fallen will do anything to hide Gabriel from the Host – even allowing an innocent girl to be kidnapped.

INSTRUMENT OF CHAOS

The long hidden heart of the Twisted Curse had been found, concealed in a realm that no angel can enter, where magic runs wild and time is just another direction. The Twisted Curse is the key to ending the Eternity War and it can only be broken by someone willing to traverse the depths of Faerie.

Unfortunately, Mitch has other things on his mind. For reasons that currently escape him he's going to university, making regular trips to the Netherworld and hunting down a demon. The Academy might have prepared him for university but Netherworlds and demons were inexplicably left off the curriculum, not to mention curse breaking.

And then the Angels return, and this time they're hunting his best friend.

Visit bit.ly/SymphonyCursed

Now available as audiobooks from Tantor

THE MAREK SERIES BY JULIET KEMP
BOOK 1:

THE DEEP AND SHINING DARK
A Locus Recommended Read in 2018

"A rich and memorable tale of political ambition, family and magic, set in an imagined city that feels as vibrant as the characters inhabiting it."
Aliette de Bodard
Nebula-award winning author of *The Tea Master and the Detective*

You know something's wrong when the cityangel turns up at your door
Magic within the city-state of Marek works without the need for bloodletting, unlike elsewhere in Teren, thanks to an agreement three hundred years ago between an angel and the founding fathers. It also ensures that political stability is protected from magical influence. Now, though, most sophisticates no longer even believe in magic *or* the cityangel.

But magic has suddenly stopped working, discovers Reb, one of the two sorcerers who survived a plague that wiped out virtually all of the rest. Soon she is forced to acknowledge that someone has deposed the cityangel without being able to replace it. Marcia, Heir to House Fereno, and one of the few in high society who is well-aware that magic still exists, stumbles across that same truth. But it is just one part of a much more ambitious plan to seize control of Marek.

Meanwhile, city Council members connive and conspire, unaware that they are being manipulated in a dangerous political game. A game that threatens the peace and security not just of the city, but all the states around the Oval Sea, including the shipboard traders of Salina upon whom Marek relies.

To stop the impending disaster, Reb and Marcia, despite their difference in status, must work together alongside the deposed cityangel and Jonas, a messenger from Salina. But first they must discover who is behind the plot, and each of them must try to decide who they can really trust.

ISBN: 9781911409342 (epub, kindle) / ISBN: 9781911409243 (272pp paperback)
Visit bit.ly/DeepShiningDark

BOOK 2:

SHADOW AND STORM

"never short on adventure and intrigue... the characters are real, full of depth, and richly drawn, and you'll wish you had even more time with them by book's end. A fantastic read."
Rivers Solomon
Author of *An Unkindness of Ghosts*, Lambda, Tiptree and Locus finalist

Never trust a demon... or a Teren politician
The annual visit by the Teren Throne's representative, the Lord Lieutenant, is merely a symbolic gesture. But this year the Lieutenant has been unexpectedly replaced and Marcia, Heir to House Fereno, suspects a new agenda.

Teren magic is enabled by bloodletting. A Teren magician will invoke a demon and bind them with blood. But demons are devious and if unleashed are sure to create havoc. The Teren way to stop them involves the letting of more of the magician's blood – often terminally. But if a young magician is being sought by an unleashed demon, their only hope may be to escape to Marek where the cityangel can keep the demon at bay. Probably.

Once again Reb, Cato, Jonas and Beckett must deal with a magical problem, while Marcia must tackle a serious political challenge to Marek's future.

ISBN: 9781911409595 (epub, kindle) / ISBN: 9781911409496 (336pp paperback)
Visit bit.ly/ShadowAndStorm

Reimar Breaking
The Prelude to the Iberan War

Jonathan Rivalland

Of all the known worlds, of all their nations and all their peoples, there is little rarer than the Helions. Each of these ancient structures is a vast, freestanding portal to other worlds; made by an unknown hand long before humanity arose. Those who control one can claim vast wealth by means of trade and movement through these portals. And on the world of Brisia, it is controlled by the nation of Reimar.

Through both scheming and conflict, Reimar won out against its competitors to claim the territory in which the Helion stands. But Reimar's rivals do not sit idle, and should widespread conflict break out between the more powerful nations, even the smaller countries have grudges to settle. Reimar's wealth and prestige flows from trade, especially cross-world trade through the Helion. But there are signs of an imminent rebellion, especially among the younger members of more distant noble houses, and some rival nations are eager to take advantage of any internal distractions. Princess Siera du Tealdan has shown herself to be a strong and innovative military commander, while her older brother Ramiros enjoys life at the court of their father King Abarron du Tealdan.

When the situation in Reimar takes a shocking turn for the worse, Siera's military expertise is desperately needed. With no mercenaries available for hire, Siera must pull off a miracle. Having only one skyship armed with ballistae and an under-strength Royal Guard, she must fend off the rebellion, while at the same time dealing with Reimar's old enemy Iln, that has declared an opportunistic war in order to raid and pillage across the border. If the rebels gain control of the Helion, the kingdom will suffocate.

Reimar Breaking, the Prelude to the Iberan War, is the first volume in *The Iberan War* series.

ISBN: 9781911409106 (epub, kindle) / ISBN: 9781911409007 (320pp paperback)

Visit bit.ly/ReimarBreaking

About Mark Montanaro

Mark has always been a man of many talents. He can count with both hands, get five letter words on Countdown and once solved a Rubik's cube in just 5 days, 13 hours and 59 minutes.

His creativity started at an early age, when he invented plenty of imaginary friends, and even more imaginary girlfriends.

As he got older, he started to use his talents to change the world for the better. World peace, poverty reduction, climate change; Mark imagined he had solutions to all of them.

He now lives in London with his Xbox, television and non-imaginary girlfriend. He has recently embarked on his greatest and most creative project yet: a witty novel set in a fantasy world. *The Magic Fix*, Mark's debut book, is set to be his best work so far.